D0851228

A Dream Within A Dream

by

Hal McFarland

authorHOUSE®

AuthorHouse™
1663 Liberty Drive, Suite 200
Bloomington, IN 47403
www.authorhouse.com
Phone: 1-800-839-8640

First published by AuthorHouse 12/3/2008

ISBN: 978-1-4389-1208-0 (sc)

Library of Congress Control Number: 2008907837

Printed in the United States of America
Bloomington, Indiana

This book is printed on acid-free paper.

Acknowledgements

Writing about events that occurred so long ago, events whose reality exists only in the headlines of yellowed newspapers and the fading memories of octogenarians presented an interesting choice: wing it or dig for the truth!

Having lived on a farm for many years, I was quite comfortable with a shovel, so my choice was easy. I would dig for the truth.

Now, digging can be a lonely pursuit. Fortunately, I had the help of many wonderful people, and my thanks go out to Kenton County Library's reference assistant, Jan Mueller, to Boone County Library's own Laurie Wilcox and to the very senior citizens across Boone County whose memories I sought to stimulate.

And, of course, to my wife, Barbara, a psychologist, whose genius I sought when trying to understand the power of Joan's night terrors. Having worked with adolescent girls and their mothers for nearly 30 years, she had a perspective on Joan and her mother that was extremely useful to me. Her collaboration was crucial in exploring Joan's psyche, as well as her relationship with Jennie. Barbara's curiosity about the case resulted in many late night discussions. Her opinions about aspects of my approach to the book generated countless thought-provoking debates and invigorating conversations. Serving as my co-editor, confidante, typist, and critic she has been my greatest source of support and encouragement. Also, because Barbara has published eight books of her own, she was instrumental in guiding me through the publishing process.

Two conscripted editors, Shirlee Williams and Alissa Groth smoothed out the rough spots in the book, making its reading a much more civilized undertaking.

And last of all my thanks to Fred who would walk with me on a moment's notice when I became frazzled or had writer's block: a faithful dog can do wonders to restore man's confidence in himself.

The book, "Images of America—Burlington," written by Matthew E. Becher, Michael D Rouse, Robert Schrage and Laurie Wilcox, with its historic pictures of people, places and events and its enlightened sidebars regarding their contributions to the town, aided me enormously.

I was surprised at the reaction of many of the people whom I interviewed when I would ask if they remembered the murder trial of Joan Kiger. "I remember it as though it happened yesterday!" they would say. The women could remember what Joan wore each day of the trial: the dress, the shoes, as well as the accompanying purse! They would comment on how "sweet" she looked and how dignified she carried herself.

The men, on the other hand, observed another side of Joan: "She was as cute as could be," one gentleman said, with a twinkle in his eye, "but she was no little girl, no sir. Now I know that lawyer of hers kept calling her 'that little girl,' but, I'll tell you, she was as grown a woman as I've ever seen!" His brother then chimed in, "...and I wouldn't mind that 'little girl' turning down my sheets, any time!"

A Dream Within a Dream

Edgar Allen Poe

Take this kiss upon the brow!
And, in parting from you now,
Thus much let me avow-
You are not wrong, who deem
That my days have been a dream;
Yet if hope has flown away
In a night, or in a day,
In a vision, or in none,
Is it therefore the less gone?
All that we see or seem
Is but a dream within a dream.

I stand amid the roar
Of a surf-tormented shore,
And I hold within my hand
Grains of the golden sand-
How few! yet how they creep
Through my fingers to the deep,
While I weep- while I weep!
O God! can I not grasp
Them with a tighter clasp?
O God! can I not save
One from the pitiless wave?
Is all that we see or seem
But a dream within a dream

Prologue

In August, 1943, during the height of World War II, an event occurred in Boone County, Kentucky that put the war news on page two from August 17 until the 21st. The headlines throughout the nation focused on the murder of Carl Kiger, the Vice-Mayor of Covington, Kentucky and his six-year old son, Jerry, who were shot fifteen times.

Human nature is a strange beast: at the same time that thousands of American service men were dying in Europe and the Pacific, much of our nation was talking about only one thing, the murder of two people in a county of barely ten thousand.

This book is an attempt to explain the fascination with these killings, to review the murder trial of the sixteen year old daughter, Joan Kiger, and to suggest the parts which the Cleveland Syndicate and the Chicago Outfit may have played in these two murders.

In order to promote the various theories regarding the reasons for Carl's and Jerry's Kiger's murders as touched upon in the newspapers during the fall and winter of 1943 and the spring of 1944, it was occasionally necessary to create characters, events and plot lines leading toward conclusions which the author chose, based upon his research, interviews and his instincts; and although the timeline for the major events surrounding Joan Kiger's life is basically accurate, the author wishes to invoke his creative right to digress and, occasionally, to enter the realm of fiction; and as an active participant in this process, the reader is free to decide "which is real and which is the dream."

Chapter One
The Awakening
August 16-17, 1943

1

Joan awoke fitfully, breathing very hard. Her heart was pounding; her head was on fire. Gradually, and with some effort, she passed from her nightmare world to reality. Often, when she made this journey, she would not know where she was—but at least this time, she knew— she was in her own bed. As she looked around her room, the dream-state receded and the brightness of the overhead light hurt her eyes. Her breathing was fast and deep. She could not get enough oxygen. Each time she broke the nightmare's bond it was like this. Awakening would require fighting for air, struggling to reach the surface of some tormented lake—and through this subconscious battle, Joan had divined a way of escaping her dreams and returning to the real world as those dreams drifted toward experiences which she was incapable of maintaining. She learned that when she simply held her breath long enough, her survival instincts kicked in, forcing the nightmares to fade.

This time she found herself sitting bolt-upright in bed; and as she glanced down toward her hands, she was startled to see that she held a gun. The shock was so great that her right hand flexed, involuntarily, and the gun fired.

Her senses were overwhelmed. The sound of the .38 going off so close to her body caused excruciating pain in her ears and her head. She coughed violently—the inhaled gunpowder constricting her breathing.

The slug had pierced the screen in the open window to the left of her bed.

When she turned to see where it had exited, the warm night air washed over her, causing her sweat-soaked pajamas to stick to her heaving breasts. Glancing down toward the gun, lying in her lap, she noticed the blood stains on the sheets.

She jumped from the bed, thinking that, somehow, she had shot herself. Frantically, she opened the closet door revealing a full-length mirror. The bare wooden floor was reassuring to her feet, but she was shivering violently. Slowly removing her pajamas, she let them fall in a wet heap at her feet and carefully scoured her body to see if she were injured. Viewing her pale skin, auburn hair, full breasts and lithe body had, in the past year, brought her a growing sense of pleasure and she was beginning to feel an increased titillation in her nakedness—but not tonight—not when she was in the throes of one of her nightmares—nightmares which always coincided with her menstrual period, an advent which began three years ago when she was twelve. Relieved to find that she had no self-inflicted wound, she relaxed a little and found her robe.

Daddy's going to be upset when he sees that bullet hole in the window screen, she thought. Then, looking at her bed where the pistol lay, she said aloud, "And he's really going to have a fit about his gun!"

She recognized it as the one he always kept in his bedroom, under his pillow.

"What was I doing with Daddy's gun?" But she knew—or at least thought she did. "I must have been sleepwalking again."

After returning from the bathroom where she cleaned herself up and put on a fresh pad, she stood perfectly still in the hall way, listening intently for any sounds in the house. Maybe no one had heard the gunshot. Maybe she could sneak the gun back under her father's pillow. The old farm house, a former log cabin that had been enlarged and modified throughout the years, creaked and groaned, confessing its advancing age.

Going back to her room, she decided to change her sheets. She was embarrassed by her stained linens and always had extra sheets in preparation for these infrequent accidents – sometimes her period was early, sometimes it was late. Her mother had admonished her for not keeping better track of her cycles. Going to her closet, she pulled down a fresh set of linens, pillow case and all, changed the bed, quickly, but meticulously, covering it finally with a Chenille bedspread. Joan then threw the stained linen into the clothes hamper in the rear of the closet. She also picked out another set of pajamas, her blue ones, and put them on. Noticing the open window, she decided to shut it. Removing the iron bar (actually, a large silo wrench) which was used to prop the window open, she closed it gently and returned the bar to her dresser drawer. She sheepishly looked around to make sure no one was watching this nefarious activity. Joan was well aware of her father's penchant for closed and locked doors and windows, but some nights were so hot that she just had to break this house rule. Then, picking up the .38 from the night stand where she had placed it while changing the sheets, she flipped open its cylinder as she had seen her father do.

That's funny, she thought. There were five chambers with spent cartridges visible and only one live round left. Daddy must have been out practicing today before I got home. But he always reloads before he puts his gun away. He likes to say that an empty gun is no more than a big stick. Oh, well, she continued to muse, if I reload the one round that I fired, he'll never know that I've had his gun out. I'll sneak it back under his pillow, and he won't be mad at me. Joan's father was already really angry with her because she had spent the night in Newport, Kentucky with her friend, Mae, and failed to show up for his and her mother's 24th wedding anniversary.

Remembering his explosive temper, she reflected, I sure hope he doesn't find out about my shooting his gun. Joan tried to remove the empty casing she had fired, but her lush auburn hair kept falling over her eyes. Grabbing this shock of unmanageable mane with her left hand, she tried, with just her right, to reload. It was than that she noticed that the nail on the thumb of her right hand had been torn off and the thumb was oozing blood. "My gosh! How did that happen?" After bandaging her thumb, she remove the casing, but with some difficulty.

Now that she was aware of her injury, each step she took down the stairs toward the kitchen caused her thumb to throb. She began tiptoeing toward the wall cabinets where her father kept two extra guns and a box of .38 shells. Turning the kitchen light on, she headed for the top shelf of the cabinet to the right of the sink where she knew they would be, but her gaze was drawn to the kitchen table. Behind a bushel basket, containing a few red and yellow tomatoes, was a partial box of .38 shells. I wonder why Daddy would leave these out, she thought. He was always so careful to keep them away from her, but especially from her six year old brother, Jerry.

She was preparing to replace the one round in the pistol when she thought she heard her mother moan. The sound was one she had never experienced before. It frightened her. Joan grasped the pistol tightly in her right hand and headed for the stairway. Half way through the unlighted entranceway, her foot struck something. It caromed across the floor making a terrible racket. By the light coming from her upstairs room, she could see the object, dimly. She picked it up. Another pistol! While she stood holding both guns, she heard a sound—she couldn't tell what sound, but it was coming from her parents' bedroom.

Quietly she headed upstairs, a pistol in each hand. Leaning in the open door to her parents' bedroom, she stood, listening. Not a sound. She stuck her head inside. All was peaceful. Silently, she walked over to the bed. Her father was on his back, his face turned away from her, and her mom was facing her with one leg thrown over her dad's torso. Joan eased the .38 under her dad's pillow and, relieved, returned to her room.

Now that Joan's bedroom window was closed, the heat began to build up; she started to sweat—and she was confused. Wiping the sweat from her face, she paused. None of this made any sense. Maybe she was still dreaming. This kind of dream within a dream feigning reality she had experienced before. "How do you ever really know?" she asked herself, "How do you ever really, really know what's real and what's not?"

Thinking that she would just go back to bed, she started to turn off the ceiling light, when she caught sight of herself in the full length mirror. Her screams stung the eerie silence in the house. Her face and hands, as well as the remaining gun, which she held, were covered with blood. Panicking, she hurried to her parents' room, yelling, "Daddy, Daddy, help me!"

She went over to the bed. Neither her father nor her mother had moved. She shook her father gently. "Daddy, there's something wrong with me! I'm bleeding. Help me!"

Neither parent stirred. Joan turned the night stand light on and what she saw sent her running from the room, wild thoughts racing through her head. "My God! My God! He was right! He was right!" Her father was constantly worried about someone breaking in—someone killing him. It had finally happened. Her father was dead.

She ran, screaming, down the stairs and into the night.

Chapter Two
The Crime Scene
August 17, 1943

2

Jake Williams had been High Sheriff of Boone County, Kentucky for the past three years. The four years prior to that, he'd been Sheriff Frank Walton's deputy; so in his seven years in law enforcement, he'd seen almost everything that happens in the county. Today, August 16, 1943 had been a fairly normal day: a farmer who'd had one of his sheep killed, wanted Jake to look at the carcass to determine if it were attacked by an animal or if it was something else that had killed it. A neighbor, down East Bend Road, asked him to pick up a dog that had been hanging around her house, acting strange. An irate taxpayer who felt that his farm taxes shouldn't have gone up, especially since his smokehouse had burned down the previous summer, called to complain.

Nothing out of the ordinary, yet, by the end of the day, Jake was tired. He was fifty-two years old, and his early years as a sun-up-to-sun-set farmer had taken its toll, not to mention the hardships of his World War I experiences. By ten that evening he was asleep.

At about twelve-fifteen in the morning the phone rang – and rang. Jake did not respond. A short time later, someone was banging on his front door. Struggling to shake off the remaining bonds of sleep, he stumbled toward the sound, cursing in a raspy nocturnal voice. It was Lucille, the local telephone switchboard operator. When she could not rouse him by phone, she got in her car and drove to his house.

"Jake! Jake!" she shouted, pounding on his door. "Answer your phone. My God, there's been a shooting!"

"What?" Jake sleepily said, not comprehending that for Lucille to leave her post at the telephone exchange in Burlington was a major indication that something very extraordinary was happening.

When he opened the door, Lucille stood there sheet white. "There's been a shooting," she said again, breathlessly. "Out at Rosegate, the Kiger place, on Highway 25."

"Okay! Okay! Lucille, call Deputy Rouse. Tell him I'll pick him up in half an hour."

"Now Sheriff," Lucille said, still panting heavily, "I'm going to call you in a few minutes when I get back in touch with Mr. Mayo. He wants to talk to you before you go out there."

Jake's mind raced with the news. Shooting? Was someone killed? He quickly got dressed and picked up the phone on the third ring.

"Yup," he said into the receiver. "Mayo? What's going on out there? What? It's hard to hear you. Your neighbor's been shot?" While trying to strap his watch on, Jake grasped the two-piece phone between the fingers of his left hand..

"Uh huh, uh huh. I'll be right out there. Make sure no one touches anything."

*   *   *

Irvin Rouse was out in front of his house, waiting, when Jake arrived. Yawning, he asked, "What's going on, Jake?"

Deputy Rouse was an energetic forty-eight year old, about five foot ten, and 200 pounds. His years working for the State Highway Department had kept him in good shape; and in spite of too much inside work lately and a lot of driving around the county since becoming deputy, he still had a muscular upper body. Because of his missing right hand, he always wore a long sleeve shirt, the right sleeve neatly pinned over his stub. He had a way of turning his left hand upside down in order to shake hands with the voters, and he loved to shake hands, no doubt, in part, due to his intense desire to become the next sheriff in a little more than a year from now, when Jake's four year term expired.

"I didn't bring my gun, Jake. Do you think I'll need it?"

"Don't think so. From what Robert Mayo said, all the shootin's over. Seems that someone killed the Covington Vice-Mayor, Carl Kiger. Also shot his wife, but she's still alive. Sounded like a lot of voices in the background, so I couldn't catch everything he was saying. Sooner we get there, the more likely the evidence won't be disturbed too much." At least he hoped that was the case.

At one o'clock in the morning there was no traffic. Jake pushed the old Chevy for all it was worth. The trees and fence posts flew by, and within fifteen minutes, they were pulling up in front of Rosegate.

Jake noticed that there were already several cars parked haphazardly in the front yard, two with Kenton County plates. They walked past a crowd of strangers and were greeted at the front door by Robert Mayo, Sr. a Kenton County Constable.

"This is terrible. I've never seen anything like it! Sheriff, you've got to come upstairs with me. There's blood everywhere."

Deputy Rouse watched Jake and Mayo go upstairs. He was, at the same time, struck by the smell of the old house – and the heat. Looking around, he noticed that all of the windows were closed. It was a hot August night; yet everything was battened down as though it were the dead of winter. The house also smelled of sweat, stale sweat and of something else.

"Gunpowder," Irvin said aloud. "That's what I smell: foul air, stale sweat and gunpowder."

Looking around the first floor living room, he noticed an emaciated gray-haired lady partially hidden in the corner of the library by the bookcases. In the center of the room, two men in suits were looking at a pistol.

Just as he headed for them, to see if the gun was part of the crime scene, the front screen door opened and Louis Henderson, the Grant County Sheriff, entered the room. He and Irvin knew each other from other cases over the past few years.

The burley sheriff said, "What the hell is goin' on, Irvin? This better be good to get me out of bed in the middle of the night!"

Irvin gave Sheriff Henderson one of his up-side-down handshakes and adjusted himself before speaking: "Sheriff Williams is upstairs where the murder took place. What are you doing here?"

"Well, I got a call from Bob Mayo that there had been a shooting here at Rosegate. I knew the place, of course – one of the nicest farms on the highway. Tell me what you know, Irvin," he said, looking around the room and, at the same time, pulling out a crumpled and stained handkerchief to wipe the beads of sweat that were trickling down his face.

Irvin adjusted himself again.

"I just got here. When Jake comes downstairs, I guess we'll know more. We better look around and keep things as they are, don't you think?"

Rosegate had the floor plan of many of the older homes in Boone County: coming in the front door, the stairs were on the right, a spacious living room on the left, with a small foyer between the two. The back rooms consisted of a library with wall-to-wall bookshelves, a large modern kitchen with a breakfast area, a dining room that could entertain ten for dinner and, under the floor of the utility room, a cistern.

Irvin had been on his way over to the men who were examining a pistol, so he resumed that unfinished business. He introduced himself, as did they, showing him their identification and explaining that they were Covington detectives. The taller of the two handed Irvin a Smith and Wesson .38, indicating that Mr. Mayo had brought it from upstairs, having taken it from Mrs. Kiger. "Take a whiff of the barrel. It smells like it's been fired recently."

Irvin took the gun by the trigger guard, hoping that he was not disturbing any fingerprints that would help identify the shooter. As he accepted the weapon, he realized that these two so-called detectives had been handling this pistol with their bare hands. "Damn," he said out loud. What chance would there be of finding finger prints? He stuck the gun in his back pocket and headed toward the kitchen.

As he did, he passed a young bare-foot auburn-haired girl who'd just come from the second floor landing. The gentleman who accompanied her down the stairs guided her just to the other side of the hall door frame into the living room where she leaned against a wall that was dotted with family pictures.

"Wait here," her escort said. "Don't move."

Her head rested next to a family photo that depicted a little boy's birthday party. Irvin was struck by the fear and confusion he detected, not just from her face, but from her entire body. Wearing a velour robe over a two-piece blue pajama set with the top piece hanging outside the waistband, the girl covered her face with her hands.

Not knowing who she was or where she fit in this case, if at all, he eased past her into the kitchen. Fresh tomatoes were piled in one of the sides of the double sink. On the kitchen table was a bushel-basket with tomatoes in the bottom; behind the basket, on the edge of the table, was a box of .38 cartridges – half empty.

Definitely evidence, Irvin said to himself.

By the time Henderson sauntered back to the kitchen, Irvin was on his hand and knees by the table. "What you lookin' for, Irvin?"

"Anything that seems out of place," Deputy Rouse said, as he spotted some live ammunition on the floor beneath a kitchen chair. "Hmmm," he murmured

"Hey, Irvin, is this anything?" Henderson asked. He was pointing to the cistern lid which was not quite covering the opening.

Irvin walked over to it. "That's just the cistern," he said. "You ain't that much of a city boy. I know you've seen 'em. It's for the drinkin' water. Water comes off the roof, goes down into this underground tank."

"Of course I've seen them! I've got one behind my own house – most of us around here have a cistern. But we keep the lid closed tight. If you don't, snakes, moles, bugs and all kinds of crazy stuff can fall into your drinking water. Nobody would leave the lid half-way off."

"Well, pull the lid back, and take a look; but I'm tellin' you, it's just a cistern."

Henderson, using both hands, eased the lid back. It was actually a manhole cover that was used as a substitute for a cistern lid, the type often used in roads to cover sewers and, therefore, was very, very heavy.

"You got a flashlight, Irvin?"

"No," Irvin said. "Look around. There ought to be one somewhere. I'm going to check the windows to see how someone could break into this place."

Henderson rummaged through the kitchen drawers and cabinets and finally found one. Returning to the cistern, he shined the light toward the opening. As he dropped on his hands and knees, he noticed something reddish on the edge of the cover. A fingernail! "Well, hell. You never know," he said, aloud. "You never know what's important. Hey, Irvin, I just found a fingernail—looks like a woman's. It has red nail polish on it." Irvin yelled from another room, "Well, hang on to it—it may be important." Henderson placed it to the right of the lid and leaned into the opening of the cistern. Nothing but darkness peered up at him. He knew he had to get his head and much of his upper body into that cavity in order to be able to see bottom. As he squeezed further into the hole, his elbow caught on the fingernail and, without noticing, pulled it over the edge. It fell, unseen, and sank to the bottom.

Henderson was motionless now, waiting for his eyes to become accustomed to the darkness. There were only about three feet of water, so the light beam easily penetrated to the bottom. The floor of the cistern was almost black from the decaying leaves washed from the roof during recent rains. Sure needs a cleaning, he thought.

A couple mammoth water spiders were darting around, excited by the light. A tree frog was suctioned to the side of the wall, his eyes squinting, furtively.

"Oh, shit!" Henderson shouted. "Oh shit! There's a pistol down here!" 'down here, down here....' the echo from the cistern replied.

He pulled his head back through the opening so fast that he cracked it on the concrete, but he hardly felt the pain, he was so excited.

"Irvin," he shouted. "Come here! Come here!"

Irvin was in the library when he heard Henderson shouting. He hurried in.

"Irvin, I told you, you just don't leave your cistern lid off. There's a gun down there!" he said, pulling his worn and wet hanky out of his rear pants pocket.

Irvin took the flashlight in his left hand, braced his stub of a right arm on the floor and tried to peer into the cavity. His upper body was too massive to fit.

"You sure you saw a gun?" he asked.

"Damn straight I did," Henderson said, feeling insulted that Irvin doubted him.

"I'd better go tell Jake about this," Irvin said, walking toward the stairwell. "We probably need to call the fire department – get them out here to pump out the cistern. I'll see what Jake wants to do."

*   *   *

When Sheriff Williams reached the top step, he heard a woman crying and moaning at the same time. Strangest sound he ever heard coming from a human being. All the lights upstairs were on: the hall light, as well as the ceiling lights in all three bedrooms.

Walking into the Kiger bedroom, he saw two men huddled around the wailing woman in bed. She was half crying, half screaming while one of the men tried to apply pressure to a hip wound that was bleeding profusely. In between her moans, the words "Jerry—Jerry," were barely audible.

Having been raised on a farm and having participated in many hog killings, Jake was accustomed to the sight of blood, but not human blood – and not in such a bizarre setting.

Carl Kiger was lying on his back on the right side of the bed, his face turned toward the center of the bed, toward his wife, Jennie. It looked as though he had been shot multiple times: once or twice in the head, in the arm and in the chest. He was covered with blood, as was the bed on all sides. Jake put his finger on Carl's neck, sticky with blood, trying to feel a pulse. There was none.

Addressing the man who was attempting to bandage Jennie's right hip, Jake asked, "Has an ambulance been called?"

The man nodded in the affirmative. "We called immediately. It has to come all the way from Covington, so we're trying to do our best 'til it gets here."

As Jake glanced out the window, he saw that two other vehicles had pulled off the road in front of the house.

About that time Deputy Rouse entered the room. "God damn!" he exclaimed, shocked by what he saw. He put his left hand over his mouth, hoping he wouldn't embarrass himself. The waves of nausea grew as he looked over at the bed.

Jake took Irvin by the arm and walked him out of the room.

"Irvin, we've got to secure this crime scene as best we can. Check the other rooms on this floor. Let's see what we've got. I'm going downstairs to find out who all is here and try to keep them from messing with the evidence."

Irvin turned to the right and entered another bedroom. It was very orderly. The bed was made and covered by a pink flowered spread. The window to the right of the bed was closed. He still was puzzled as to why all the doors and windows were shut. The night was so hot. For the first time, he was aware of the wetness under his arms. Perspiration was beading down his back, as well. The inside of the house was like an oven. The closet door was ajar and when he opened it, he was startled to see himself in the full length mirror; it was obviously a woman's bedroom: dresses, skirts, blouses and scarves were hung in a neat row. Five pairs of shoes were lined up on the floor in the back of the closet. A laundry basket was on the left side, slid behind the hanging blouses.

Irvin looked again at the bed. It had obviously not been slept in. He made a mental note of that.

Walking into the hallway, he turned to his left and headed for the remaining room. The door was fully open. Irvin noticed that the ceiling light was on. The window in this room was closed, as well. Lying on the bed was a small child – five or six years old. Again, more blood, but this time mostly on the child, not so much on the bed, itself. The little boy had been shot in the head and in the chest. Irvin put his hand to his mouth again and looked away. Shutting his eyes, he took several long deep breaths. "Oh, my God. Who would do this to a child?" He stepped back and turned away from the grisly scene.

"C'mon Irvin, you're a police officer. You can do this. You can do this," he chanted, out loud.

He walked toward the bed continuing to talk to himself. When he felt more in control, he touched the boy's skin. It was slightly warm. There was still the distinct smell of gunpowder in the air. "This murder was pretty damn recent," Irvin said.

As he slowly circled the little boy's room, he carefully examined the walls, the ceiling, the floor, looking for – he didn't know just what. And then his eye caught the "just what" at the base of the bedpost: a small hole with a circle of gray surrounding it – a bullet hole. Reaching for his pocket knife, he opened it with his teeth and carefully dug out the slug. Not wanting to lose it, he stuck it in the watch pocket of his trousers.

He headed back downstairs to tell Jake about the little boy, and, passing the second bedroom, the one with the full length mirror, he noted that the door was now shut.

Turning the knob, he was surprised to find it locked. Puzzled, he mumbled to himself, "Did I lock that door? I don't think so." But he was so intent on telling Jake about this second murder that he did not, at that time, investigate what was going on behind the closed door.

Jake was in the corner of the living room talking to a gray haired lady and a younger gentleman. "Well, that's real neighborly that you'd come over here when you saw all the lights on; but, Mrs. Hitzel, you best go home now." About that time, Lucille Carpenter, another elderly neighbor interrupted. "Now Sheriff, if you want us to testify, we will. Oh, is it okay if we tell our friends about what went on tonight?"

"Now y'all just go home, and the less that you say, the better it will be." Jake sounded a little tense – and he was. Too many people. Too damn many people, he thought.

"Okay, Sheriff, we'll go," Mrs. Hitzel said, looking intently at the staircase. "Oh, by the way, maybe I should give this to you." She pulled a shell casing out of her pocket.

"Where did you find this?" Jake asked, his exasperation showing.

"It was on the floor in the kitchen," she said, coyly.

About that time another car pulled up.

"Irvin," Jake yelled, "Whoever that is, keep 'em out!"

"Where is Joan?" Jake asked of Al Schild, the police chief of Covington, who had been talking with her earlier.

"Oh, she's upstairs in her bedroom with Jack Maynard."

"Isn't he Covington's City Manager!" Jake yelled. "When the hell did he come in? And what's he doing with Joan?"

Earl Christophel, one of the Covington detectives, came over to Jake, holding out his hand.

"What's this?" Jake asked.

"Lt. Tiepel of the Covington Bureau of Investigation gave me these slugs. Said he found them in their beds while taking pictures of the bodies."

"Bodies? There are other bodies?" Jake asked, his eyes widening.

"Yes, little Jerry, their son, was also shot and killed. Tiepel is upstairs taking photographs."

"Taking photographs!" Jake bellowed. "I'm in charge of this investigation. This is my case. This is my county! Who told him to take any pictures?" Jake was incredulous that this was happening under his watch.

Climbing the stairs two at time, he shouted, "Irvin, clear this house of everyone! You hear me? Everyone! I won't have Kenton County's police overrunning Boone County's crime scene—they've messed with me one time too many." Jake continued to rant as he headed toward the flashes of the camera.

Irvin looked around at the group in the living room who were now glaring back at him. He wished he'd brought his gun – or at least his badge. Taking a deep breath and standing as tall as he could, he turned to the on-lookers and said in his most sheriff-like tone, "Okay, everybody. Out! You heard the Sheriff."

No one moved. They all stared at him as though he had no credibility whatsoever.

Irvin was angry. With his heart pounding, he shouted, while waving his stump toward the front door, "Go on, now. This is Boone County jurisdiction. We're just trying to preserve the crime scene. Everybody out!" Swelling his chest, he started moving people out the door.

Louis Henderson, the Grant County Sheriff, supported him, "Okay, everyone, the deputy is right. This is Boone County's case. Let's go."

That seemed to do it. As Schild walked over to Irvin, handing him some additional slugs; another detective handed Irvin some shell casings. Lt. Huff, of the State Police, counted out the $1440.00 found under the library couch, as well as the Kiger will, and put them all on the coffee table.

One by one they left the house – but they did not really leave. They stood around in the front yard, smoking and talking quietly.

Jake gasped as he walked into Jerry's room – the boy was so small, lying lifeless like a crumpled and bloodied rag doll. All he could think of was his daughter, Osceola, when she was that age—so innocent and so full of life. Anger rose within him and stopped at his throat, causing him to feel breathless.

"Irvin," he tried to shout, but the word spilled over his lips in a whisper. He swallowed hard and took several deep breaths.

"Irvin," his voice boomed.

Running up the stairs, Irvin rounded the corner and collided with Jake. "Why didn't you tell me about this?" Jake demanded. "I told you to check the other rooms. Did you?"

"Of course I did." Irvin was distraught that Jake thought he hadn't followed his orders. "I was just coming over to tell you when you yelled for me to throw everyone out of here," Irvin declared, while wiping sweat from his face.

Knowing that this deputy was the most loyal and hard working individual he had ever encountered, Jake took a step back and said in a conciliatory tone, "All right. Good job. Make sure everyone is out of the house."

Irvin felt relieved. As he started down the stairs, the front door swung open and several people walked in.

"Stop!" Irvin shouted, as he blocked the entrance way with his body. A slight gentleman dressed in a black suit, carrying what looked like a medical bag was trying to push past him. Just behind him was a visibly distressed couple who appeared to be in their fifties. The woman was shouting, "My God. Let me through. Let me through! Jennie! Jennie!!" Her body shook with each sob. "Fred...Fred," she looked to the man at her side, pleadingly.

"Eva," the man said, as he stepped in front of her and the other gentleman, "Eva, calm down. Let me handle this."

"Look, I'm Fred Williamson and this is my wife, Eva. We're family. Eva is Jennie's sister. And this is Doc Ertel, the family doctor. For God's sake, please, let us through."

Irvin didn't know what to do, at first. The scene was getting out of control, as Fred pushed past him, holding onto Eva's hand and yelling at Dr. Ertel to see what was going on.

Hearing Irvin shout, "Stop! Stop right there! Only the doc can come in," Jake was startled to see that the commotion at the front door was become increasingly chaotic. He briskly walked over and said, "Hold on, here. I'm the Sheriff. Doc, go on upstairs. Who are you?" he asked, glaring at Fred.

Eva Williamson began to scream at him, as she grabbed his arm, "I'm Jennie's sister! Where is she? Where is Joan? Jerry? Carl? Please tell me what's happening!"

Fred once again took Eva by the shoulders and tried to soothe her. "Eva, you have to calm down. This is getting us nowhere. So, please, stop. Just stop. Let me talk to the Sheriff. Can my wife please sit down over there?"

Jake had never seen such fear in a human face before. "Of course, of course." He stepped aside while Fred led Eva to the sofa, but he followed them closely.

As Eva sat there, she glanced around the room. Her tears had reached her lips where she was startled by their saltiness. My God, she thought. We were all in this room just forty-eight hours ago – laughing, reminiscing and celebrating. She shook her head, as though she could somehow turn the clock back. Carl was particularly excited as he talked about his future in politics, about becoming Mayor. Jennie was stunning in her silk azure dress, the color of which intensified her blue eyes. With her dark, wavy hair pulled back and held in place with a rhinestone clip, she looked much younger than her forty-eight years.

Eva's thoughts rippled back to when they were little girls. Being the oldest, Jennie would sometimes yell at her younger sister because she was such a pest; but most of the time, she was protective of her, partly because Eva was incredibly shy. Their mother frequently had to admonish Jennie and tell her to stop speaking for Eva. These reprimands yielded no compliance. Since the two of them felt like twins in spite of the difference in their ages (not in the sense of any physicality but more in spirit), Jennie could feel the self-consciousness that enveloped Eva. This expectation and need for Jennie to speak for Eva continued into adulthood.

Almost everybody—teachers, family and friends considered Jennie to be a particularly loving youngster – she was patient and kind, eager to please. The counterpart to Eva's shyness was her fiery temper often triggered by her impetuosity. Their mother often told them that they needed to make trade-offs with one another – Eva needed some of Jennie's patience and Jennie needed some of Eva's verve.

Eva absently looked up and noticed that Fred was leaning against the piano, talking to the Sheriff.

"So you're Jennie's brother-in-law?"

Fred nodded. The Sheriff told Fred the events of the night. Wanting to make sure Eva couldn't hear, he whispered that both Carl and Jerry were dead and that Jennie was seriously wounded. Fred felt a wave of nausea rip through his stomach.

"What about Joan?" he asked, not really wanting to hear the answer.

Joan, the Sheriff thought, as he looked up the stairs, wondering why Maynard had sequestered the two of them in her bedroom. Once he finished with the family, he was going to find out.

"The girl's fine but shaken up. Since she's the only one in the house who wasn't shot, we have a lot of questions for her; but she's not hurt in any way."

Fred was relieved, but for only a moment, as the nausea returned with its original ferocity.

The Sheriff assured him that they would do everything they could to find out who had committed this heinous crime, and that the person or persons responsible would be brought to justice. Jake didn't want to indicate that he already had suspicions as to who the perpetrator was. One shock at a time, he thought to himself, as he glanced over at Eva who was sitting on the edge of the couch, her eyes darting around the room.

Fred thanked Jake and walked over to his wife, experiencing a trepidation he had never felt before in his life. Jennie and Eva were more than just sisters, and Carl was so much more than a brother-in-law. Their four lives intertwined in the most intimate of ways: births, birthdays, holidays, anniversaries, the simple day-to-day routines. They were a tight- knit group. Carl had shared with him some of his dealings as the Vice Mayor which, up until now, had not worried Fred. Politics was politics. But tonight, as the horrors of Rosegate unfolded, all that he had been told began to suggest a more sinister reason for Carl's murder.

Fred approached Eva, ever protective of his fragile soul-mate; she pleadingly looked into his eyes. Kneeling down, he took both of her hands in his and revealed that Joan was unhurt and that both Carl and Jerry were dead and, without taking a breath, told her that Jennie was wounded but alive. She buried her head in the four hands that were lying on her lap. Fred comforted her, fighting back his own tears – tears that surprised him, not because of the feelings he was having but because he couldn't remember a time in his adult life when he had ever cried. He was a man who took pride in his ability to remain in control and rational, no matter what the situation.

In between sobs, Eva demanded to know what had happened. Fred told her what he knew and said they would just have to wait and see how this would all unfold.

Just then the ambulance arrived. The Sheriff pointed the medical team in the direction of the stairs, yelling "First bedroom on the right. She's been shot in the hip."

Rushing up the stairs with a stretcher, the ambulance driver and his partner simultaneously shouted to their co-worker who was just behind them to go back to the vehicle and get some more dressings.

Bolting from the couch, Eva ran to follow them up the stairs. Fred grabbed her arm and pulled her back. "Eva, don't interfere. They need to get her out of here as quick as they can and to the hospital." He was surprised to find himself shouting at her and grasping her arm so tightly that she winced.

Eva stopped, and a wave of sobs overtook her.

After some minutes, Jennie, tied on the stretcher, was carried down the stairs and out the door before anyone could even catch a glimpse of her face.

The surreal sound of the siren faded into the night; Fred walked Eva back to the sofa and gently sat her down.

Suddenly her demeanor changed. "Where's Joan?" she asked, looking around the room; she pushed Fred away and got up from the couch. "I want to see Joan."

Fred searched the living room with his eyes and eventually saw the Sheriff standing at the bottom of the stairs with the one-armed fellow who had been blocking the door when they first arrived. They were in an intense discussion.

"I ain't gonna search no girl!" Irvin said, shaking his head vehemently. "No siree."

"Irvin, someone has to search Joan. I've got to talk to Maynard and find out what he was doin' upstairs with her."

"Hell no!" Irvin said in a loud whisper. "I ain't gonna do that."

Fred was surprised at what he heard. He politely interrupted Jake and Irvin, apologizing for eaves dropping, and asked why they intended to search Joan.

Jake was caught off-guard and annoyed that Fred had overheard their conversation. But when he looked at him and saw that he was quite worried, his irritation waned. As he patted him on the shoulder, he assured Fred that it was just the usual procedure in a situation like this.

Fred was a man who had a knack for recognizing opportunities that he could shape to his advantage.

Knowing that Eva wanted desperately to see Joan, he said, "You know, if you need to search Joan, my wife can do it. That way no one is embarrassed."

Irvin grinned and immediately agreed, "That's a great idea!" He felt relieved that he wasn't going to be responsible for that part of the investigation.

Jake wasn't so sure it was the right choice and hesitated; but as he looked around the room and mentally reviewed who might still be in the front yard, there was no woman there, other than the nosy neighbor ladies; he would never ask them.

"Well," he said, with some reservation, "All right. After all, I don't want anyone to feel embarrassed." And as he said that, he gave Irvin a disparaging look.

Thanking the Sheriff, Fred walked toward Eva, reaching for her arm. He told her that Joan needed to be searched, explaining that this was only routine, in a situation like this. "The Sheriff will tell you what he wants done," Fred said, trying to smile.

Eva had a difficult time processing what she had just heard. "Search Joan?" she asked. "What in God's name for? Why aren't they looking for the killer instead of wanting to search a fifteen year old girl who had just lost her father and brother and whose mother had been seriously wounded?" She began to feel the heat of anger in her belly.

Fred stepped closer to her and re-assured her that this was just what had to be done—that it was the only way she would be able to see Joan at all. Eva's anger softened as she thought of poor Joan who must be absolutely terrified and grief stricken.

"Well, if that's the only way, then, of course, I'll do it." She looked past Fred, trying to locate the source of the sobbing that she heard coming from the library. When she saw Joan step into the living room, something within her died and withered. As she rushed toward her niece and they embraced, Eva knew a piece of her self was forever lost. This wonderful family she had so long ago come to love as her own was now fragmented; and although she had no reason, at this point in the evening, to foresee the degree of self-denigration, melancholy and suspicion that they would all live under for the rest of their lives, she instinctively was aware that the future would hold no happiness for any of them –ever again.

Chapter Three
The Cleveland Syndicate
1920-1943

3

Beverly Hills Country club was opened in 1937 in Newport, Kentucky, as an illegal gambling house which gradually morphed by the 1950's into a high rolling Las Vegas style dinner club and gambling casino, attracting big name entertainers such as Jerry Lewis, Phyllis Diller, The Righteous Brothers, Liberace, The Everly Brothers, Steve Lawrence and Eydie Gorme, Ray Charles and John Davidson. In fact, John Davidson was to perform the night of May 28, 1977, when a fire engulfed the club killing 165 people.

Beverly Hills traced its roots back to the bootleg and gambling syndicates of the twenties and thirties. Pete Schmidt, who early in his career drove for George Remus, a Cincinnati bootlegger, opened the Beverly Hills club on the site of a former speak easy called the Kaintuck Castle in Southgate, near Newport, Kentucky. Schmidt's club did very well, but in the gambling world that could be good news or bad news. Moe Dalitz visited the club, liked what he saw and decided it would be a profitable acquisition for the Cleveland, Ohio Syndicate. Dalitz made an offer in 1935 but was rebuffed by Schmidt. The Cleveland Syndicate did not take this rebuff kindly, and the next year the casino was destroyed by fire.

Undeterred, in 1938 Schmidt rebuilt the club and called it the Beverly Hills Country Club. Unfortunately Moe Dalitz was not deterred either. He continued to pressure Pete Schmidt until Pete was finally beaten down emotionally. He sold out to the Cleveland Syndicate in 1940.

Pete still had his gambling house in Newport, called the Glenn Hotel; he modernized it and changed its name to the Glenn Schmidt Rendezvous. The Cleveland Syndicate continued to run Beverly Hills and other clubs in Covington and Newport, Kentucky and to influence politicians through money and threats.

Although Moe Dalitz left his mark on Northern Kentucky, his businesses were spread out from Cleveland to Florida to Las Vegas. It is said that at the top of his game he was worth well over one hundred million dollars. In spite of his wealth, however, and unlike the people who worked for him, his mode of transportation was a well worn VW; and this car of choice, he drove himself.

Moe witnessed it all. Born in 1899 he saw and influenced the major part of the twentieth century, dying in 1989. By 1943, he dominated the gambling world well beyond Kentucky; and being the savvy business man that he was, he preened the brightest and most ambitious young men he could find to run his far flung empire. If they were loyal and if they made money for him and the Cleveland Syndicate, they often became millionaires themselves.

Cleveland's crime families came under Dalitz' influence in 1931 when a Cleveland mafia boss, Frank Milano, joined the national crime syndicate, a group controlled by Moe Dalitz, along with Charles Luciano, Myer Lasky and Tony Accardo. This group also allied itself with the Genovese family.

All of these leaders were shrewd business men with a penchant for solving problems with either a car bomb or a gun. They rewarded success magnanimously, and they saw that those who were responsible for failures did not have an opportunity to fail again.

The stock market gurus are always expounding on risk: the greater the risk the greater the reward. This philosophy was also true for anyone working for the Cleveland Syndicate.

Chapter Four
The Messenger
(August 16, 1943)

4

Nick LaSita had driven down from Cleveland – driven all night, arriving in Covington in time to stop at the York Hotel for breakfast. He grew up here, attended Holmes High School but dropped out during the Depression. "A man has to live," was his motto. Translating this for Nick would be, "Accept any assignment and do it well." And that's how Nick became the Messenger.

In those times, as it is even today, the telephone could be a dangerous place to conduct certain kinds of business. Nick provided the privacy and the assurance that a message was not only delivered but properly understood. He carried with him to Covington a job description and a list of names, mostly in his head. "Little in writing; nothing over the phone" had kept his boss's business off the radar. And it was the Syndicate's operating principle that each human cog in the wheels of this ever expanding machine had information given to him strictly on a need to know basis. Only the Committee had all the pieces of the puzzle. And Nick was okay with that. "If you know too much, you think too much. You hesitate." Hesitation, in his profession, could get one in trouble.

So he drove here to Covington to deliver a message. He didn't know too much, but he did know that the Cleveland bosses were worried about their little moneymakers in Newport and Covington. The war had brought prosperity to the Cincinnati-Newport-Covington triangle. Money was in the hands of everyone, and the population was willing to spend it as though they had no memory of the lean times of the 1930's.

The Cleveland Syndicate had gained a toehold first in Newport, before the war, and now had expanded its services into Covington. In fact one third of the total number of slot machines in the state of Kentucky was in these two cities – a total of over 4000 slots nicknamed, in earlier times, the one armed bandits.

The Syndicate provided the slots to such local establishments as Beverly Hills, Glen Rendezvous, York Café, the Merchant's Club and others; and the take on these machines was doubling every year. The owners complained because they were only allowed to keep half the proceeds; but, after all, as the Syndicate explained, a payroll had to be met and this Cleveland organization was responsible for providing hush money or, as some locales would call it, "look the other way" money.

Charles Lester, Jr., a Newport attorney, was pushing Newport's mayor J.M. Morlidge to spearhead a move to tax the slot machine business. His argument was that the federal government taxed the owners of slots, so why shouldn't the city of Newport also levy a tax?

Mayor Morlidge was digging in his heels. Although it was true that the operation of slot machines broke no federal laws, it was also true that in the state of Kentucky these business activities constituted a felony.

Lester would have none of that argument. He threatened to place the proposed tax on the ballot for the fall elections if the mayor did not cooperate. He also knew that the Covington commissioners had been discussing a similar tax. The competition between these two cities for the gambling revenues was intense. There were spies in both camps, each trying to stay one step ahead of the other.

The voters of both cities, encouraged by the owners of businesses which provided what they fondly called their "coin operated amusement devices," could more than likely be convinced that this extra revenue would be beneficial to their schools, roads and community projects.

The owners themselves had grander plans. They knew that if slots were taxed by their governing bodies and the revenues from these taxes became a necessary part of running a progressive city, no one would ever try to shut down their operations. Also, these local taxes would lend an air of legitimacy to the slots; and since local businesses would no longer have to depend upon the syndicate to provide "look the other way" money to the appropriate people, they would not have to accept syndicate slots. Places like Beverly Hills could buy their own slots, pay their tax and keep all the profits – no more fifty per cent for Cleveland.

The thinking of Charles Lester, Jr. was that the city would place a $250.00 per year tax on each slot machine in Newport. He calculated that the estimated 3000 slot machines would generate annual revenue of $750,000.00 for Newport. Now who could object to that?

The simple answer, of course, is no one. But objections there were; and Nick's reason for his all night drive to Covington was to see that every city official was aware of these objections and was aware, too, of the appropriate actions which should be taken regarding attorney Lester's attempt to make the city tax on slots legal.

After checking in to Covington's York Hotel, Nick made a phone call to the local provider, Justin Jenkins, suggesting that they have dinner that evening at The Mounds. He then had breakfast, showered and, before going to bed, brushed his grey fedora gently and placed it, with care, on the dresser. His most prized piece of male accouterment always received this special treatment.

Although Justin was not Italian and was not a gambler, he had one strong suit which the syndicate appreciated: he could be trusted with family business. Born in Harlan, Kentucky thirty years ago, he was, by the age of 14 working for his dad as a carpenter, building barns, houses and sheds, a skill he was becoming quite good at. His tall angular frame was made for work; his disposition, however, was not; and as the depression deepened, he left the family's floundering business to find work in Cleveland.

He did not bring his resume to Cleveland; and even if he knew what the word meant and had actually constructed one, he would not, in all likelihood, have included the one thing which made him employable in certain parts of this huge city: he always carried a pistol, and no one but no one could use it better.

Cleveland was not kind to Justin. With $23.00 in his pocket, he arrived with a great feeling of optimism about his new home. But after three weeks of competing with the thousands of other newcomers to the city, all looking for the same job – anything that would alleviate the hunger pangs and promise a brighter tomorrow, he took matters into his own hands or, more aptly phrased, into his gun hand.

He held up a grocery on Mayfield road. Well, actually, he didn't hold up a grocery but he tried. Pointing his gun at the clerk, he yelled at him to hand over his money. The old man had his hands up and was saying something in a language Justin did not understand; the last thing he remembered was reaching into the man's apron pocket which he used as a change purse. At that point, his head exploded.

*   *   *

Raw and primeval in appearance and furtive in demeanor, Justin, unlike Nick, would subconsciously draw attention to himself when he entered a room; and the people would react as would a herd of deer when they saw a wolf. They were afraid to look at him but were more afraid not to. Justin was accustomed to this response and came to revel in the feeling of power and energy he experienced each time he sensed the crowd's reaction. He did not try to mitigate it; he could not, because his *were* the eyes of the wolf, of the hunter stalking his prey. And his comfort zone was the wolf's stalking distance

On the other hand, bring Justin up close and personal with one individual, and his manner changed. He would become uncomfortable and self-conscious. Unable to make direct eye contact, he would sweat profusely. What pained him the most was when his victim would stare at him. Justin hated that. It was as though, by looking directly into another person's eyes, he would reveal his very soul; and just as Dorian Grey's vulnerability was in his attic, Justin's was in his eyes.

Nick was Italian, through and through, but not robust or menacing. He was a scrawny, five feet five inches 135 pounder, including the snub nosed .32 he carried; but he had a smile and a handshake and way of saying "I like you" without saying a word. He was also very discerning. He could pick up on body language easily and adjust his approach to an individual based upon what he perceived, without missing a beat.

In Justin's case only a moron could not see that he was repelled by eye contact. Nick could talk with Justin for an hour while staring into his coffee; and he was perfectly happy, also, letting Justin direct the conversation.

Justin had never met anyone like Nick, and he was drawn to him increasingly as they would meet to discuss business. This friendship grew as Justin became an integral part of the Syndicate's enforcement staff. As with many businesses, each staff member was responsible for an assigned territory: Justin's was Kentucky and each of its contiguous border states; and this was an ideal set up because it allowed him to maintain contact with his parents, his brothers and sisters, as well as his extended family. There is no more miserable a person than a Kentuckian denied the rejuvenating experience of frequent contact with his family. In addition, his parents were quite old and not in good health – his father's teenage years in the coal mines had come back to remind him of the life-threatening dangers of that occupation.

When Justin got the call from Nick to meet him at The Mounds for dinner, he was pleased that he would be seeing his old friend again. Justin flagged a taxi and, within a few minutes, arrived at the restaurant. Checking his watch, he was satisfied he would be on time to the minute. This punctuality fetish would probably drive a wife crazy, but Justin had no wife, no girlfriend. Yet, he felt complete. He had family and he had a well-paying and respected job. Respected, of course, depends on one's point of view. But if one limited that point of view to those in the Syndicate, Justin was respected. He had never failed them. His services were always timely, efficient and impossible to trace.

The August evening was hot and muggy, and the sports coat Justin was wearing was already becoming uncomfortable. Adjusting his shoulder holster, he headed for the front door of the Mounds; and as if on cue, when he entered the main dining room, patrons noticed him and the turbulence of talking and laughter gradually subsided. Nick, who was sitting at a corner table, a curtain separating him from the central part of the restaurant, stood up and waved Justin over. He had not seen his friend enter the room but, by the change of the sound level, he knew he had arrived. Justin smiled and briskly came toward Nick, holding out his hand. Nick took it warmly, fixing his gaze on the handshake, not making eye contact.

They were genuinely happy to be in each other's company. After the usual greetings between friends, Nick ordered a Brock beer and a Courvoisier from the waiter who was scurrying past their table. Justin's intense gaze caught his attention and stopped him short in his tracks.

"Bring us some of those peanuts you have at the bar." The server, who was more interested in his tips than he was his customers, sensed that this guy wasn't someone you screwed around with. He said with a smile, "Yes, sir."

Eager to get business over with so he could relax and enjoy his dinner, Justin asked Nick what the job was.

Short, sweet and to the point, he only wanted the barest of details.

This "let's get down to business" attitude of Justin's was an area Nick always had trouble with. It wasn't a big issue; but unlike Justin, Nick wanted to relax, talk, drink and enjoy dinner and then, over a Cuban cigar and Courvoisier, he would be in the mood to talk business. He always felt better on a full stomach.

But Justin was Justin and there was no changing that.

"Interesting deal," he said to Justin, and reaching in his coat pocket for his note pad, he gave it a cursory look. It contained only five letters, one below the other. This was his cheat sheet.

"I've got five names for you. The boss doesn't care which one you choose. You can write them down or memorize them."

Justin did not reach for a pen and Nick knew he wouldn't because, unlike Nick, who had to carry some form of pneumonic to nudge his memory, Justin had what Nick called a "phonographic memory" – If he heard it, he remembered it.

Pulling a thick envelope from his coat pocket, Nick placed it on the table, next to Justin's napkin. Justin nodded. No words needed to be spoken – he took the envelope and placed it in the breast pocket of his blazer.

Justin did not count the money. There would be time for that when he was away from the crowd; and he knew, from past arrangements, the envelope would contain $500.00 – a half year's salary for folks back in Harlan. Justin was the oldest of ten and the first to strike out on his own, from his insular, safe and very poor home; and as was usually the case for mountain families, when the eldest found employment, part of the paycheck was always sent back home. When Justin returned to Harlan, after every job, he would always give his daddy $50.00 to help with the bills. His folks, of course, were not aware of what he did for a living; and although Justin would like to give more to help out, he did not want them to become suspicious; he figured $50.00 was about right.

As Nick swished his brandy several times, he inhaled its fumes and then, as if he were having a religious experience, rolled his eyes back into his head as he sipped the golden liquid from the crystal snifter. Justin knew better than to interrupt Nick with any conversation while he was imbibing his brandy.

As he finished, Nick uttered a sensuous "Ahhhh," and said, with great emotion, "That's almost as good as an orgasm."

As much as Justin liked his booze, he could never get his mind around that comparison, thinking Nick needed to meet some of the Harlan whores he knew.

With his cigar protruding from the corner of his mouth, Nick resumed their business conversation and instructed Justin to call him from a pay phone and wish him a Happy Birthday – that way he'd know the job was done.

Justin nodded.

Business was over.

*   *   *

What began as the usual dinner repartee, gradually morphed into personal experiences never previously shared. As they chatted about the War, Nick could feel the effects of the brandy warm his entire body. During a lull in the conversation, his mind drifted back a few weeks to his last job for the boss, a particularly messy one which called into play Nick's religious beliefs and resurrected some self-doubt as to the kind of work he had drifted into. This reflection led the conversation into deeper waters.

"You know, what we do for a living sure isn't for everybody. And it's not something you plan to do when you grow up or to keep on doing as you grow older. I don't know about you, Justin, but I'm kind of tired of it all." He knew his zeal was waning – after this last job, he felt particularly depleted. It no longer gave him a major adrenalin pump.

Justin was not surprised or perplexed by Nick's question. Lately he, too, had wondered after almost every job how much longer he could continue making hits. In the last year, every time he killed someone, he would feel that he, himself, had been diminished. He intuitively knew that this was not what most of his counterparts experienced.

Nick ordered another Courvoisier for himself and one for Justin. Ignoring Justin's protestations, he waved the waiter on and told Justin that if he didn't like it, it wouldn't go to waste.

As he popped some peanuts into his mouth, Justin looked intently at Nick and realized that the two of them had never really talked much about their line of work. They both knew that they were but two members of a vast secret society; and initially, each had felt a degree of pride in being part of such a select group; however, as of late, this gratification had come to be more of a burden than a satisfaction.

"You a religious man, Nick?" Justin queried.

"Hell, how could anybody do what we have to do without being religious?" Nick's hand automatically caressed the small worn gold crucifix that hung around his neck day and night. His grandmother had placed it there at his First Holy Communion, and he never removed it.

"Sure, I consider myself a practicing Catholic. I go to Mass every Sunday and to Confession after almost every job."

Ever since he was a little boy, Justin had a curiosity about the Catholic religion. It had often been discussed in his own church but in very disparaging terms. He had never ever known a Catholic in his life, let alone talked to one about any of their clandestine rituals. Deep inside, he felt a surge of excitement as he looked at Nick. A real Catholic, he mused.

The waiter, trying to move the meal along so he could prepare the table for its next group of diners, hovered over the two, refilling their coffee, asking if they'd like dessert and, in general, making it obvious that their time was running out on this table.

Justin suddenly stood up, grasped the man by the elbow and whispered with clenched teeth so close to his ear, the server could feel his spittle spray his eardrum, "I don't want to see you again until I lift my right hand and summon you with my index finger." He demonstrated what this cue was going to look like. "Do you understand?"

In his preoccupation with his other tables, the server had completely forgotten his first impression of this man. Gazing into his eyes, he was jolted into a level of fear that reverberated all the way to his bowels. They did not see him again for the rest of the evening.

Nick was relieved that Justin got rid of that schnook. As soon as he thought of this word, he laughed out loud. One of the boss's right hand men, Manny, a Jewish guy, taught it to him on one of their jobs. Justin didn't seem interested in that story but pressed Nick more about his Catholicism, especially about confession.

Never having had anyone interested in his religion, Nick was enjoying Justin's inquisitiveness. Nick explained that confession was a sacrament that people used in order to get back into God's good grace—it was a way to be forgiven.

"So you go in this box…." Seeing Justin's eyes widen, he clarified. "I mean it's not like a coffin for God's sake, but it *is* a box. There's this center door that the priest sits behind. On either side of his door are two other doors," taking a pen from his inside coat pocket and yanking the cocktail napkin upon which his Courvoisier rested, Nick drew, in his best three dimensional fashion, what he was trying to describe. "See here. That's where the sinners go, one on each side. So, let's say I go into one of the side doors. It's dark in there. Sometimes, if I strain, I can hear the mumbling of the other sinner spilling his guts. I kneel down and wait until the priest slides open a....well, it's like a little screen that rests between his face and mine. That's my cue to start rattling off my sins."

Justin was totally intrigued with this description. As he began to take a sip of his brandy, Nick immediately held up his hand and corrected his faux pas.

"Swish, Justin, swish. Then sniff, sniff deeply. Then take a sip."

Justin did as he was told but found the brandy, no matter what the initial ritual was, to be most unappealing to his palate. He was a Brock beer man, but so as not to offend Nick, he followed his directives, smiled and nodded his head. Nick was pleased.

"So where was I? Oh yeah, I forgot to tell you that it's so closed in this confessional that sometimes I can smell the booze on the priest's breath! Father Paul was the boozer. Father Bill....now he would stink up that box with garlic so bad, I would gag. And I'm a Dago!" Nick emitted a belly laugh, one that brought tears to his eyes.

"So then what? What does the priest do? Just sit there and smell?" They both laughed, heartily.

"Well, see, the priest is like a stand in for Jesus. He hears your sins and then he—he's kind of like a judge, too. He sentences you."

Once again Justin's facial expression moved Nick to be more precise.

"Well, not like you go to jail. It's really called penance. But he might tell you to say a rosary for a month or to say three Our Fathers or three Hail Marys. I think the toughest penance I ever got was when I confessed that I blew away the Lombardo brothers. Father Paul told me in no uncertain terms to get down on my knees every night for an hour and say the rosary out loud. He wanted me to do that for one whole year! Of course, he also wanted me to make a big contribution to the Sunday basket. Anyway, before you leave the confessional, you're supposed to say an Act of Contrition."

"Shit, what's that?" Justin asked, with a slight slur to his words.

This inquiry took Nick back to Sister Philomena who pounded this prayer, along with the Hail Mary and Our Father, into the heads of all the little sinners of St. Robert's second grade class. He smiled.

Glancing around the room to make sure no one was eavesdropping on this most personal revelation; and with some embarrassment, Nick recited in a sing song fashion much as he did when he was seven: "'Oh my God, I am heartily sorry for having offended Thee, and I detest all my sins, because I dread the loss of heaven, and the pains of hell; but most of all because they offend Thee, my God, Who art all good and deserving...' Ah, ah, wait a minute....'and deserving of all my love.'" Nick smiled as he was able to joggle his memory for the final words.

"'I firmly resolve, with the help of Thy grace, to confess my sins, to do penance and to amend my life. Amen.' And when you're done with that, you walk out and sin no more!" Nick laughed as a way to return to his more macho nature.

Justin was beginning to feel the effects of the brandy; and although he didn't like the taste, he was certainly enjoying its aftermath. "I've never heard about that before," he said, with some excitement. "So, as long as you go to confession after every job and say this contrition thing, then it's okay to keep doing what you do."

"No, Justin, that has nothing to do with it. Don't you get it? It's about forgiveness."

Frankly, Justin didn't get the whole picture, but he was young enough and still had an open mind to new ideas. Following a few minutes silence, he said, "You know, Catholics aren't that much different from us Holy Rollers. *You* have to go to confession after every job, and I have to return to Harlan."

"Holy Rollers?" Nick said, incredulously. "Is that like a religion?" Justin nodded and finished his drink.

"So, what does going back to Harlan have to do with your religion?" Nick had heard about many variations of non-Catholics, but this Holy Roller thing was a first.

"Haven't you ever wondered why I go down home?"

"I figured it was a good place to hide out while the heat blows over; and from what you say, your mamma's a great cook."

Uncomfortable with sharing something of such a personal nature as his deeply held beliefs, Justin began by hedging his description, not wishing to reveal in too much detail, the inner workings of his religion. His daddy always told him to be cautious in talking too much about his faith with outsiders who would think that he was an ignorant hillbilly.

"Well, it's more than that. I have to meet with the Twelve Elders and take the Test of Faith."

"Okay, I'll bite. What's the test of faith?"

"I remember my first time. I was 15 and my daddy took me to the Elders who always met an hour before church started to administer the Test to anyone who showed up. Daddy told me I had to take it, and that I had to explain to one of the Elders, the one who was called the Keeper, what I had done—and tell him the question I wanted the Test to answer. You know, Nick, how you have to meet with the priest? Well, I have to meet with the Keeper."

Justin could tell that although this was new to Nick, he was receptive to what he was hearing. Feeling less guarded, he explained that the Keeper is similar to the Catholic priest, and that he's the Keeper of the faith and also the Keeper of the serpents.

This really got Nick's attention. "Serpents?" he asked in amazement.

Justin nodded his head and said, "In our religion we get the word of God through the Keeper – well, actually through the serpents that he cares for. We're a religion that tests our faith by handling rattlesnakes and copperheads."

"Holy shit. Why would anybody do that?" Nick felt goose bumps forming on his arms.

No one had ever been that curious about Justin's religion before, so talking with Nick helped him clarify his own thoughts about it. Recalling the time his daddy took him to the Elders, he told Nick about his first meeting with the Keeper when he had to tell him what he had done wrong. Justin's father, Walter, escorted him into the small clapboard church that had once served as a gas station, over to a makeshift altar where Mr. Isaacs, a tall, gangly bearded old man, looked down at Justin with piercing black eyes, roughly grabbed his shoulders with his strong, gnarly hands, glared at him and shouted, "Do you need forgiveness, son?" Justin thought that a strange question, since if he didn't want forgiveness, he wouldn't have come; but instead, he nodded his head. The Keeper, without blinking his eyes, continued to gaze into Justin's and asked him if he had a question that needed answering. Unsure as to what he meant, Justin looked over at his father and shrugged his shoulders.

Before he could look back at the Keeper, the old man pulled a large diamondback rattler out of its cage and said, "Well, you might ask God if He would forgive you. Then you hold the snake for a few minutes and wait for God's answer."

"How will I know what His answer is?"

Mr. Isaacs eased the snake back in its cage; and as the diamondback rattled its warning, he turned to Justin, saying, "If the serpent don't bite you, the answer is Yes—I reckon its about the simplest test a man can take."

"And if it bites me?" Justin asked, shaking all over. "What does that tell me?"

"At that point, it really don't matter none," the Keeper said, smiling, knowingly.

Justin told Nick about having to stand in front of the church at the altar facing the entire congregation of about seventy-five fellow believers and asking for forgiveness as he handled several snakes, one at a time, which the Keeper passed to him from their cages. The worshippers did not know the sin which required forgiveness or the question which Justin had asked. The purpose of the congregation was like that of the Greek chorus; and like the chorus, it sometimes reflected the joys or fears of the sinner or commented, through repetitious chants, on the situation the sinner finds himself.

Nick was attempting to understand all of this; but being a very concrete thinker, he tried to summarize what he was hearing. "Okay. Let's take me, for example. If I went to your church, I'd have to tell everybody who I hit and then handle a snake to be forgiven?"

"No, it's the same way as with your priest. *Only* the Keeper knows your confession. The rest of the congregation understands that you're in need of forgiveness, but only the Keeper knows the question that you need answered. Are you getting this, Nick?" Justin asked.

"So, if I want to be forgiven, I tell the Keep what I did; and then, if the snake doesn't bite me, I'm forgiven."

Justin smiled and held up his brandy snifter for a toast. As he clinked Justin's glass, Nick asked in lowered tones, as if he were in a church, "Now, what *was* your question?"

There was silence for a few minutes.

Nick thought that perhaps he was getting too personal. Looking at him intently, Justin explained, "My question is the same every time I go home for forgiveness."

As though he were in a trance, Justin went on and talked about the feelings of being forgiven that came over him each time he returned the serpents to the Keeper and heard the congregation, in unison, shout, "Amen." It was as though he had been washed in the blood, baptized in the spirit each time he survived this cathartic ritual, this Test of Faith.

Nick was struck by Justin's demeanor as he shared his beliefs. It was one of sincerity, honesty and integrity. This snake handling religion was something that Justin would risk his life for every time he posed a question to the Keeper. Ordering another brandy, Nick thought that Justin had some real balls to be fooling around with snakes, religion or not.

Nick pressed him again, "But what was the question you told the Keeper you needed answered?"

"It's always the same," Justin replied, "Can I be forgiven if I were to commit the same sin again?"

Their table was silent for some time, as Nick absorbed this message. That Justin would risk his life for forgiveness was a sobering thought. He had never seen any evidence that Justin was particularly religious, and he certainly wouldn't have taken him for a snake handling lunatic. Yet, there was something compelling and noble about this branch of the Pentecostal religion that required a life or death faith. Nick knew that he would not risk his life to have any question answered, and he wondered, now, if being a Catholic wasn't just for sissies.

Nick broke the silence and changed the subject, "You know what I'd like to buy you, Justin? A Sidecar."

Justin laughed, enjoying the foggy feeling of already having had one too many. "A Sidecar? What the hell would I do with a Sidecar?"

"You ever have one?"

"No."

"Before the war I went to Naples to visit my family. While I was over there, I took a bus trip through France, and I stopped for a week in Paris.

"Did I ever tell you how I started working for the Syndicate?"

Justin hated this. He was a very lineal thinker. He liked to proceed from A to B to C; but when Nick had a few too many drinks he would hop scotch from different time periods and different topics in the middle of a conversation. And although this made Justin anxious, it was one of the things he was willing to put up with. When drunk, Mr. Stream-of-consciousness Nick could take you around the world and back while talking about a trip to the dentist.

"No, Nick, how did you start working for the Syndicate?" Justin asked, trying to disguise his lack of patience.

"Well, I was a bartender in Cleveland where Louis Carusi liked to eat. He would come in and order a brandy, every day at 6:00 p.m. Well, this one day, he comes in, sits down at his table, doesn't come to the bar first to get his drink. So I go over to him, 'Mr. Carusi,' I say, 'You want your brandy?' I could tell he was distracted. Something was bothering him. You know how it is. You can just tell."

"So," Justin said, encouraging him to get on with the story.

"So I go over to him and he says, 'Yeah, Nick. Bring me a drink. But surprise me.' "

"I thought, oh shit, this is not a man who likes surprises. But I figured, if he liked brandy, he just might go for a Sidecar.

"Hey, Justin, did I ever tell you, Nick LaSita isn't my real name?"

"No, Nick you didn't. But first finish your story about the Sidecar."

"Well, like I told you, I stopped in Paris for a week. I saw all the sights, and I would stop everyday for lunch at this same little bistro. You know how I enjoy having a cigar and brandy when I finish a meal. Well, this day, I guess it was the second day I had stopped at that place, the bartender told me he was just about out of brandy. Can you beat that? I was a little pissed. But the guy says, 'Let me make you a Sidecar, on the house.'

"Hell, I was like you are now. I didn't know what a Sidecar was, but it was going to be free. So I said, 'What do I have to lose? Sure. Make me a Sidecar.' You know what, Justin that was the best damn drink I'd ever had. It was so good, I had the guy write down everything that went in it. And I watched everything he did to make it – which is a big part of the secret."

Justin closed his eyes. He was sure he was about to hear how to make a Sidecar, and he was not wrong.

"Remember this, Justin. Here's how to make the best drink you've ever had.

"Use two ounces of brandy, one ounce of lemon juice, one ounce of Cointreau. Put it all in a mixer with ice. Stir it real good. Then on your cocktail glass, don't coat the rim with sugar. A lot of people make that mistake. No, No. The secret is this. Coat half the glass rim with a lemon rind and the other half with an orange rind. If you drink on the lemon side, you'll smell the orange; if you drink on the orange side, you'll smell the lemon. It's that surprise – the mixing of the taste and the smell – that plus the drink, itself, of course.

"I asked the bartender why they called it a Sidecar – strange name for a drink, don't you think?"

But not pausing for Justin to reply, Nick continued. "Seems that in World War I there was this Colonel who had his aide drive him to this very bar where I was sitting.

He came on a motorcycle, in the sidecar. Well, it was winter, and by the time he got there, he was freezing his ass off. He kept asking the bartender for something to thaw him out. The bartender just keep experimenting until, finally, one of his concoctions did the job. The Colonel thawed out, and he came back every day until that damn war ended – and he had a Sidecar everyday. That's a helluva story, don't you think?"

Justin wanted to move the story along – get Nick back on track, so he said, "So you made the boss a Sidecar?"

"So, yeah, I made a Sidecar for Mr. Carusi – gave it to him and went back to the bar. I wanted to watch him. I'm good at figuring what people are thinking or feeling just by watching them. So, I watched Mr. Carusi. He was still distracted by something in his head. He didn't drink for a few minutes. Finally, not even looking at the glass, he picks it up and takes a sip. Nothing, no reaction."

"Ok," Justin interrupted, "What does that...."

"No, no. Wait. About ten seconds later, he snaps out of his mood. He looks at the drink. Really looks close. Then he takes another swig. His face had the strangest expression.. He looks over at me, 'Hey Nick, come here.' "

"I thought I was in for it. But you know what? He wanted another!"

"When I took it to him, he said, 'What is that? It warms me all the way down to my flat feet!' That's how we became friends. He had me come to some of his parties, you know, bartend for him. Gradually, he had me work for him full time – doing all kind of stuff. Finally, after a couple years, I became the Messenger."

After a moment of silence, Nick said, "That's my story. Now how the hell did you start working for the boss?"

Justin felt very comfortable with Nick – always had and would confide more with him than he ever did with his own family. So, he shared his story: he told Nick about his first botched hold up in Cleveland – that old Italian grocer.

"When I came to, Nick, there were these two big goons sitting in the back of the store, just looking at me. They reminded me of Oliver and Hardy – one was real fat and the other guy was a bean pole. My gun - a really nice long barrel .38 revolver was being fondled by the fat guy.

"Where did you get this, kid?" he asked.

"It's my daddy's gun," Justin said; and feeling the warm and sticky blood on the side of his face; he immediately understood the reason for the throbbing pain in the back of his head.

The bean pole laughed, mimicking his accent, "My daddy's gun." The two laughed, disparagingly, at him.

"Look, hillbilly boy, my friend and I are trying to decide whether to dump you in the river or not. Now, what do you think we should do?"

Justin told Nick how much the word "hillbilly" piqued him, especially when it came from an asshole like this. Given the fact that his gun was in another man's hands, however, he held back his anger and told this guy to dump him in the river because all hillbillies are good swimmers.

Fatso became irritated with Justin's cockiness. "You don't get it, hillbilly boy, we plan to shoot you first. How well do hillbillies swim with holes in 'em?"

Recognizing that he was in a very dangerous situation, Justin became more conciliatory. "Not so good," he replied, lowering his eyes.

The odd couple laughed again.

"You know how to use this gun?" one of the men asked.

"They say I'm real good with it, down home," Justin said, exaggerating his Kentucky twang. In his job hunting days, he learned quickly that by turning it on, some people from the big city either felt sorry for him or thought he was just plain stupid. He was getting good at figuring out who would respond which way.

"Ever killed with it?"

"Sure. Used it to kill hogs back home."

That brought more laughter.

The bean pole handed Justin his billfold, telling him what he already knew – that he was dead broke. Surprised that these two characters were walking out the door without following through on their earlier threats, Justin struggled to stand up. The fat guy suddenly turned on Justin, pointing the .38 at him. Moving his body into a defensive posture, Justin thought for sure he would feel the slug rip into him.

"If you want to make a few bucks, come back here tomorrow. Same time," the fat guy said, taking some pleasure in seeing Justin flinch.

"Do I get my gun back?" Justin's daddy had given him that gun for his 16th birthday, a family ritual. Every male Jenkins gave his first son a firearm on this rite of passage celebration for generations.

"Look hillbilly boy, you don't get to ask any questions. Get it? Just come back tomorrow and find out."

By then the Sidecars had arrived and Justin took a big drink – one doesn't do that with a Sidecar, as he immediately found out. His mouth and throat burned. He coughed, instinctively.

"Good, huh?" Nick smiled, knowing what Justin was experiencing.

Since the drinks he liked required great ceremony, Nick once again explained a step-by-step ritual in drinking a Sidecar. "Sip it, Justin. Sip it. Smell the orange. Smell the lemon. Let the liquid just trickle down your throat."

After following Nick's drinking tips, Justin had to agree. The combination of the smell, the taste and the warmth, as it headed for his stomach, was all quite pleasurable; but it was time to go. He looked at his watch. Nick caught the look and wanted to continue the conversation a little longer. "Wait, Justin. You haven't finished your story. Did you go back the next day? Did you get your gun?"

Oblivious to Nick's questions, Justin was already anticipating his assignment. In the past, he had enjoyed the stalking process—researching his job and picking the right time and place. He worked best at night, learning that by a very early failure: approaching his first mark, with his gun cocked and ready to fire, Justin was startled by the man, as he turned and eerily stared directly into his eyes. Justin just froze. Although *he* had the gun, Justin was the one who felt vulnerable. Averting the man's gaze, he fled. Justin could not shoot a man who was intently looking directly into his eyes. Strange, but that was who he was. His solution was to work at night; he didn't have to worry as much about his target's glaring eyes. This early problem came before he began working for Carosi—a good thing, because the boss would have had Justin disappear, if he had failed him.

"I'll call you, Nick." Justin said. "I want to get started. What's my lead time on this job?"

"Two weeks."

"Good seeing you again, Nick. Thanks. I'll be in touch." And with that, Justin was gone.

Nick straightened his tie and reached for his grey fedora on the vacant chair to his right. This assignment was now officially over.

Chapter Five
The Chicago Connection
(Early to Mid August, 1943)

5

In the 1940's, the windy city, as Chicago was called, not because of the breeze coming off Lake Michigan, but because of the verbosity of its politicians, was a booming war town of over three million people. In fact, it was here that the World War II Manhattan Project got its impetus when Enrico Fermi, a physicist at the University of Chicago, conducted the first controlled nuclear reaction, resulting, a few years later, in the dropping of atomic bombs on Nagasaki and Hiroshima, ending the war with Japan.

Chicago had come a long way from the 1920's when Al Capone and other gangsters turned parts of the city into a war zone; but in the '40's they still controlled vital sections of Chicago's infrastructure—and since Italians represented one of the largest ethnic groups in the city, they still played a prominent role in its future.

The Poles also constituted a large ethnic block, there being almost as many Poles in Chicago as in Warsaw!

Stanley Lukazewski was born and raised in the windy city, and as one might assume, he was Polish. He grew up on the northwest side of town, attended Taft High School and even spent two years at Loyola University. But World War II intervened, and Stanley was no hero. He simply disappeared. Chicago was an easy place in which to do that because of the thousands of immigrants and rural hopefuls coming to work in defense plants. Stanley's only requirement in his job search was that no one asks for a birth certificate or other proof of who he really was.

He was young and eager, and the underground took him in. Being six foot three made him physically intimidating and helped launch his career with a local crime family, a group loosely connected to the Chicago Outfit. Although Stanley was given a pistol to carry, most of his jobs involved bullying local shopkeepers who were late with their contribution to the Businessmen's Protection Association. These were a small time group of thugs who would agree not to rob or hustle local entrepreneurs for a monthly contribution of $100.00.

It was such an insignificant scam that the Outfit tended to ignore them. However, as in professional sports, those at the top are always looking for up-and-coming young talent. That's how Stanley Lukazewski came to the attention of Joseph Rizzi; and at their first meeting on August 1, 1943, Stanley was given the job of roughing up a Covington politician who was resisting the Chicago Outfit's attempt to infiltrate the slot machine business in Northern Kentucky.

Stosh, as he was called, locally, had a simple M.O: he would follow his mark for a few days until he had an idea of his habits, his hangouts. And then he would choose a place where the victim was vulnerable, usually a parking lot, a deserted section of road, anywhere he would have sixty seconds alone with his target. One minute was plenty of time to deliver a message: a few blows to the ribs, the kidneys, but leave the face alone.

So Stosh followed Carl Kiger the first week of August and chose the spot, a little gas station near Devon on Highway 25 not far from Carl's summer home at Rosegate. Carl was easy to follow because he drove a 1940 Oldsmobile. Since 1941, no cars had been produced due to the war; therefore, most vehicles on the highway were from the 1930's or earlier.

Carl was a big man, himself, and from having worked on his farm at Rosegate during the summer, he proudly maintained his athletic build. But the element of surprise generally overcomes all else, and sixty seconds was all it took. A few well placed punches and Carl was down. No blood, no marks – but the message was delivered.

When Carl arrived home, at Rosegate, a few minutes later, he did not share this beating with his wife, Jennie. He drew a long hot Epsom Salt bath and spent an hour soaking, trying to soothe his aching body. As he considered the implications of this encounter, he knew he had to follow through with the Outfit's demands because, if he did not, the next visit from the Chicago boys would be much more serious, possibly even involve his family. That was the part that worried him the most. His two oldest boys, John and Joe were in the military, ready to be shipped overseas, a worry in its own right; but not one he could blame himself for. His immediate problem involved the safety of Jennie, Joan and Jerry. Who knew what the Outfit might do next?

His mind drifted back to the 1930's. As hard as they were, it was a happy time. Jennie was a wonderful and compassionate companion, a stern but fair mother; and the interesting spread of children over more than a decade kept him young and invigorated by life. His family gave him reason to work hard—to burn the candle at both ends.

Thinking back to the days when he was a candy salesman, pounding pavements calling on drugstores, restaurants, filling stations and mom and pop shops, he wondered how he was able to make any money at all. Life became much more predictable once he became a Covington City Commissioner and then, with the help of two friends, Jack Maynard and William Beutell, he was appointed Vice-Mayor. The salary of $125.00 a month was not great, but he was a candy salesman no more! Carl quickly discovered that if one knew how to manipulate the system within the bounds of legitimacy, other business opportunities became available. He felt that if he could make a living selling sweets door-to-door, he could sell himself; he could sell cars; he could sell anything! And it was with that ambitious attitude that he began a relationship with the Studebaker dealership, on Madison Road, in Covington. A buck here and a buck there all add up. Carl nodded, agreeing with his unexpressed thoughts.

As the hot water and Epsom salts continued to ease his pain, he tried to think of ways to reduce the threat against himself and his family. He was carrying a gun now; but he realized after today's encounter, that a gun was not the answer. His second line of defense was the installation of dead bolts on all the doors at his Crescent Avenue home. He had even begun this process at Rosegate. What else could he do? Knowing that he couldn't run from the Syndicate, and he probably couldn't lock them out gave him pause. There did not seem to be an answer. What a mess he had gotten himself into and all with the best of intentions. He had accepted money from both the Chicago Outfit and the Cleveland Syndicate; but these funds were given freely to him as, no strings attached, contributions for his campaign; and he had believed them. What does a candy salesman know of the ways of the mafia? He was basically an ambitious but honest man. Now he must decide whether to cross the line or not. He must join with the crime families or risk his life and the lives of those dearest to him.

His musings were interrupted by Jennie, banging on the bathroom door, "Carl, you've been in there long enough. Dinner's ready and we're all hungry."

Quickly, but painfully, he stepped out of the tub and dried himself. Throwing on a pair of slacks and a shirt, he joined his family at the dinner table. Everyone was in good spirits, chattering about the day's events.

As he glanced around, he noticed that Joan was wearing a yellow sundress, her long auburn hair glistening in the late afternoon sun; she was the joy of his life, his only daughter, bright, ambitious and engaging. The thought of anything happening to Joan or to Jerry, all energy and mischief, was more than he could bear. Jennie, scurrying around, placing a platter of freshly picked tomatoes, as well as steaming bowls of corn and green beans from their garden on the table, was his anchor, his best friend. As she sat down to dinner, she looked at him and winked. After all these years, theirs was still a love affair.

At that very moment, he knew he could not jeopardize their lives or their happiness. As the family laughed and talked about the routines of their separate lives, he made his decision. He did hope, however, that he could postpone the implementation of the Chicago Outfit's request of slot machines in Erlanger until after the elections. By then he would be able to better leverage their demands. Surely they could wait until then.

Chapter Six
Don't Kill The Messenger
(August 17, 1943)

6

Louis Carosi was larger than life—over six foot tall, and because of his many years of eating and drinking whatever pleased his eyes and his palate, he was overweight. But, at 63, he could still move surprisingly fast. What kept him secure in his mid-level position in Cleveland's Syndicate, however, was that he could think even faster. His judgments were always swift and sound.

He wore several hats in this growing organization; to generalize, he received orders only from the top men in the Cleveland Syndicate, such as Moe Delitz or Alfred Polizza. Carosi was the implementer of these orders. Because he had done this so well over the years, he was recently rewarded with the slot machine business in Kentucky.

Today, he had dinner in Cleveland's Little Italy, as the area around Mayfield Road and Murrey Hill Road was called, at Guarino's, a restaurant which specialized in dishes native to southern Italy, his parents' homeland. The ambience was particularly inviting with its quaint bar, cozy booths and tantalizing aromas. The outdoor summer patio, where he could feel the heat of the sun and the frequent gusty breezes whip against his face, was Carosi's favorite. I shoulda been a farmer, he sometimes thought; I just love being outside. The second reason he came here to Guarino's was to keep up on the family's gossip. Since its inception in 1918, this establishment had been the favorite hang out of the Costa Nostra's finest.

Mariano, the short, pudgy owner, would treat the usual patrons with a reserved affability; however, when his special and regular guests arrived, his cordiality and service knew no bounds. Others in the restaurant thought for certain that these patrons were Mariano's own family – blood family. His face would light up and his yellowed and crooked teeth would protrude from his thick lips as he bellowed, "Buona sera!" in the evening and "Buon pomeriggio!" at lunchtime. Waving his stubby arms, he would personally seat these favored guests in the farthest and darkened corners of the restaurant and closely shadow the waiter to make certain he moved in and out of his serving duties with as little intrusion as possible. Under Mariano's protective eye and the watchfulness of his staff, everyone knew there was no safer place to conduct business. He knew who should be here and who should not.

As he sipped his brandy, Louis Carosi inhaled deeply, knowing that he was at the top of his game, at the zenith of his power. The family businesses were successful, bringing in so much money that even the nay sayers of the Committee were silenced.

Today, August 17, 1943, Louis Carosi had only one worry, and it was not a major one. It regarded some rumors coming out of Kentucky. He understood the problem and since his motto was, "Don't let little problems become big ones," he had sent The Messenger to Covington, yesterday, to begin resolution proceedings.

Carosi's messenger had returned in time to drive him here to Guarino's and was now sitting at the bar, reading *The Cleveland Plain Dealer*.

Just as his dinner was served, Carosi heard Nick exclaim, "Son of a bitch!"

Nick was a talker but not given to excitement and certainly not to shouting, so the outburst did catch Carosi's attention. He glanced toward the bar and saw Nick headed in his direction, still looking at the newspaper and shaking his head.

"Quiet down," Carosi said, waving his hand.

Nick looked around the room, sat down and in a hushed tone said, "You hear about this, Boss?" The color was draining from his face. He did not want to be the one to break this news to Carosi.

"What's the problem, Nick?" Carosi mumbled, as he shoved a forkful of spaghetti into his mouth.

"Boss, someone shot and killed Covington's Vice-Mayor, Carl Kiger!"

"What? Let me see that," Carosi grabbed the paper.

"God damn! God damn—he's shot Kiger; he's shot his wife; he's shot their six year old son! Has he gone crazy?" Realizing that his voice had reached a level that was causing a stir among the other diners, he leaned forward and with a forced whisper continued, "Kiger wasn't even on the list of five that I gave you! You didn't screw up did you, Nick? You didn't give him Kiger's name?"

"Hell no, Boss. I gave him the five names you told me to. Justin couldn't have done it – it's too soon for one thing, and for another, my God, he doesn't shoot whole families—unless, of course he's gettin' paid to." Nick's voice had lowered to the point that Carosi had to strain to hear him.

"All hell is going to break loose down there, now. Justin was supposed to take out a minor politician—a nobody—just to get their attention. Not the Vice-Mayor. Damn! How can I keep the family's name out of this? Says here they were both killed with a .38. What does Justin carry?"

"A .38," Nick all but whispered.

Carosi continued reading. "Justin does all his work at night. This shooting took place after midnight. Oh, yes, it was Justin—it was Justin!" Carosi's beet red face reflected the rage growing in his body. His anger had nothing to do with the Kiger family being murdered. No, he was terrified that the ensuing investigation would lead back here to Cleveland, and that it would jeopardize his slot business in Kentucky—and maybe his own job.

"What you want me to do, Boss?" Nick was really uneasy, thinking that somehow he might take the fall for this mistake.

"It's done, Nick—it's done!" Carosi said, resignedly.

"Want me to go talk to Justin?"

"You know where to find him?"

"Yeah, he always goes back to his family in Harlan, Kentucky after a job."

"Go down there and put him away."

Nick flinched. "You want me to take him out?" He was hoping to talk Carosi out of this directive or at least buy some time for Justin. Not wanting to overstep his bounds, he said, warily, "How about if I go down there and see what the story is. After all, I can't believe he didn't follow instructions. I mean, I know the guy real well, and he's good at what he does. Hard to find someone you can really trust. How about it?"

The boss looked up at Nick, suspiciously. "I said get rid of him."

"Whatever you say, Boss," Nick said, wishing he hadn't challenged him.

Carosi's dinner sat untouched. For the first time since taking the reigns of power for the Kentucky region, he was baffled. It was so easy. His instructions were so clear. What had happened?

"When you want me to go, Boss?"

"Right now! Leave right now! And get back here as soon as you get the job done. I've got something else for you to do."

Chapter Seven
An All Nighter To Harlan
(August 17 – 18, 1943)

7

The Messenger didn't even stop to change his clothes or pack his suitcase, so urgent were the vibes he was getting from his boss. He headed out of Cleveland on Highway 3 toward Harlan, stopping only long enough to fill his gas tank, check the oil and grab a Coke and a Baby Ruth.

As he headed south, Nick was distraught about what he had to do. There were many things about Justin that Nick always admired: he was someone you could count on. He always did what he was told, and he had been willing to share so much of himself, over the years. Nick just plain liked him. He felt they were more like brothers than just friends. The two had had quite a few conversations about where they came from, their families and how they ended up in this business.

He tried to put Carusi's orders out of his mind as he thought about this trip to Justin's home town, a trip Nick had wanted to take for a long time. Although he had never been farther south than Covington, he felt he knew Harlan pretty well. After all, his buddy had talked about it often enough. It sounded like a great place to grow up, surrounded by the hills of Appalachia, the Cumberland and Black mountains looming in the distance, preceded by vistas of green fields. According to Justin, you never met a stranger – everyone in town, whether he knew you or not, would say howdy. And if you were a lady, men would tip their hats in respect. The many shops in town contained the latest wares and fashions, just as one would find in Chicago or New York. The school system was first rate, though Justin admitted he was not directly familiar with that fact. This was Justin's vision of his hometown.

Although Nick had, for some time, been looking forward to visiting Harlan, going as Justin's executioner was not what he had in mind. But he understood what his job was; he knew that in this all night drive, if he did not come up with an alternative, he would have no choice. He would have to kill his best friend.

Finishing off his candy bar, he pulled out a map and, with a quick look, decided he'd stop for dinner at a place in Florence, Kentucky which Justin had talk about – a greasy spoon that served steaks the size of your plate for only 50 cents. It was dark and late by the time he pulled up to the Stringtown Restaurant, a name reflecting the town's original beginnings – Stringtown on the Pike. Sizing up the outside of the place, Nick had his doubts about the fare within: an old two story brick building on the corner of Youell Road and Main Street, a brooding structure with one naked bulb illuminating a sign hanging precariously by what looked like a frayed extension cord.

Nick was not one to appreciate history. The here and now was his game. The Stringtown Restaurant had been serving customers since 1932 and was the longest lasting and most successful restaurant in the county, the building itself dating back to 1869, originally having been built as a hotel.

But Nick was thinking steak, not history, and even when he was stressed, as he was now, nothing ever interfered with his appetite. "If this place is shit, I'm going to give Justin hell." He walked in, resigned to his culinary fate. To his surprise, the restaurant was packed. The smells of bacon grease, hot biscuits and coffee made the Baby Ruth seem like a long time ago. A dark haired, dark eyed waitress, about fifty, came over quickly. "Coming for dinner? We're just about ready to stop serving."

"Yeah, dinner," he replied, as he followed her to a counter stool. "My name's Estelle. I can seat you here or you can wait for a table," she said, eyeing him, curiously.

"Here's good. Thanks."

He grabbed a menu from between the sugar container and a large greasy salt shaker.

The man at the next stool looked over, "You're new here, aren't you?" he said, obviously trying to draw him out.

"Grew up in Covington," Nick said.

"Then I guess you heard about the murders," the man offered, adjusting the bib on his overalls.

"Can't say I have," Nick replied. And then, his curiosity growing, "What murders?"

"Oh, there's been a couple big murders here! If you're from Covington, you probably know the family, the Kigers."

"No, I've been away for awhile," Nick replied. "Do they know who did it?"

"Well, we interviewed the Sheriff. We're going have his picture on the front page. He says they have their suspicions."

Nick, becoming even more curious, said, "Who's this 'we' you're talking about?"

"Oh, I'm sorry." The tall slight build man said, extending his hand, "I'm Ty Combs. I work for the local paper, the *Boone County Recorder*. My boss – he'll be in here shortly – his name is Pete Stevens." Suddenly Ty felt self-conscious as he began to smell the perspiration that stained his shirt. "I know I look like a mess. You'd never guess I was the typesetter and editor for the paper. But I like to do carpentry work on the side. I bought an old abandoned Negro Church in Burlington, and I'm tearing it down. Lots of good lumber in that old church. I'm going to build myself a house out on Belleview Road."

Nick thought to himself, so who gives a damn? But he said, "So you're interviewing people about the murders," trying to get back to the topic which had brought him on this road trip.

"Well, Pete and one of our reporters did most of the interviews. It's a strange case. The deputy – that's Irvin Rouse – thinks the teen-aged daughter did it." Sipping his coffee, Ty shook his head. "I can't believe that. She's only fifteen. Our jailer, Elmer Kirkpatrick, says she's as cute as can be. The Sheriff thinks it's some kind of gang killing. He suspects that it has something to do with Kiger's job. He was Vice-Mayor of Covington, you know, and he may be right; after all, the Sheriff found $1400.00 hidden under the couch. That's a lot of money."

Given the notoriety of the case, Ty was surprised that his counter companion hadn't heard a word about it.

The waitress plunked an over-sized white plate down; but the steak on it was so large, it dangled over the sides, touching the counter top. Nick smiled as he looked up at her and said, "I need some more coffee when you have time." His mouth watering, he attacked the steak voraciously, cutting it expertly into large pieces. The juices seeped into his mashed potatoes, making them pinkish around the edges.

"How do you like that steak?" Ty asked, although it was obvious that Nick was really enjoying it.

"Big and really good," Nick replied, between bites.

"Stel, I want the same steak," Ty said, eyeing Nick's plate, enviously

"Hey, Pete, over here." Ty welcomed his boss to the counter. "Did you get everything all set up?"

Pete was a stocky man – still had a spring in his step and looked to be in his early thirties – too young to be a boss, Nick thought. He sat to Nick's left (Ty was on Nick's right) and they leaned forward and talked around him. As Pete reached for a menu that was lying on the edge of the counter, Nick noticed that his large hands were black and stained with what looked like ink. Makes sense, Nick thought. He's been setting type.

"Got everything but the front page ready," Pete said, as he scanned the bill of fare. Ty always thought it strange that Pete would bother to look at a menu, since he ordered the exact same thing every time he came here; and everyone knew Stringtown listed its daily specials on the chalkboard near the front door, so there was nothing new to consider.

"I'll have fried chicken, green beans and mashed potatoes," Pete shouted to Estelle who was at the other end of the counter. Ty grinned and shook his head.

"What you grinning at?" Pete leaned over, talking past Nick.

"You know what I'm grinning at. You always order the same damn thing, so why do you bother looking at the menu?" Ty asked. "You could recite that thing by heart."

It was obvious to Nick and to any other stranger that these two men liked each other. Not only were they friends, but they worked well together. Each could do the other man's job; and although Pete owned the paper, he enjoyed getting his hands dirty and loved the smell of ink even better. In fact, much to Ty's chagrin, Pete preferred doing Ty's job – setting the type.

Since this had been a rough week for Ty, with all the pressure of getting the old church torn down so that work could begin Monday on his new house, Pete had done most of the typesetting.

"I guess you come here a lot to eat?" Nick asked Ty.

"Every Monday. Pete and I come here every Monday."

"Then you know what the best dessert is, "Nick said, anticipating something great after that most satisfying steak.

"Peach cobbler," Pete said, grinning at Nick. "Get the cobbler."

By that time the waitress was refilling his coffee again.

"Your food is comin' up," she said.

"And I'll take that Peach Cobbler," Nick chimed in. Pete leaned forward, speaking to Ty again. "I think we'll go with the two inch banner. JOAN KIGER JAILED FOR MURDER. What do you think of that, Ty?"

"Well, it would sell papers but, Pete, is it true? The Sheriff didn't say she murdered her father and brother."

"Yeah, true – give me a better one."

About that time Albert Weaver walked over. He had just finished eating and he, too, worked for Pete. "Well, boys. Did Joan pull the trigger?"

"There's your headline, Pete. 'Is Joan Kiger the Killer?'"

"Too sensational," Pete said.

"Sit down, Sickem," Ty motioned to the third stool. Weaver was a fourth generation Burlingtonian, a local who had worked for the Recorder most of his life. A deacon at the local Baptist Church and a thirty-third degree Mason, he knew everybody and everything that went on in Burlington.

Nick dug into the golden plump peaches that rested on a brown, crisp biscuit. So absorbed in the pleasure of his dessert was he that he lost touch with anything going on around him. As he gulped the last of his coffee, he looked up to see that the three journalists seemed to be talking over and around him. Scraping the remaining crumbs from his plate, he slipped off the stool. Glad to be on his way, he waved and said, "So long, fellas. It's been nice talking to you." Burlington hospitality required that each of the three shakes his hand and wish him a safe trip.

What a bunch of hicks – really strange people, Nick thought, as he returned to the main highway; but then he reconsidered—sounds a lot like the way Justin describes the people 'down home': "In my town, nobody can be a stranger for long."

This restaurant conversation resurrected the urgency of Nick's trip. So the Sheriff thinks it a gang related murder….and the money found under the couch…sounds like Justin's really screwed up.

He guided the Buick through the night, its headlights slicing a path toward Harlan and a final meeting with Justin.

At Richmond, Kentucky, he turned on to Highway 52 and took it until he hit 155 South, and then he got lost. Finally, after hours on the narrow back roads of Eastern Kentucky, he saw the sign to Harlan. What a drive, he thought to himself. If this is God's country, as Justin says, why does God make it so damn hard to find the place?

The sun was beginning to come up on his left, a beautiful sight to anyone who had not driven all night. Nick's eyes were gritty and tired. He blinked to bring into focus what looked to him like a huge snake crawling up the two lane road ahead. As he slowed, he could see the coal trucks as they began rolling by empty, headed for the Blue Gemmy Mine. Justin had nothing good to say about the coal company. They worked his friends until their bodies gave out and then found some excuse to let them go. He also told about his own uncle, Andy Cox, who worked for a small independent company and, when the foreman told him to take out some extra support columns, the roof collapsed. These types of columns had been named, years ago, "Dead Man's Columns." Cox had been in a wheel chair for about five years since that incident, until he finally got tired of living and killed himself.

But Justin's stories were mostly upbeat, so Nick was anxious to experience Harlan. Justin was always saying to him, "Go down home with me. We'll skin a few cats." Nick never knew what that meant, but he was ready to find out. Justin told him to go to the General Store and ask for his dad, Walter Jenkins. Everybody knows where he lives. Nick thought, how hard can that be in this hick town? He didn't figure that the General Store would be open at sunrise, so he drove around looking for a restaurant. Justin had always talked about the biscuits and gravy his mother made – said that the only ones that came close were at the Green Parrot restaurant. So Nick made a circle around the town—and sure enough, there it was. Coal trucks were lined up in a haphazard fashion all across the parking lot. He finally was able to squeeze in between two behemoths and crack his door enough that he could slide out.

As he walked toward the front entrance, breakfast smells insinuated themselves upon his senses. No, more than insinuated – they pounded on the door. His steps quickened, but he had to give way to two huge men coming toward him. Letting them pass, he eased into the smoky and noisy restaurant.

"Rose, bring me some more coffee," one voice boomed from the farthest corner of the dining room.

"Hey, Rose, some more gravy," another shouted from the counter.

Nick was conspicuous: a 135 pounder in this land of giants – a stranger, wearing a suit, in a room filled with tired faces and coal blackened clothes.

He sat at the counter, hoping not to draw attention to himself.

"What'll you have," Rose barked.

"Bacon and eggs, black coffee – and some directions," Nick said.

He had decided not to go for the biscuits and gravy which Justin recommended, having heard that gravy was made out of milk and flour. It sounded more like a recipe for making paste, he thought.

When she brought his order, Rose asked, "So, where do you want to go?"

"Walter Jenkins' place," he replied.

"I don't know the Jenkins' place. Hold on, I'll find out."

She took a large pot and, with a gravy ladle, banged on it for all she was worth; that got the intended result. Talking stopped and everyone turned, looking at Rose.

"Who knows the Walter Jenkins' place? This guy here's lookin' for Walter." Nick had to strain to understand her through her eastern Kentucky twang.

There was a murmur and then a couple of hands went up. "Hey Rose, I'm going down that way after I eat."

"Here's your man," Rose said as she pointed to Nick with her gravy ladel.

Finishing his breakfast, Nick kept an eye on the tour guide; and in a few minutes, he came over. "I'm Jericho," he said, in that peculiar mountain drawl. "What ya'll want with ole Walter?" He continued picking his teeth with his little finger, as he talked.

"Well, it's not really Walter I'm looking for; it's his son, Justin." Nick said, as Rose grabbed his dirty dishes and dumped them into a pan of soapy water.

"Sure, I know Justin. My older brother went to school with him. What you want with Justin?" Jericho eyed him, suspiciously.

"We were friends back in Covington," Nick said, wondering at the third degree.

"He ain't here. Don't you know that? Well, I guess you don't since you're lookin' for 'im," Jericho chortled.

"Sure he's here," Nick replied, with some concern. "He has to be here."

Jericho was the only one so far in Harlan who did not tower over Nick. He was about five foot six, skinny as a rail, round shouldered and was wearing glasses. Not a coal truck driver, Nick guessed.

"He ain't here," Jericho said again. "I oughta know."

"Why ought you to know?" Nick asked, feeling, for the first time, a little combative. The .32 under his armpit egged him on.

"Well, I reckon, 'cause I'm seein' Walter's younger sister's girl – and she's been stayin' at the Jenkins, takin' care of Walter. Ya know, he's bad off with the black lung."

"I'd like to go out there, anyway, just to be sure," Nick countered.

There was a long silence as Jericho gazed at Nick. "Ok, by me. Just follow my truck. I'll let you know when we get there."

And with that, Jericho headed for the parking lot, pausing in front of the coal truck parked next to Nick's Buick.

"Some damn Buckeye parked his car in here so tight I can't open my door. I'll give that bastard a message," Jericho said, angrily, pulling out an iron pipe from his truck's tool box.

"Wait, wait, that's my car," Nick bellowed.

"Your car? Whatcha doin' with Ohio plates?"

"It's a long story. Just let me get in my car, and I'll get out of your way." Squeezing into his front seat, Nick slowly backed, out waving for Jericho to get in front of him. These hillbilly boys sure seem strange, he thought. "Justin must have been adopted," he said out loud and laughed at his own joke.

Nick followed the lumbering coal truck up Highway 421 and they turned off on 119. Then Jericho stopped his truck in the middle of the road and, getting out, jogged back to Nick's car. Still picking his teeth, he mumbled, "The next road, turn right. Walter's back about a half mile. The only house on the road." Nodding his head and returning to his truck, he got in his vehicle and sped off.

Nick watched the truck disappear around a curve. He turned off where Jericho had indicated and followed the road until it came to a dead end at a coal tipple.

"What the hell....?" Nick exclaimed; and retracing his path, he looked carefully down both sides of the road. There wasn't a single dwelling to be seen.

So intent was he in his search that he almost collided with a coal truck which was blocking his path.

Suddenly, two men jumped out of the cab, their shoes scattering the gravel on the road.

Oh, shit. Wouldn't you know it, Nick thought. A couple of really big ones.

Nick quickly got out, too. He could sense the seriousness of his predicament, and he knew he needed some maneuvering room.

One of the men was clutching a tire iron in his right hand while the other had a crow bar. Nick was no stranger to this kind of threat. He had grown up with it. He, in fact, preferred it to some slick lawyer picking his pocket.

He pulled out his .32. The men stopped.

"You sons of bitches want to live? Turn around and back toward me." To emphasize his command, he cocked his revolver and pointed it right at their stomachs.

Nick was surprised that they were surprised. It showed in their faces. They turned around meekly and backed toward him. He shouted for them to drop the tire iron and crow bar and spread out, face down. They quickly complied.

Walking over to them, he asked, "What the hell have I done to deserve this welcoming committee?" The larger of the two turned his face sideways and said with a tremulous voice that Jericho told them he was looking for the Jenkins'.

Nick was perplexed. "Yeah. So?"

The big guy gave him an introductory lesson on the suspicious nature of mountain folks by telling him that his Ohio plates were a sure sign of trouble.

"So you were going to trash me because I had Ohio plates?" Nick wasn't getting the picture.

"We don't like outsiders here," the other prone man yelled.

"Got any rope?" Nick asked, nudging the talker with his foot.

"In my truck."

Nick walked toward the truck but spun around quickly; and sure enough, one of the men was reaching for the tire iron. Nick fired a shot in his direction. "You that anxious to die, asshole?"

Finding the rope, Nick returned and tied both securely.

"Now, you two roll out over the road down in to that ditch and don't you move from there."

From the iciness in Nick's voice, the two realized their lives were hanging by a thread. They rolled and rolled and rolled.

Nick went to the truck, pulled the keys from the ignition and tossed them into the field; and returning to the Buick, he was able to maneuver around the coal truck and head back to town.

By now, the General Store was open. He went in, cautiously, beginning to doubt Justin's stories about Harlan's being a piece of heaven.

"Yes sir. Can I hep ya?" An older gentleman with one leg and two crutches came out from the back room.

"I'm looking for Walter Jenkins," Nick said. Glancing around the store, he noticed the place had a unique mélange of smells – a mixture of tobacco, gasoline and baked goods.

"Sure," the man replied. "C'mon inta the back room."

Nick was not happy with that request. Sounded a little too much like, "Turn right, the Jenkins house is the only one on the road."

But he followed, keeping his right hand inside his jacket.

They walked through the shop and stepped out onto the back porch which seemed unstable, even to Nick's slight weight. "See that house over yonder. That's the Jenkins." The old man turned and spat into an empty five gallon lard can. Just missing his aim, the brown liquid slid down the side of the greasy container, following the tracks of previous attempts. "Gul dang," he muttered.

"Thanks," Nick said. He spun and hurried through the store and out the front, letting the screen door bang behind him. He wasn't sure how long it would take his trucker friends to untie themselves, but he wanted out of there before that time.

Jumping into his Buick, he followed the road until he came to a gravel path which he thought would take him back to the Jenkins' place. The road was slick from a recent rain and the creek alongside it was just now beginning to recede. Nick could see toilet paper hanging from the tree limbs that leaned over the creek. "Damn," he said, "their toilets must flush out right into the creek. Some Paradise."

As he turned a sharp corner, he saw a coal truck parked in front of the Jenkins' house, an ageing structure that looked like it could blow over with the slightest of winds.

"Jericho, I bet," Nick said. "Well, I want to meet that bastard again."

Leaving his car in the roadway, he began walking very deliberately, taking a circuitous route to the back door. The house was lifeless and bleak – eerily silent. Expecting trouble, he drew his revolver, slowly opened the back door and stepped quietly into an empty hallway. An unnatural darkness caused him to pause. He cautiously closed the door, only to feel cold steel against the back of his neck.

"Don't move a muscle," the man said, reaching for Nick's gun hand.

Jericho appeared on the right side of Nick and, grabbing him by his shoulders, shoved him into a bedroom.

As Nick turned to face the men, he said, "Oh, shit, Justin, you scared the hell out of me."

Justin was standing there, not smiling. Jericho handed him Nick's gun which, along with his own .38, Justin quickly pointed directly at his buddy's face.

"You son-of-a-bitch. I never thought it would be you, Nick. It never occurred to me. We were friends." Justin looked deeply into Nick's eyes, something he had never been able to do with an assigned mark – his anger over Nick's betrayal erased his usual aversion of the probing nature of his victim's gaze.

Nick pretended to be baffled. "What the hell is going on, Justin? Two bruisers down the road tried to waylay me, and now you're acting like I'm your worst enemy."

"Aren't you?" the words spat out between clenched teeth.

Nick began to experience what all of Justin's prey felt in their final moments. Looking into his eyes, a pervading sensation of fear filled Nick's belly; so much so, his heart beat quickened, his hands became unusually clammy and small beads of perspiration dotted his brow. Nick knew he had to buy time.

"Justin, can we talk alone? I've got some questions. Mr. Carusi sent me down here...."

"Yeah, I'll bet he did," Justin interrupted, derisively, as he cocked his .38.

The sound of the hammer locking in position is usually one of the last things a victim hears. Trying desperately to conceal the inner workings of his body, Nick said, in a tone louder than he intended, "Can't we talk alone?" His eyes darted between his two captors.

Justin continued to glare at Nick. His anger at his buddy's betrayal enveloped the room. This was the first time in Justin's career that he actually knew who he was going to kill. With Nick, however, it went far beyond just knowing him; he was Justin's first and only friend. At this moment, he despised him for his perfidy. This heightened emotion pushed Justin to step closer to Nick. When he saw him flinch, Justin felt a momentary wave of compassion.

He released the hammer on his .38. Handing Jericho Nick's gun, he told him to leave.

Feeling the cadence of his heart slow down, Nick took a neatly pressed handkerchief out of his breast pocket and wiped his face.

Justin's tone of voice re-ignited his fear. "I'm listening. What questions?"

Nick's words came staccato fashion, "Well, yesterday we read that you hit Kiger. Damn it, Justin, he wasn't even on the list!"

Nick wondered if he needed to be more conciliatory. He could see Justin's eyes turning a dark blue, and he was squinting. Nick had observed him at work, and he felt he didn't have much time to talk.

"Mr. Carusi sent me here to find you – to find out why you hit Kiger – and my God, why the little boy? And don't tell me you didn't do it. You always come here after a job. You're here. You must have done it." Nick knew the truth of his trip here would get him killed.

Again, silence from Justin. Taking a few steps back from Nick, he leaned on a pine dresser that had loose change, odd assortments of paper and old photographs sprawled on the top. Taking a cigarette out, Justin opened the top drawer and rustled its contents until he found a book of matches.

Striking the match, he said methodically, "Why would I take out someone I wasn't hired to hit? And why would I shoot a little kid? Does that sound like me, Nick?" Taking a long deep drag, Justin felt the bitterness rise up within. "Shit. I read about it in the paper. That was the first I heard of the murder, but I knew Carusi would think I did it."

Emboldened by Justin's openness, Nick asked why he had returned to Harlan if he had not killed Kiger.

"Pretty fucking obvious, my friend." Nick winced at Justin's profanity. Not one to use that four letter expletive easily, Justin would only resort to its use when he was especially angry.

"I knew that if Carusi thought I had screwed up, I was a dead man. When I got word from Uncle Billy that an outsider was on the way over, I knew what I had to do. You could have knocked me over when I saw you. How the fuck could you take this job?" He tossed the half-finished cigarette on the floor and crushed its embers with the heel of his boot.

"My job was to come here and talk with you. Look Justin, if you tell me you didn't do it, that's good enough for me." Nick scooted back on the bed and leaned against the hand carved headboard. "I met some newspaper guy in Florence who was working on the story, and he said that Kiger's fifteen year old daughter was the shooter. If that's the case, you're off the hook."

Justin paced in front of the closed door. "Are you fucking kidding me? A fifteen year old broad killed her old man and brother? I'm finding that one hard to believe."

Opening the door, Justin told Jericho to get his truck and meet him out in front of the house. "Well, I'll tell ya what I'm gonna do. 'Cause we *were* friends, I'm gonna keep ya here until we get this afternoon's newspaper. I hope you're not lying to me, old buddy, 'cause if you are, you know what that means." Nick knew all too well.

He had to spend the afternoon tied to the bedpost, waiting for the *Knoxville New Sentinel* to be delivered; and as hour after hour passed, he began fantasizing his own end. Knowing that it would be quick and painless did not help, but he replayed his death over and over in his mind's eye. Justin would probably take him to some remote wooded area and put a bullet through the back of his head. His demise certainly wouldn't get the kind of attention that the Kiger murders did. Who around here would care that a 40 year old Dago had died in a violent way? Who would miss him? There had been very few times in Nick's life that he had to think about the possibility of his own imminent death. But this ranked pretty high in those times.

There was no guarantee that the afternoon paper would even mention the Kiger case; and if it did, would it have the latest information about the Deputy's suspicions that the girl killed her old man? What if....What if....

As his thoughts rambled, he wondered if he could have really come down here and killed Justin? Never before had he been ordered to end the life of a friend. Could he really do it? He asked himself if Justin would have killed him—but from the look in Justin's eyes, there was little doubt. In one of the dinner conversations they had several years ago at the Mounds in Covington, he had asked Justin how old he was when he first killed someone.

Justin's answer was a curt, "Fifteen." And Nick remembered his own reply, "Holy shit....you were just a kid! Were you a hit man at fifteen?"

Justin did not respond right away, seemingly lost in his own thoughts. "That was a long time ago, Nick, a long time."

By 1941 these two men had become close enough that they were able to kid each other, saying things that, to a casual acquaintance, might offend.

"So, you were hit man at fifteen. What was your first job?"

"It wasn't a job, Nick."

Nick would not change the subject. "How much did you get? I'll bet it was a lot less than the five hundred you get now."

"You aren't going to let that go, are you?" Justin said, grinning at his friend.

"C'mon. I've told you my story. What was it like for you the first time?" In addition to hearing Justin's narratives on his Harlan life, Nick also found great pleasure in the changing speech patterns Justin reverted to when reminiscing.

Scooting his chair closer to the table, Justin moved his plate to one side and, leaning forward, began telling Nick about his and his daddy's being hired by Hen Branham, his mother's cousin, to build an underground storage area on his mountain, so he could hide his corn liquor until it was transported to Cincinnati or Knoxville.

Justin told Nick how ole Hen's moon shine was in as much demand as Coca Cola. Although there are many recipes for making moonshine, Hen's formula was one he painstakingly tweaked and mastered over many years. Moonshine begins by mixing corn meal, sugar, water, yeast, and malt into mash which is then placed in a still and left to ferment. The exact time it took for fermentation depended upon the amount of heat that was applied to the mixture. And this was Hen's secret – he nailed down a certain temperature that gave his moon shine a kick that could not be replicated by other 'shiners. Consequently, he was generating a substantial amount of money back in the late twenties and was willing to pay them – his family – more than they could ever make, working for anyone else.

Hiring family wasn't as altruistic as it appeared on the surface. Justin explained that Hen knew if he paid them each a dollar an hour, that he and his daddy would keep their mouths shut about what they were doing on the mountain. The Appalachian code that blood was thicker than water would further protect his clandestine distillery.

As they planned for the building, they all agreed that the underground structure needed cured poplar boards, sturdy and long-lasting. As a way to save time, ole Hen hitched up his mules and traipsed down to the mill in the valley to choose the strongest and most seasoned poplars while Justin and his daddy burrowed out the earth from the mountainside.

"My daddy and me dug out enough of that hillside for a building measuring twelve by twenty. Working ten hour days, we were determined to get the whole damn thing done in a month's time. Even though we were gettin' good money, Daddy was not one to take advantage of his relatives."

Hen wanted everything done in time to plant grass, wildflowers and maybe even trees, small ones like the dogwood and the redbud—anything that would hide his moonshine storage building from prying eyes, especially from the air. The mountain laurel, all white and fresh looking, the yellow colored bloodroot and those delicate yellow violets were all over the mountain sides as Justin and his father labored; but Justin, having grown up with all this, paid very little attention to the natural beauty which surrounded him. It wasn't until after years in the monochromatic cities of the 1940's that he confessed to yearning for visits down home every spring in time to share in this annual rebirth.

The biggest challenge in their current project was to make a roof strong enough to hold tons of dirt. Using shakes over tar paper, they fastidiously attached them to each other, forming the covering of the roof; then muscling whole poplar trees, still oozing with sap into position, they added additional bracing for the building As Justin and his daddy were about ready to bury the whole structure, except for the secret entrance way, John Finn, a moon shiner from the other side of Branham's Mountain, walked into the clearing.

" 'I declare,' John said, laughing, 'Walter, what kind of shit work are you doin' now?' Without bothering to look up, Daddy said, matter-of-factly, 'Just puttin' up a barn, a place for Henry to cure out his tobacco. What are ya doin' over here? I thought he tole you what'd happen if he caught ya snoopin' on his mountain agin?'

" 'Well, this time I brought me a friend along,' John said, holding up his rifle. 'I'm thinkin' my friend oughta convince ole Hen that I ain't such a bad neighbor. Ya don't mind if I take a look inside what you're callin' a tobacco curin' buildin'? I might just like you boys to build me one of these things.'

" 'Now ya know Henry ain't gonna 'preciate your comin' around his barn. Why doncha just go on your way,' Daddy said, walking toward John.

" 'Stop right there, Walter. I aim to see this barn. So you just git outta my way.' John's tone became menacing.

"Nick, you sure you want to hear all this?" Justin asked, hoping to go to a more pleasant subject.

Although Nick could see this topic was uncomfortable for Justin, he had to hear it all. "Then what happened?" he asked, encouraging Justin.

"Well, I was inside the barn, building shelves for ole Hen's moonshine jars. And when I heard John's voice, I stopped and listened; and I could tell by the way Daddy talked, he was not gonna let John in the barn. I also knew that Daddy's .38 was there in the barn with me and that Daddy was just going to have to *talk* John out of trying to come in the barn. Pretty unlikely, I thought, since John had a gun. I'd heard about John's reputation as a brawler, especially when he'd had a little too much of his own shine; so I figured I was gonna have to do somethin'. I don't know about you, Nick, but I've been shootin' a pistol since I was ten; so when I pulled Daddy's .38 out of its holster, I had no doubt that, if I had to, I could do whatever was necessary. I heard my daddy say, in a loud voice, 'John, doncha come any closer to this here barn. I don't want no trouble, but I ain't gonna let ya in there.'

John had a nasty temper and was known to lash out at man or beast when the mood overcame him. It was a fact that he had once killed his only mule with a mattock handle when it veered out of a field that John was plowing, trying to get to some water.

His neighbors also tell a story about his first car, a ten year old Ford. It seems that he got up one morning to go to town for supplies; and to pay for them, he had loaded the car with eggs, handpicked blackberries and ginseng root. When he went to the front of the Ford to crank the engine, it backfired; and the crank handle hit his wrist, almost breaking it. In one of those dark fits of temper, he used that handle to completely destroy his car.

It looked as though he was working himself into one of those moods again. "He snickered. 'Oh, you ain't gonna let me in, huh? What ya figurin' to do—you gonna talk me to death?'

"Raising his voice, my daddy said, 'My boy's inside the barn. He's got a gun on ya right now, so why doncha just go on home? We don't want no trouble.'

"Well, Nick, when I heard that, I knew what my daddy wanted me to do. I quietly climbed up by the roofline and looked past the overhang. I could see Daddy's back, and I could see John facing him. When John cocked his rifle and pointed it at Daddy, saying, 'Well, Walter, why doncha tell your boy that he damn well better shoot straight 'cause, as soon as I hear that gun of his'n fire, I'm gonna kill you.' He seemed to be darin' me to do something.

"No offense, Nick, but your snub-nosed .32 wouldn't have been much help to me. But that long barrel .38 I was holdin' was, at about 30 feet, awful accurate. I took my time 'cause I knew I had to hit him right in the head. Anywhere else and John woulda killed my daddy."

That was as far as Justin's story went. Nick waited, but Justin had nothing else to say. "Come on," Nick pleaded, "you can't stop there."

"What do you want to hear, Nick? That I shot him between the eyes? That his head jerked back; that when he fell to the ground his whole body twitched and quivered; that, as he died, he pissed all over himself?"

Nick was surprised by this graphic description. "So is that how it happened?"

"Nick, you've been in this business longer than I have. You know what it's like."

Justin looked past Nick, still reliving that first experience. "You know how ugly death can be."

Remembering that statement from Justin returned Nick to his current predicament—that of being tied to a bedpost in the Jenkins' home. Yank, and pull and twist as he might, the ropes held. His salvation lay elsewhere, and that's what worried him.

Based upon his religions beliefs, he knew that, unless he could locate a priest, the afterlife would not be a pleasant place. Since his last confession with Father Paul, he had been involved in some very unsavory jobs and needed forgiveness in the worst way. Can a sinner be forgiven without the presence of a priest? Nick wondered. Having always been the runt of his large Italian family, he had become very assertive, very aggressive to compensate for his size; and he had always been willing to take a chance – especially if the payoff would justify the risks. Therefore he took a deep breath; and although he could not assume a prayerful position, he began his one-on-one meeting with his Maker.

"God, I've never really thought I'd need your help for anything. I've always been good at figuring out things for myself." After a long silence, he continued. "...but this time I can't make it alone." The thought of his own death terrified him. He always imagined that when the moment finally came, he, like his father and grandfather before him, would be old and feeble, having lived a full life. Always convinced that death would meet him on his own terms, his belly quivered as the certainty grew that life was no longer under his control. Feeling the sweat of his fear under his arms, in the palms of his hands and trickling down his back, he experienced the strength of his will re-exerting itself, demanding to be heard.

Whispering, he said, "God, I need to strike a bargain with you; and I think you know, I may be a lot of things, but I am a man of my word. If I get out of this alive, I promise you, on my mother's grave, that I will change my life. I swear to you I will walk away from what I've been doing – the Syndicate, the killing, the whole bit. You have my sacred oath that I will lead a good life."

For some reason Nick's mind drifted back to a summer, many years ago, when he was on his uncle's farm outside Naples, Italy. He remembered it as one of the few times when he felt completely at peace with himself and pleasantly exhausted at the end of a long day in the vineyard. Uncle Nicholas, his namesake and godfather, was a man of few words. This uncle taught Nick the value of hard work and familial love, not by what he said, but by what he did—by the way he lived his life. When Nick was younger, he chafed at the thought that his life might become as constricted and unrewarded as he viewed his uncle's to be; but now, as his mind jolted him back to the image of his uncle's face, he began to cry. These tears were the first, as far back as he could remember, that he had ever shed. "My God, I'll live a quiet life like my Uncle Nicholas and…." His supplications were interrupted by the sound of Jericho's coal truck as it came to stop in the side yard. Justin shouted above the roar of the engine, "C'mon, c'mon, let's get this over with."

*　　　*　　　*

Before Nick left Harlan that afternoon, he bought an evening newspaper – a souvenir and a reminder of how close he'd come to being an unwilling participant in Justin's vocation. Glancing at the paper on the car seat, opened to the front page, he read those wonderful headlines: "Daughter Arrested for Kiger Murder." He hoped the girl's arrest would satisfy Carusi, as well; otherwise both he and Justin would now be expendable. Justin tried to give Nick back the contract money, the $500.00 which the Syndicate had advanced him for his involvement in this shot across the bow of Covington's ship of fools, the city commissioners, but Nick refused. Trying to sidestep the truth, the Messenger said, "Mr. Carusi didn't send me down here to take your money."

Nick thought back to his handshake with Justin, as he prepared to leave Harlan—and sadly, realized that their relationship could never be the same again.

Chapter Eight
A Dream Within A Dream:
Jail
(August 17 – 21, 1943)

8

When Joan awoke, she was frightened by a new sensation, something she had never experienced before. She felt removed from her body. It was as if she were floating above it, allowing her to observe this girl lying in a strange bed in an unfamiliar room. Watching herself, she noticed that the girl looked terribly fatigued and confused. The furrows in her forehead revealed that she was reliving the violent events of the night before. As if trying to shake the thoughts from her head, the girl quickly sat upright, rubbed her eyes, got up and began slowly pacing around the room, touching the sink, the cold steel bars and the gray sheets. Joan tried to merge with her but could not. The girl wouldn't let her—not yet.

The girl sat on the hard cot, clutching a lumpy pillow. She looked around and slowly began to rock back and forth, holding the pillow tightly. Breathing deeply, she began to recall the men, so many men, asking questions —men with shiny badges, in uniforms—others in suits. They kept parading in and out of the library at Rosegate-

- then, later, in her bedroom and again, even later, in the living room. At first they seemed to be kind and gentle; but as hour after hour passed, their demeanors became more aggressive and accusatory. Questions... "Did you kill your father and brother?" "Did you shoot your mother?" "Did you have a fight with your parents?" "What intruder?" "What did he look like?" "Who else was in the house?" "What did you do with the guns?" "Did you and mother talk before you went to Mr. Mayo's for help?" "What did the two of you talk about?" And more questions....so many that the girl drifted off to sleep as they were badgering her—and there she stayed for over an hour. No matter, they were relentless. "You killed them, didn't you?" they barked at her.

Some papers were placed before the girl, just next to her head as it rested on the desk.

"Sign it. This is what you said you did, now sign this and then you can go home." Home, the girl thought. Yes, I want to go home. Her rocking became more deliberate and feverish.

As Joan looked down upon the girl, somehow she knew—if they did not merge, she would be lost forever. Finally, Joan heard the girl say, "You can come in now and, please, don't ever leave again."

*   *   *

The next morning, the jailer, Elmer Kirkpatrick, brought Joan a breakfast of pancake and eggs. "Well," he said, jovially, "You look much better in the light of day. Want some coffee to go with those pancakes?"

The smell of pancakes and country sausage made Joan inhale deeply. It was as if she were just coming out of a deep, dark nightmare. The hunger pangs that rumbled in her stomach surprised her. She was beginning to feel more connected to her body.

"Yes, please. I'd like some coffee with lots of cream and just a little sugar." She forced a smile.

"You're going to have a couple of visitors today," Elmer said.

Joan was caught with a mouthful of pancakes whose taste was surpassed only by those made by her father. She looked at Mr. Kirkpatrick but could not respond. Understanding the situation, Elmer continued, "Judge Cropper is coming to see you. Do you know who he is?" She nodded in the negative.

"He's the county judge – awfully nice. He was upset with me when he learned that we put you in jail."

"Does that mean I can go home?" Joan asked; and then, from the change in her expression, Elmer could see that the events of the night before were flooding over her. She turned away, her shoulders beginning to shake.

"Don't you worry, honey," Elmer said, "Judge Cropper will help you."

He felt that she might want to be alone, so he said, "I'll be back with the coffee."

Elmer and his wife, Julia, really weren't sure what to do with Joan, a beautiful auburn haired 15 year old girl.

It didn't seem right that she should be locked behind bars in their Spartan jail, a young lady who had been exposed to the more affluent side of life. Her father, Carl Kiger, after all, had been Covington's Vice-Mayor, as well as a city commissioner. Elmer had seen Rosegate, the two story summer home the Kiger's owned out on the Dixie Highway, one of the finest places in Boone County. Deputy Sheriff, Irvin Rouse, had told him that the Kiger's also had a home on Crescent Avenue in Covington and that Joan attended the prestigious La Salette Academy. Carl was a rising star in local politics. It was rumored that he was in line to be Covington's next mayor.

So it was that after Boone County Judge Carroll Cropper spoke about Joan's lodging at the jail that they decided to allow her to share the jailer's private quarters. Having a girl who was accused of killing her father and brother sleep in the next room, no bars, no locks between them, for many people, might seem fool hearty; but Elmer and his wife, after seeing how well Joan comported herself and just having a gut feeling that she had nothing to do with the murders, would sleep well.

After finishing the pancakes and before Elmer had returned with the coffee, Joan walked over to her housecoat, hoping she had brought a comb. She was surprised, at first, to feel just a hole in the pocket; however, she immediately recalled that last week she had lost her favorite lipstick, only to find that it had made its way through the hole and had lodged in the lining. Pulling the hem of the housecoat up, she ran her hand along the edges and, sure enough, there was the comb – and there was something else, as well. Gradually she eased the items up and into the pocket, and her fingers touched a small and cold object. Pulling it out, she was startled to see that it was the shell casing she had removed from her father's gun last night. She just now realized that she had not put a live cartridge back in the chamber of his gun; and she had, in fact, brought the shell casing, unwittingly, to jail.

Rolling it around in her hand, Joan once again began thinking back to the previous night's horrors – an action she would repeat for the rest of her life – rolling that empty casing around and around in her hand, trying to separate the dream from the reality. She could still hear her mother pleading for her to get help, asking her, with fear in her voice, if she'd had another nightmare; and she could still see the shadowy figure in front of her, still feel the kick of the pistol in her hand as she fired it again and again. The shell casing rolled faster through her fingers. Feeling conflicted, she wondered: had she really shot those guns? She would spend a lifetime brooding over the events of that night, as she desperately sought closure: was it just a dream, a dream that was so convincing that she would never be able to separate it from what really happened?

Her family was the center of her life. From the time he could walk, Jerry was her shadow – following her everywhere she went. Could she, as Mr. Maynard suggested when he talked with her at length in her bedroom the night of …. that night ….that she was having one of her nightmares. Could she, in one of her nightmares, have shot them? She thought not—yet she'd often had nightmares which caused her to do strange things.

She remembered the shock that she felt the very first time she experienced one. It was at Rosegate. She woke up in her dad's fishing boat in the middle of the lake. Completely baffled, she rowed back to the dock, ran upstairs and tried to rouse her mother. "Mamma," she whispered, not wanting to wake her daddy, "Mamma, wake up. Something strange just happened." That was when her mother re-assured her that she was in a sleepwalking state. "Your daddy has the same problem. Just go back to bed and we'll talk about it tomorrow."

Her mother told Joan of the time she found her in the kitchen eating a snack which Joan had prepared while in one of these somnambulistic states. The strangest occurrence, Joan reflected, was when she awoke in her father's car at a stop light in downtown Covington – and this was long before she had been out with her father, learning how to drive, in anticipation of her 16th birthday.

But she'd never done anything to hurt anyone—ever. Could she have pulled the trigger fifteen times? She wavered between thinking she could and knowing that she could not. These ambivalent feelings continued to haunt her.

Another problem she had was separating the nightmare from her real life. Just like right now, here in the Boone

County Jail: was this part of her ongoing nightmare? Her tortured reverie was interrupted by Elmer.

"I told you the Judge was coming over. This is Judge Cropper. He's going to help you."

Joan noticed that Mr. Kirkpatrick opened her jail door without even unlocking it. She had been in an unlocked cell. Strange, she thought.

The Judge was a slight man with pitch black shiny hair that was slicked back into a pompadour. His eyes look kind, Joan reflected, and she noticed that he smiled easily.

"Hello Joan," the judge said, extending his hand. "I'm sorry you had to spend the night behind bars. We're going to fix that. Mr. and Mrs. Kirkpatrick have agreed to give you a room in their quarters, so you'll be moving there later today. You'll be much more comfortable in a regular bedroom."

A sense of relief flooded over her. The judge must think she's innocent to do that; and the jailer must think so to, since he did not even lock her cell door. This was quite different from that Sheriff and his deputy and all those other people last night asking question after question, making her believe she had murdered her.... she couldn't let herself even think it. Just because she had nightmares did not make her a murderer; yet, knowing that she had no control of these episodes often caused her to sink into a state of self-pity, worrying about her ability to manage the sleeping Joan, as well as the waking Joan.

Her nightmares had begun several years ago with the onset of her menstrual cycle; not every month, but the dreams came often enough that she began dreading her periods. Her friends would complain about cramps and the general discomforts of pads, stained clothes and menstrual odor. As far as she knew, not one of her friends had to deal with sleep walking; however, since she was so ashamed of her problem, she never asked.

"Joan," the judge began, "The sheriff has filled me in on what happened last night. We've been in touch with your Uncle Fred. He's going to try to arrange bail for you and will be responsible for your well-being while we sort this thing out. The sheriff and the county prosecutor think they have enough evidence to charge you and, maybe, your mother with the deaths of your father and brother."

His words swirled around in her brain…. bail…. evidence….charge you and maybe your mother…. "How is Mamma?" Joan blurted out. "Where is she? Can I go see her? Is she all right?"

The judge gently patted her hand, treating it as if it were a fine piece of porcelain. "We're going to try to arrange that, Joan. Your mother is in St. Elizabeth's Hospital. She's in critical condition because she's lost so much blood, but the doctor says she is going to make it. We're also trying to locate your two brothers. We know they're in the military, but don't know where they are."

Her other brothers – she hadn't given them a thought. They were both in the service. John was stationed at the

Great Lakes Naval Station and Joe was a marine lieutenant, who was stationed…. She could not remember. I wonder what they will make of this, she pondered.

*   *   *

Shortly after the Judge left, Julia Kirkpatrick shuffled into Joan's cell with a Coke. Handing the cold sweaty bottle to her, she told her that Elmer had to go to Gulley's to get a part for his lawnmower; and in the same breath, she notified Joan that Father Nicholas Judermann, her parish priest, was here to see her.

Joan was totally surprised with this piece of news. But after a few moments, she decided that she wasn't so surprised after all.

Father Nick was a balding, short, rotund pastor whose joviality and quick wit made St. Aloysius one of the more desirable parishes to belong to. More like a PR man than a priest, his bingo parties, carnivals and hobnobbing with the elite of Covington brought in more financial support to the church then it had seen in decades.

The Kigers went to the noon Sunday Mass without fail; and Carl, one of the volunteer male parishioners who passed the collection basket, brought the alms to the altar and kept the Communion line moving, always made sure that his Sunday envelop had a brand new crisp twenty dollar bill in it. Joan's family habitually sat in the last pew because Carl liked to be one of the first church goers out the door, so he could stand on the front steps to "meet and greet" his fellow Covingtonians. When he became Vice-Mayor and aspired to become Mayor, he took every opportunity to shake hands and get to know people, whether it was at church, the grocery store or at the gas pump.

For Joan, Father Nick was someone she knew from a distance, as she watched him move about the altar with his back to the congregation. When she received Holy Communion from him, she usually cast her eyes downward as she asked God to forgive her sins, so she would be worthy of this sacrament.

When he walked into her cell, she saw his face up close for the very first time. She was startled at how homely he was; yet, even with his pockmarked complexion, large bulbous red nose, and pencil thin lips, he still seemed to have a charismatic air about himself.

There was an awkward silence between them which was interrupted by Julia who suggested that they move into the parlor where they would be more comfortable and have privacy.

As they entered the living room, Father Nick motioned for Joan to sit on the sofa while he pushed a brightly flowered wingback chair close to her. They engaged in small talk about La Salette and Joan's Latin teacher, Sister Cornelius, who, much to her surprise, happened to be Father Nick's cousin. Telling Joan some humorous personal family stories about Lelah, the nun's baptized name, she found herself smiling slightly for the first time since that night.

When he finished with his gossip, there were a few more moments of uncomfortable silence. Finally Father Nick asked Joan if she wanted to go to Confession. For the first time in his religious life, Nick, who was never at a loss for words, didn't know exactly what to say to a parishioner, especially one so young and one who had been accused of committing the most mortal of mortal sins. So, he thought the best way to engage her would be by asking this question.

Joan wasn't surprised that he wanted to hear her Confession; and as she was about to say yes, she remembered the confession of another kind—the one she signed while she was completely physically and emotionally exhausted just a few hours ago. And after a night's sleep, she realized that confessing has its own consequences. Admitting guilt to those men yesterday was bad enough, but she knew that confessing to a priest had more dire and everlasting implications.

Since she had become a teenager, Joan, occasionally, questioned whether or not there was a God. On most days she thought there was, especially after she returned from Mass and communion when a feeling of peace seemed to fill her heart. Right now this very moment, Joan desperately wanted to believe there was a God.

Examining her conscience, the greatest and surest guilt she felt was disobeying, lying to and angering her daddy to such a degree that he repeatedly hit her the day before he died. If she could only erase from her mind his enraged face, the wicked fight they had. Dear God, please forgive me. Tell my daddy I'm sorry, she thought to herself as she quietly wept.

What else would she confess to Father Nick? If she, in fact, was responsible for what happened to her brother and father, she would need absolution—forgiveness. But, what if she didn't kill them? What if there *was* someone else in the house the other night? Why should she confess to something she didn't do? What would God think if I did confess, but really didn't do it? Does that get the real killer off the hook in the eyes of God? Joan thought, Should I confess, just to be safe? Maybe I did do it.

*   *   *

Father Nick stood up and blessed Joan when she finished her Act of Contrition. Touched by the nature of her confession, he wished they had been in a confessional rather than in such a casual environment.

"Father Nick," Joan looked at him as he was about to leave. "I'd like for us to pray to St. Jude." In one of Joan's religion classes, she learned of St. Jude who is known as the patron saint of desperate cases. When she and Mae had had a terrible fight and Mae vowed she'd never, ever speak to her again, Joan fervently prayed to St. Jude; and by the next day, Mae apologized. Joan was convinced that St. Jude worked a miracle.

Asking her to get down on her knees, along with him, he said the following prayer.

Most Holy apostle, St. Jude, faithful servant and friend of Jesus, the name of the traitor who delivered thy beloved Master into the hands of His enemies hath caused thee to be forgotten by many, but the Church honors and invokes thee universally as the patron of hopeless cases, of things despaired of. Pray for Joan, who is so miserable. Make use, I implore thee, of that particular privilege accorded to thee, to bring visible and speedy help where help is almost despaired of. Come to her assistance in this great need that she may receive the consolation and succor of Heaven in all her necessities, tribulations, and sufferings, particularly over the next few months and that she may praise God with thee and all the elect throughout eternity. She promises, O blessed Jude, to be ever mindful of this great favor, and she will never cease to honor thee as her special and powerful patron, and to do all in her power to encourage devotion to thee. Amen.

As he bade his farewell to Joan, he asked her if she wanted him to say a special prayer at her brother and father's funerals which were to be held in two days. Joan brusquely turned away from him, shaking her head.

As Father Nick drove back to St. Aloysius, he made a mental note to send Joan a St. Jude medal, one he had received when he last visited the Vatican.

*   *   *

The morning of August 19 was hot and humid. Joan hadn't slept well. Her mind would not rest. She was very excited about seeing her mother for the first time since that night. Myriad questions interrupted her every thought: "What would she say to me? Would she be really mad at me? Does she think I did it? What will I say to her?" For the first time, she felt grief swelling within her, this particular night's silence having opened the door.

Although she loved her and felt she was a solid presence in the family, Joan hadn't been as close to her mother as she had with her daddy. He was the apple of her eye, and she knew the reverse was true, as well. Whenever there was an altercation between Joan and her mother, her daddy would step in and defend Joan, often resulting in a fight between her parents.

Her feelings for her mother had been particularly ambivalent since she turned 13. When she was younger, however, the family would tease Jennie that Joan was her clone. Although they were unusually close for a mother and a daughter, the onset of puberty seemed to pull them apart.

Because Carl was so lenient with her, Jennie felt she had to be the disciplinarian, the one to tell Joan when she had too much make-up on or when she didn't like her hair style: "Those bangs are way too long!" "Joan, you look like a Maisie in that outfit."

Her daddy, on the other hand, would never criticize her directly. He was much more subtle: "Joan, I like that outfit you put together but I think another color blouse would make it look even snazzier." And these "suggestions" usually ended with a wink. He was always willing to listen to her, no matter how tired he might be: "Ok, sweetheart, come over here and tell me what's on your mind," as he patted the empty cushion right next to where he was sitting, motioning for her to join him. She looked forward to the long summer days and evenings at Rosegate for many reasons, but especially because, unlike in their Covington home, her daddy seemed more relaxed and available to her.

This reverie intermingled with her grief, and Joan began to experience short rapid jabs of guilt closely followed by feelings of intense shame: "My God, I didn't do it! Sobbing into her pillow, as though it were her closest confidante, she whispered, "My God, I hope I didn't do it."

"Joan, it's time to go. Are you ready?" Mr. Kirkpatrick asked. Without waiting for an answer, he went on, "The Sheriff is parked in the back so you can avoid the crowd out here."

When she walked outside into the stifling summer heat, she saw Uncle Fred. As she approached him, he gave her a quick kiss on the cheek and escorted her to the Sheriff's car where Aunt Eva, Joe and John were waiting. The boys were leaning up against the trunk, so handsome in their uniforms.

She froze when she saw them, eyes averting theirs, her shame sweeping over her.

Joe reached out and hugged her while John patted her shoulder. Their affection comforted Joan. Maybe they don't think I did it either, she thought.

Aunt Eva took her hand and sat next to her on the ride to the hospital. No one spoke a word. As they drove to St. Elizabeth's, the silence turned to perfunctory small talk, "How 'bout those Reds. Aren't they something" "Is this the hottest summer on record?" And of course, chatter about the war.

When they arrived at the hospital, the Sheriff turned and instructed the group. He wanted first to prepare them because they would be greeted by Matt Egan or Leslie Loud, two Covington police officers ordered by Maynard to stand guard outside Jennie's hospital room 24 hours, 7 days a week. These cops were directed not to let anyone see or talk to Jennie without Maynard's specific approval. Jake had several theories as to why Maynard was doing this. One that he toyed with was that these policemen were on a suicide watch. Another was that they were to make certain that whatever Jennie saw and heard the night of the murders stayed within Room 321. And his most favored speculation was that since Jennie was an eye witness to whatever happened that night, she needed protection. In spite of these reasons for having her so closely guarded, it irked him that he, as the Boone County Sheriff, had to ask permission to see a suspect and to jump through hoops that a Covington official established.

None of the family reacted to his disclosure that they would be greeted by a policeman who was guarding Jennie's room. Maynard had only given permission for Joan and her brothers to visit Jennie, and he had insisted that they stay for only 45 minutes, at that.

Fred and Eva were particularly miffed with this restriction because they had not seen Jennie since she was carried out of Rosegate on a stretcher. Although Jake had called Maynard, at Fred's behest, asking that they be allowed, as part of the family, to visit Jennie, Maynard adamantly refused.

As they left the squad car, the Kiger family, without realizing it, walked single file into the main entrance of the hospital and on to the elevator in total silence. Fred, Eva and the Sheriff watched Joan and her brothers walk into Jennie's room. As soon as the door closed, Matt Egan, the day watch guard, quickly planted himself in front of the entrance, hooking his right thumb in his pistol belt.

*   *   *

On August 20, another hot and humid day with the air feeling as thick as honey, Joan again left the jail, but this time to attend the funeral of her father and her brother, as well as their burial, at St. John's cemetery, in Fort Mitchell.

At first, Joan did not want to go. The dread and panic of seeing their lifeless bodies overwhelmed her. The people, the whispers, the stares – she knew it all too well. Whenever she left the jail, she was besieged with onlookers and reporters. "I don't want to go! I can't go!" She sobbed as she made this announcement to her mother and brothers on the day of the hospital visit. "Please, don't make me go!" It was the one and only time they talked about it, and their conversation never directly touched on why or how their loved ones had died.

"Joan, do it for me," was her mother's simple plea. Those words were the last ones spoken in Jennie's room that day. Joan took her mother's hand and kissed it. Although there was silence, it was wrapped in an invisible thread of love and grief, which bound them to each other.

*   *   *

The month of August saw its first gentle breezes on the 21st. Even though they were warm against the skin, they provided a slight relief from the thickness of the previous day's humidity and heat.

Elmer was still upset about the events of the day before. Joan had been acting peculiar just prior to the Sheriff picking her up so that she could attend the funerals of her father and brother. She was pacing in her room, back and forth, back and forth and mumbling unintelligible words over and over again. The sounds frightened his wife and it left him feeling edgy, as well.

"Joan, are you all right?" he asked, with real concern, not sure what kind of a response he might get.

But his question was met with silence, followed by more pacing and more sounds.

The girl wanted to detach again, but Joan wouldn't listen to her pleas, knowing that if she did, she, herself, would be lost forever.

When the Sheriff arrived, Elmer warned him that he thought something was wrong with Joan; but when Jake brought her past them on the way to the car, she looked and acted just fine – except Elmer noticed that her body seemed stiff, her eyes looked somewhat glazed, and when she smiled at them as she walked out the door, her mouth formed into a tight thin line. Elmer and his wife had generally felt sympathy for Joan; but at this moment, their sympathy was tinged with fear.

Later that afternoon, when Joan returned with the Sheriff, her demeanor was remarkably different. She was chattering incessantly about how much she loved Coney Island and of the times she went there with her best friend, Mae. The Sheriff looked bewildered as he left her with the Kirkpatricks.

So, as Elmer brought Joan her dinner this evening, he wasn't sure what state she would be in. Since this was her 16th birthday, his wife had made a special dinner for her and prepared a festive tray with her best china, some flowers in a crystal bud vase and a lace napkin.

When he walked into her room, he eyed Joan cautiously, but she turned at the sound of his footsteps and smiled when she saw the tray. "How very nice! Please tell Mrs. Kirkpatrick, thank you." He was relieved to see that she was back to her old self.

"I brought the afternoon paper along. I always liked to read a little bit after I eat, and maybe you would, too." Placing her dinner on the table, he said, "Hope you like ham, cabbage and cornbread. My wife makes the absolute best cabbage and cornbread in the county!" he said, proudly. The strong smell of the cabbage momentarily took Joan's breath away. Even though she always had this physical reaction to it, she still loved the taste— at least once her nose got used to its pungent aroma.

"Mr. Kirkpatrick, my mamma and brothers will be calling me today to wish me a Happy Birthday, so I hope you'll let me talk with them."

"Of course I will," he said.

"If Mae calls, can I speak to her?" He nodded his head. She was hoping that Mae's parents would let her call. But even so, Joan knew that Mae wouldn't let anything they said or did prevent her from seeing her or talking to her.

After she finished her dinner, Joan was curious about what was going on in the world. At La Salette, the sisters emphasized the importance of keeping up with current events. The last unit of Modern History which Sister Ignatius taught before the end of school in May was on World War II, and Joan always tried to read the *Kentucky Times Star* to find out how the Allies were doing.

Today's front page, however, told a different story. The words startled her, and seeing her name in print along

142

with the word "murder" seemed surreal. Parts of her body began to feel numb whenever she heard or saw something related to that night.

She quickly turned instead to the funny papers – anything to get her mind off Rosegate. Glancing at the images, she couldn't make herself focus on the words.

While at Coney Island last week, Mae Klingenberg and Joan had talked about going to catch a movie at the Albee or the Schubert. Leafing through the various sections of the paper, she found the entertainment page to see what was playing: *Above Suspicion* was at the Albee, starring Fred MacMurray and Joan Crawford.

"Oh, she'd like that movie," Joan said, thinking of Mae and how, in addition to her affinity for Joan Crawford, she loved mysteries. She wondered what Mae was doing. Not having talked with her since their date at Coney Island, she longed for her company. Mae was almost like a missing part of herself. When they were together, Joan felt complete. There was nothing they disagreed about – well, except maybe who was prettier, Joan Crawford or Bette Davis. Mae was a Crawford fan while Joan adored Davis. So their only quarrels had to do with who was the more stunning of the two actresses. Usually after about 10 or 15 minutes of bickering, they would start laughing and agree to move to a topic they were in agreement on. They both were crazy about John Garfield.

Joan looked up as she heard Elmer walk through the door. "Well, little lady, wait 'til you see what we've got for dessert." He realized almost immediately that he shouldn't have brought the newspaper to her since it was filled with pictures and descriptions of the Kiger murder; but it was just a habit that he had developed after becoming jailer. When Julia and he finished their paper, they would share it with whoever might be in jail at the time.

"Do you like strawberry shortcake, Joan?"

"Oh, yes, we raise strawberries on the farm. I love fresh strawberries with ice-cream. Thank you, Mr. Kirkpatrick."

Elmer felt a little better. It seems that the paper did not upset Joan. He would not want to do that.

"Joan, if you like to read, my wife has some magazines you might enjoy. I could bring you some."

"That's awfully nice of you. Maybe later. I don't feel much like reading now. I think I'll work the crossword puzzle in the paper. That's Daddy's favorite...." She trailed off, her eyes looking into a world Elmer could not see.

*   *   *

As the sun began to set on the 21st day of August, on Joan's 16th birthday, this distraught teenager looked from the jail, toward the court house, across the street, and wondered when the nightmare would end.

Taking a deep breath, she held it, thinking that if this were but one of her dreams, she could force herself to wake up, as she usually did, by just refusing to breathe. She reflected, I must still be in my nightmare world: the day before yesterday I visited Mamma in the hospital.

Yesterday, I attended the funeral of Daddy and Jerry, and today, my birthday, I'm still in this awful jail. Will I ever wake up? Finally, the burning sensation in her lungs became too great—she had to exhale.

Chapter Nine
Mae
(August 17 - 19, 1943)

9

Mrs. Klingenberg just didn't know how Mae would take the news of the murders. Joan had been her daughter's best friend since they were in elementary school. When Joan told Mae that she was going to attend La Salette Academy upon eighth grade graduation, Mae begged her parents to send her there, as well. At first, the Klingenbergs said no. They couldn't justify that kind of tuition when there was a fine public high school nearby. But Mae was persistent, telling them she would go to work, scrub floors or do anything to get the money, so she could go to La Salette with Joan. Mae did have a bit of drama to her personality and was often described by teachers and other adults as immature for her age. Her parents finally relented and carefully altered their family budget to allow for the additional expense.

So the girls took the entrance exam together, were measured for their uniforms at the same time and planned their freshman schedule of classes. When Joan was placed in higher level algebra and English classes, Mae sulked and sulked; but once her father told her she'd better stop this nonsense or she'd be going to Holmes High School, she changed her attitude immediately.

Joan was the more outgoing of the two and definitely prettier. Tall, thin with long wavy auburn hair, she would turn the heads of many a young boy and some not so young. By contrast, Mae was shorter, and although she wasn't fat, she had a round figure with small breasts and large hips. Her wide face and high forehead, although not unpleasant to look at, further detracted from the totality of her physiognomy. No matter how much time Mae spent fixing her hair, she always looked as though she just came in from a rain storm. They were an odd pair.

The Kiger family's resources afforded Joan the ability to buy the latest fashions of the time, as well as sundry other adolescent female necessities. Her vanity was strewn with mascara, lipsticks and nail polishes; and her jewelry box was laden with sparkly earrings, necklaces and bracelets. This disparity between the girls would intermittently pull Mae into an envious mood, but it never really lasted very long. Joan was very generous and would share anything she had with Mae. Mrs. Klingenberg would frequently see Joan's clothes in Mae's closet, as well as her nail polish bottles and lipsticks strewn all over Mae's bedroom. At least once a week she would make Mae go through her closet, pick up everything that belonged to Joan and return it to her.

"Joan doesn't care!" Mae would insist. "We're like sisters – what's hers is mine and what's mine is hers."

"Seems to me that you got the better deal on that one," Mrs. Klingenberg would say. She worried that Mae depended too much on Joan, not only for personal items but for academic help, as well as for friendship. Not having the self-confidence that Joan possessed, Mae seemed to be socially inept when meeting new girls; however, with Joan nearby, a buried side to Mae's personality surfaced. She became quite the jokester, making everyone around her laugh. Nothing made her feel better than to have an audience who appreciated her humor. Her heart swelled with pride, especially when she could make Joan laugh.

Although Mae and Joan were in the same Latin class during their freshman year, Joan was the star pupil. Every quiz, every test yielded her nothing less than an A. Mae, on the other hand, was struggling for every D she got. Translating Hannibal's address to his soldiers as they marched into southern Gaul left Mae totally overwhelmed.

"I'm never going to pass this test," she lamented, as they lay on Joan's bedroom floor which was scattered with papers, note cards and books. Here and there were a few empty Pepsi bottles.

"Sure you will," Joan said, shoving some flash cards in front of Mae's face. "Here let's go over these again."

On the day Sister Cornelius returned the graded exams to the students, most of the girls wanted to see how everyone else had done. Mae shrank down in her seat and stuffed her exam paper in her notebook. But

Betty Cummings, who sat directly behind her, saw the red D- and laughed, "Well, as usual Hannibal is Mae's worst enemy! She got the lowest grade, a D-." The rest of the girls chortled and snickered.

Joan said, in a loud voice, "Well, now. That makes two of us who don't get Hannibal."

"You got a D-!" Betty chirped. "Joan, I thought you were the Latin scholar."

"Well, no one's perfect, and this was a very hard exam," Joan said, defiantly, as she grabbed Mae to leave. Silence filled the room, as the other students filed out for their next class. Mae never asked Joan what she really got on that exam. She knew.

Although Mae and Joan had a small group of friends at La Salette, Mary McDermott, Joan Theissen, Marcella (Mickey) Straehle and Dorothy Mae Jones among them, they would generally spend their week-ends alone with each other. Frequently Mae would spend the night at Joan's house – her bedroom was more spacious and luxurious. The girls never experienced a dull moment, as long as they were together. While curled up on Joan's bed, munching on potato chips and pretzels, they swooned over their favorite movie stars while leafing through Photoplay Magazine. Mesmerized by the magazine's Hollywood gossip columns, they could sit for hours reading, without saying a single word to each other. Just being in each other's presence was all they needed.

At one of their overnighters at Joan's house, they smoked their first cigarette together. When Joan saw

Bette Davis and Paul Henreid in *Now Voyager* share a cigarette in the last scene of the movie and Bette says, "Oh, Jerry, don't let's ask for the moon . . . we have the stars," she left the theatre in tears; and it was then she knew she was destined to be a smoker.

So one night, under Joan's tutelage, Mae took a puff of a Lucky Strike and imitated her favorite star, Joan Crawford, as she blew the smoke from her mouth.

"Mae!" Joan said as she cracked her bedroom window open, "That isn't what you do! You have to inhale. Watch me." Grabbing the cigarette from Mae, she took a long drag and inhaled deeply. Even though a wave of nausea made her feel woozy, she smiled at Mae in triumph.

"See," she said, pointing to the smoke that surrounded her, "when you inhale you take the smoke into your lungs, and when you exhale the smoke comes out with more of a haze. Try it again."

Mae was getting a headache but took the cigarette from Joan anyway and did as she was told. As the smoke began to fill her lungs, she felt quite sophisticated and very grown up and then, suddenly, her lungs seemed to rebel and close down. She started choking and gasping for air.

Joan shoved a pillow over her face to stifle the sounds.

Opening her bedroom window even wider, Joan looked below and when she saw that no one was in the backyard, she snuffed the cigarette and tossed it out the window.

"Will you be quiet! My mother will never let you spend another night if she catches us." Suppressing her cough, Mae vigorously nodded her head. "Okay, Okay." She struggled to breathe normally and was finally able to talk.

"Joan, I feel like I'm gonna throw up," she said, as she ran to the bathroom with her hand cupped over her mouth.

In order to keep Mae as a smoking partner, Joan had to find another brand that wasn't so strong. Willie the Penguin won her over. Once she tried Kool cigarettes, she knew immediately that she would never have to smoke alone again.

So on any given Saturday afternoon, they could be found writing fan letters, painting their fingernails, sharing a Kool in secret, fussing with each other's hair or, if they were at Mae's, walking up to the pharmacy for a cherry phosphate. The one activity that would get them shrieking with excitement and out of Joan's bedroom was going to a movie; however, they could only do so when their parents approved of their movie selection. The girls were greatly disturbed when they were forbidden to see Joan Crawford in *The Women*. But no matter how much they balked and sulked, they couldn't win on that one.

So, when Mae's mother told her about Joan and the murders, she became hysterical, screamed and then collapsed right at her mother's feet. After several cold compresses were applied to her forehead, Mae revived, somewhat, but didn't speak one word. Frightened and not knowing what to do next, Mrs. Klingenberg called Dr. Ertel, who was their family doctor and asked if he could come over and talk to her.

Whatever Dr. Ertel said to Mae seemed to comfort her a bit. After he left, she went downstairs looking for her mother who was cooking dinner. The smell of liver and onions made Mae gag.

"Mom, I have to see Joan," she said, trying not to inhale the horrible smells in the kitchen.

"What did Dr. Ertel tell you?"

"Well, he said that Joan is in jail and that her dad and Jerry were murdered. Mrs. Kiger was wounded but..." she put her hands to her mouth and began to cry. "Joan didn't do it! I don't understand this. Joan could never do anything so terrible....never!" her crying swelled into deep heavy sobs. All she could think of was Joan sitting in a jail cell all by herself. The thought terrified her.

Mrs. Klingenberg's heart seemed to split in half as she witnessed her daughter's pain. She, herself, had been stunned with this news about the Kiger family. In the last year or so, there had been some gossip about Carl's entanglement with syndicate types. Many of the neighbors and parents at La Salette wondered how they were able to afford Rosegate, the academy, the new car and all of the other luxuries.

Her mind took her back to the day before the murders when Joan and Mae went to Coney Island and didn't return home until after eleven that night. When Mae announced that Joan would spend the night, Mrs. Klingenberg told Joan that her dad had called earlier quite miffed and was worried about where she was. She told Joan she needed to call her dad; but Joan refused, saying, in what sounded like a manipulative tone, that her parents were having an anniversary party and she didn't have to be there. Joan did assure Mrs. Klingenberg that she would call before she and Mae went to bed.

Mrs. Klingenberg recalled that Mae had revealed to her that Joan and her father weren't getting along so well. It seemed that Mr. Kiger was blaming Mae for Joan's rebellious behaviors. This irked her because it was always Joan who was the instigator of their outings to Coney and their broken curfews. Everyone knew Mae deferred to Joan.

I wonder if she ever did call her father that night, Mrs. Klingenberg pondered.

"Mother," Mae's voice broke into her reverie. "Did you hear me? I have to see Joan."

"Mae, that isn't possible, right now. I'll see if you can write her, but you can't talk to her. She's in jail, for gosh sakes, and I have no idea what's going to happen," she said, putting her arm around Mae and wiping her tears with the hem of her apron.

Mae looked up at her mother and nodded her head. She slowly walked upstairs to her room. Throwing the clothes and magazines that were scattered on her bed to the floor, she lay down and put her pillow over her face, just above her mouth. Darkness was all she could tolerate right now.

Her emotions were spinning out of control. What a horrible mistake this was. She desperately wanted to hold Joan and tell her everything was going to be all right-- that no matter what, she would always be there for her...no matter what.

*   *   *

The sound of her mother's voice calling her to dinner startled her.

"I'm not hungry. Please, just let me be," she said, as she sat up. Mrs. Klingenberg would normally insist that Mae join the family for dinner; under these circumstances, however, she left Mae alone.

Mae went to a small card table that served as a desk next to her dresser. It was in such disarray with note cards, pens and composition books that it took a minute or so to find a clean piece of paper. Making a space where she could write unencumbered, she sat down and began.

Dearest Joan,

I hope you are all right. My mother told me about your dad and Jerry and your mom, too. I am so sorry but I am also so grateful that whoever did this, didn't come after you. I don't understand why you're in jail but I'm sure it's because they want to protect you. After all, whoever did this is still out there. My mom says I can't come and visit you right now but as soon as I can, I promise I'll come and see you. I'm so sad for you and, remember, I think about you constantly. You're not alone...I'm there in jail with you. Until I see you and know that you're all right, I can never be happy again.

We'll have to postpone your 16th birthday party but Happy Birthday from me. I'll give you your gift when I see you.

> *Your best, best friend,*
> *Mae*

PS I'll be sure to take notes in History and Latin class so you won't be too far behind when you come back to school.
PSS I heard that Betty Cummings transferred to Holmes. We won't have to put up with her anymore!!

Mae felt better after having written the letter. Tearing a photo of Bette Davis from Photoplay, she carefully folded it and placed it along with the note in a pink envelope from her stationery set – a gift from Joan. So as to moisten her tongue, she took a swig of Pepsi and then licked the envelope. When she went downstairs, she handed it to her mother and asked her to mail it for her.

*   *   *

Mae's parents didn't want their daughter associating with Joan any longer. Based on what they heard and were reading in the papers, they both believed that Joan was guilty. They wanted to protect Mae from the suffering they knew she would face as the days and months of the trial wore on. And even if she were found not guilty, they certainly didn't want their daughter spending time with someone as emotionally unstable as Joan.

"I just know Mae is going to have to be a witness. After all, she was the last person with Joan the morning before the murders. I just hate to see her have to go through all that interrogation and badgering," her mother said to her dad. Changing the subject she added, "Well, we're just going to have to see that Mae gets involved in other activities and with other kids at school. We have to break off this friendship, but we have to be very, very careful how we do it."

"Yup, I agree," said Mae's father, as he was reading the evening paper. "Every day there's a new headline. Now they're going to indict the mother. Can you believe that? Maybe the two of them planned the whole damn thing," he said, moistening his thumb and forefinger with his tongue as he turned to the next page.

"Maybe. I talked to Sister Virginia Marie, the principal at La Salette, today; apparently the nuns agree. Mae needs to be kept busy and distracted. Everyone knew how inseparable those two were. The first day of registration for the school year was devastating – no one talked to her 'cause those girls didn't know what to say!

The nuns should have prepared those kids. Sister Jean Marie, Mae's English teacher, called. Asked how Mae was doing and said that they had a prayer service at school for Joan and her family. That girl is gonna need all the prayers she can get."

Chapter Ten
The Psychiatrists
(August 24 – September 15, 1943)

10

True to his word, Judge Cropper, on Tuesday, August 24, with the cooperation of Fred Williamson and Jack Maynard, facilitated Joan's release from jail on a $25,000.00 bond. At the recommendation of Dr. Ertel, she was then seen by Dr. John Romano at Cincinnati's General Hospital Psychiatric Unit. Having never talked to a psychiatrist before, she was on guard and hesitant to share much of herself, particularly the events of August 17. All of her other interrogators had been law enforcement personnel; yet, opening up to a "shrink" was much more threatening to her. But after a few hours, Dr. Romano's avuncular nature gradually won her over, and she began to feel safe. She was struck by his compassion and kindness and his willingness to genuinely listen to her every word. Whenever she began to cry, Dr. Romano would stop his questioning and give her time to fully experience her emotions. No one had ever done that before – not even Mae.

Dr. Romano noticed that Joan was tiring, so he concluded their session and told her they would meet again tomorrow morning, saying that he would order a dinner tray and send it up to her room immediately. Joan felt a twinge of relief and not nearly so alone. It was then that she decided she would confide in him about the times she felt separated from herself, as though she were watching herself outside her body. This was something she had never revealed to anyone.

That same evening, Cincinnati's City Manager Sherrill learned of this placement and immediately called Dr. Romano, at his home, demanding that Joan be removed at once from General Hospital, saying that for a resident of another state to be admitted required the City's approval; furthermore, he stated that Kentucky had many of its own facilities to treat disturbed people. (A more important fact, not lost on Sherrill, was that this case would draw national attention to this area and that, financially, Cincinnati did not need to use its resources to treat Joan or, at the trial, to lose man hours and money in testifying because of a subpoena.)

Although distraught, Dr. Romano realized there was no fighting city hall: at 4 a.m., Joan was removed from the hospital, and her Uncle Fred managed to sneak her out the back door and to hide her successfully from the paparazzi of the time.

Upon hearing that Joan had been prematurely discharged from Cincinnati General, Dr. Ertel was outraged. Never having had experience with such political maneuvering and manipulations, he was momentarily unable to decide what next to do for Joan; however, after some research and forethought, he decided the next place for her would be Eastern State Sanitarium, in Lexington, Kentucky. One of his colleagues highly recommended Dr. Walter Sprague who was an expert in adolescent psychiatry.

*   *   *

Joan found herself sitting before yet another psychiatrist, one that Dr. Sprague assigned as part of her treatment team. This one looked rather strange to her – a short man with bushy eyebrows, a shock of curly black hair, a thick mustache that matched his eyebrows, greasy skin and, of all things, a monocle! He looked like Groucho Marx in *A Night at the Opera*. The only thing missing was a tuxedo. Whenever she looked at him, Joan tried to control her giggling. All she could think of was how Mae would find this man so funny!

During their sessions, he would ask weird questions and take copious notes, rarely giving her eye contact. She didn't mind that, actually, since she was afraid that if he did look directly at her, she would burst into laughter. Well, she thought to herself, this may be therapeutic after all. She had not felt laughter, even the faintest jollity, since before that night.

After leaving the Cincinnati hospital, Joan initially thought she was finished with doctors. On the contrary, it was just the beginning. On the way to Lexington, Kentucky, Uncle Fred, Aunt Eva and her mother repeatedly assured her that this was going to help, and they made her promise that she would cooperate with the nurses and doctors. Nonetheless, she felt frightened, going to a strange place, not knowing what to expect. Their re-assurances did not diminish her anxiety in the least. So, here she was again. What upset her most of all was that she really felt safe with Dr. Romano and believed he could help her; and now she was on someone else's couch, being showered with questions about her early childhood, her mother and everyone else in her family. This doctor seemed to focus quite a bit on her anxiety, having her describe it in great detail, trying to determine the times and events that seemed to trigger it.

The more she met with "Groucho," her moniker for this psychiatrist, the less she liked him. Sister Auxentia's biology class came to mind. Joan felt as though she were an amoeba being scrutinized under a microscope; and to compensate, she became increasingly guarded and disingenuous within the sessions. Rather than being honest and open, she began responding to his questions based on what she determined he wanted to hear.

In addition to her individual sessions, she was required to attend group therapy with other patients, and she was grateful for these interruptions to her daily routine. These girls were, in Joan's opinion, a lot more troubled than she was. At least she thought that on most days.

The month at Eastern Sanitarium seemed like an eternity. Joan was allowed to have only one phone call per day, and it could only be in the evening. During the first few weeks, she cried to her mother every night, begging her to please come and get her. "Mamma, I'm not crazy. Why am I here for such a long time? Why can't Mae call me? Have you talked to her?"

Jennie would ignore any questions about Mae since her conversation with Mrs. Klingenberg a few weeks ago. Knowing that Joan needed to hear from Mae to provide some normalcy to her life, Jennie had called Mrs. Klingenberg to see why her daughter had dropped out of Joan's life. Within a few short minutes and in no uncertain terms, Mae's mother stridently informed Jennie that Mae was not allowed to see or talk to Joan.

"If you were in my shoes, would you let your daughter be friends with someone as disturbed as Joan? I think not." And with that she hung up the phone.

So, during those first weeks, whenever Joan would beg to come home, Jennie, Uncle Fred and Aunt Eva would each take turns talking to her on the phone, reassuring her that this is what was best for her. Joan's questions regarding Mae were ignored.

"Be sure to tell the doctors of your sleepwalking – be very honest about that," Jennie would say, supportively. She wanted Joan to get the help she needed, so she could live a normal life.

"Mr. Smith, your attorney, says we have to do this in preparation for your trial. So, Joan make the best of this," Uncle Fred would say, and he would always follow up with, "Remember, I love you."

And then there was Aunt Eva who would chatter about movies and other superficial topics, reminding her that she would have her favorite cake waiting for her on the day she came home.

Joan and Mae once saw a James Cagney movie where he was in prison for a crime he didn't commit. As a way to cope with the injustice, he marked off each day on his calendar with a huge black X, keeping his eye on his final release date. Joan felt a special affinity with Cagney as she placed a calendar above her bed.

Chapter Eleven
The Lawyer
(1883 – August 18, 1943)

11

One of the success stories that every school child learns is that of Abraham Lincoln: his Kentucky birth, his lowly upbringing, his studying by the light of the fireplace and his using the back of a shovel to practice writing. His is an inspirational story—but there were thousands upon thousands of these versions of a young person pulling himself toward a better life, using only his own well-worn boot straps. This was the scene being played out across America in the eighteen hundreds.

These successes were not dependent upon great universities in America, although, in 1883, when Sawyer Smith was born, there were many such institutions. It was just as common for small schools in small towns to produce great men and women.

Sawyer was born in Barboursville, Kentucky, a tiny rural town in the eastern part of the state. For his family, there were no books, no radio, not even a daily newspaper. Education was tolerated by the local citizens; but it was generally accepted that when a boy was old enough to work, his school days were over. Coal mining was the backbone of this Appalachian area; and it was here, "where the sun don't shine," that youth labored and youth died. Emphysema, black lung, cave-in's and, of course, poverty were this region's gift to its youth; and yet, there were those born and raised amongst this English, Irish and Melungeon mix that made it out – and Sawyer Smith was one of these.

Sawyer was an under-clothed but undeterred scrawny youngster whose only distinguishing characteristics were his smile and a fire burning behind those dark eyes. As a teenager, he was a tall gangling sight; but his unquenchable passion for learning was his saving grace. He completed high school in Knox County and attended the nearby Cumberland College where he was trained as a public school teacher. Upon graduation, he accepted a position in Knox County. Thankfully, there was no challenge he would refuse; and this characteristic played well into that first teaching job, which included being responsible for multiple grades, being the janitor, the painter, the repairman, as well as the counselor of those with big dreams and of those with none. He later graduated from law school at Valparaiso College, in Indiana.

It is hard for us, today, to understand the grip that home and heart exerted on those folks in Eastern Kentucky and the disappointment of the brave souls who dared breach the county line or the state borders only to return, all too often, with tales of discrimination and ridicule.

What the local population did not know at the time was why they were so easy to spot in the big cities and to what degree the people outside their insulated world looked down upon them. The Appalachians did not recognize their uniqueness nor did, for the most part, the rest of America. The cities were happy to get their coal; but they recoiled at these backwoods people with their restrictive religion, their fatalism and their speech, which appeared to be a cacophony of illiteracy.

The rest of America did not know and did not appreciate the historic importance of the long dead language that these people spoke; but scholars in London, at Cambridge and Oxford Universities, heard rumors of this language pocket which represented the voices of another century and were soon traveling across the Atlantic to study and to be amazed by the purity of speech of these insulated and isolated peoples: they were speaking the language of fifteenth and sixteenth century English, the language of Chaucer and Shakespeare.

These scholars realized that they had a once in a lifetime opportunity to be able to step back in time and hear Elizabethan speech: pronunciation, accentuation, sentence patterns, even the meaning of words as the Elizabethan's would understand them. All these academic titillations were locked away in this isolated region and this was exactly why those from Eastern Kentucky and surrounding contiguous regions stood out when they left home. The more "advanced" cultures that they were trying to enter coined the word "hillbilly," not a kind word today – nor was it meant to be kind then.

And when Sawyer Smith packed his suitcase with his one suit and his few books and headed "up north," his bag was also packed with all these ingredients which could damn his future.

He was awarded his law degree from Valparaiso; but his experience there was so traumatic that he returned home, to Knox County, Kentucky and, in 1906, opened a law office in Barboursville. His law partner was a kindred spirit named Flem D. Simpson, a young man whose ambitions were no less than Sawyer's. Flem rose over the years in Kentucky politics and eventually became the governor of this great commonwealth.

Sawyer's star was also ascending. Because he was able to win case after case in Knox County, as a prosecuting attorney, he came to the attention of Warren G. Harding, President of the United States, who appointed him as a US Attorney for Kentucky's eastern district. He held this position until 1933 when he returned to private practice. It has been said that in the 12 years that he represented the eastern district, he was responsible for 17,000 convictions.

As his success continued, his confidence grew; and his ability to face and confront the world beyond the shackles of his provincial upbringing helped him make his decision to open a law office in the vibrant city of Covington, Kentucky.

Destiny was nudging him ever closer to his most challenging and famous court case, the murder trial of Joan Kiger.

Chapter Twelve
Night Terrors
(August 18 – October 16, 1943)

12

When Sawyer looked at his appointment book, he saw that Fred Williamson was scheduled on the docket for 10 a.m. Sawyer was aware of the Kiger case and felt that he must be here to ask for help in defending Joan. Recent headlines had proclaimed that the girl's mother had indicated that Joan was sleepwalking while committing the murders. That fact intrigued him immensely; therefore when he saw that name, his heart skipped a beat, something that hadn't happened to him since his very first murder trial.

When he greeted Williamson, they shook hands and walked into Sawyer's office. Although there were stacks of papers, files and books everywhere, the room didn't appear cluttered. The vestiges of past cases, research reports and old magazines were piled neatly like cords of firewood. The walls were bare with the exception of a framed law degree which was coated with a thin layer of dust. No family photos graced his desk, but it all had the air of familiarity: an old converted student lamp, several folders of current cases, a silver cigarette box and a cracked green ash tray.

The dark brown leather chair Sawyer pulled out for Fred had countless spider veins creeping over sections of its seat cushion and arms, suggesting its impending retirement. After the usual formalities, Fred and Sawyer discussed the case. Sawyer's pace and energy was charged and excited while Fred's was deliberate and precise. While going over what Fred knew, Sawyer sat on the corner of his desk, swinging his leg and listening intently. Sawyer was waiting for a formal request to be Joan's defending attorney.

"As you can imagine, this has devastated our family. My wife and Jennie are sisters and are as close as can be. We've always been a pretty tight knit group. I've stepped in to do whatever I could to help get this tragedy behind us. Jennie is desperate to make sure Joan is found innocent, and we all agree that you're the man to make it happen," Fred said.

Sawyer nodded his head and waited in the silence, waiting for a direct invitation to defend Joan.

Fred looked down at the floor, wondering at the growing silence. What was Sawyer expecting that he was not providing? After a moment, he looked up and said, "My family and I hope you will take the case."

"Yes, I would be interested; but, of course, we need to discuss my fee." Sawyer stood up, secretly elated by the offer; but he was concerned that this family would not be able to afford his services. However, he had in the past, with cases he particularly wanted to defend, either waived the fee or negotiated it.

"About the only money my sister-in-law has is tied up in her two houses. We may have to sell Rosegate to meet the expenses of the funerals and the trial. Can you give me an idea as to what you would have to have to accept the case?" Fred asked, knowing that most attorneys were bloodsuckers and would take him for anything they could get. He did not, at this point, realize that the Kiger murder was the type of case which any criminal lawyer would negotiate for, understanding that it would greatly enhance his reputation.

Sawyer replied, "We could do this in stages. I would need $500.00 up front so that I can begin my investigation; and from that point on, my fee will depend on the expense of the investigation and the length of the trial itself." Although the fee he quoted was considerably less than what he generally charged, he wanted this case and was willing to negotiate even further, if necessary.

Fred did not reply immediately. He was no beginner at negotiating, himself. After an appropriate pause, he said, "I'm not sure Jennie can afford that. Can you give us time to come up with additional monies because, as far as I know, she does not have much in savings?"

"I think as long as you agree to pay in full within 12 months from today, we can move forward."

Fred stood up, asking, "When would you like to see Joan?"

"I'll arrange that quickly. I'll be back in touch with you with additional questions, as well as actions you should take. I also need your permission to see Jennie. I understand that she is still under guard at St. Elizabeth's Hospital."

As Fred walked out, he thought to himself, I have found the one man who may save Joan.

* * *

As the days and weeks of meeting with Joan went by and as Sawyer saw the physical evidence piling up against her, he realized that it would be very difficult to mount a defense based upon the premise that she did not commit the murders. Whether she actually killed her father and her brother was not, at this point, the focus of Smith's thinking: he had to construct his case in such a way that the jury of reasonable citizens could find Joan "Not Guilty."

After reviewing the clinical evaluations and summaries of Cincinnati's Dr. Romano and of Lexington's Dr. Sprague, Sawyer balanced one report against the other. They were at times conflicting, yet shed considerable light on how he would proceed.

Psychiatry is such a pseudo-science, he muttered to himself, as he read the page upon page of detailed psycho-babble from the Eastern State Sanitarium about Jennie's pregnancy, Joan's birth and early physical and cognitive development, along with the dynamics of her family relationships, particularly with her mother. That information, coupled with the results of projective techniques – the Rorschach being the one he was most familiar with – and myriad other assessments, made him think long and hard about Sprague's copious clinical notes which indicated that he suspected Joan might suffer from dementia praecox. The final diagnosis, however, was one corroborated in Dr. Romano's report : "Severe Anxiety—one manifestation being episodic sleepwalking which can result in highly complex behaviors that could be dangerous to the sleepwalker or to others." The frequent references in his clinical notes regarding dementia praecox had Sawyer contemplating how he might use or defend against such a diagnosis.

After chatting with his good friend, Dr. Al Spekler, who was an adolescent psychiatrist at Cincinnati General, Sawyer learned that there was ongoing research about dementia praecox and that its newer label, schizophrenia, was used more frequently in psychiatric circles.

Smith interrogated Spekler for nearly half an hour and the conversation ended with the good doctor rattling off the symptoms of schizophrenia, much like an auctioneer, eager to move on to the next item: "….delusions, hallucinations, racing thoughts, flat affect or apathy, disorganized thoughts, problems concentrating or following instructions. My next patient is here so I have to go. Good luck with this one, Sawyer!"

Schizophrenia, he said to himself, as he looked out what he often referred to as his "thinking window."

Whenever he was stumped or seriously doubtful about an aspect of a case, Sawyer would peer out that window which framed the branches of a nearby towering pin oak and just let his mind flow into a stream of consciousness. After about 30 minutes, he stood up and said out loud, "Nope, I don't buy that one."

Sawyer had a gut feeling about Joan; and although he sensed that she was a troubled young lady, he never ever once thought she was crazy; and of course, his prejudice against psychiatry and all psychiatrists – except maybe Spekler—only fueled his variance with the report.

"Margie," he yelled from his desk. "Margie!!" he shouted, even louder.

"Mr. Sawyer," Margie said, as she leaned into the room, "you know you don't have to shout. We do have an intercom system…and yes, I know, you want coffee and lots of it." Margie had worked for Sawyer for the past five years; and from the day he hired her, she had this uncanny ability to read his mind and finish his sentences.

"I also will need…."

"Yes, I know, a ham and Swiss cheese on rye, hold the mayo," and, as she shut the door, she added, "and I won't forget the potato salad."

Without missing a beat, Sawyer returned to his window. A meeting he'd had with Joan when she returned from The Eastern State Sanitarium kept cropping up.

"You know, Mr. Smith, I didn't like that place. It was dreadful. I mean the people were nice but kind of phony nice. Always smiling and saying things like 'How are *we* doing today?' The nurses would use the pronoun *we* when they were only talking about me. 'Would *we* like some hot tea?' '*We're* going to see the doctor today.' It all felt very condescending," Joan stared at him, eager for some assurance.

Sawyer nodded his head, encouraging Joan to continue.

"What bothered me the most was the way the doctors treated me—and they all did this in their own way. When I first met Dr. … oh, I can't remember his name, but he was really rather funny looking. He was a very short man with these bushy eyebrows and thick mustache and a monocle that kept falling off. A monocle!—can you imagine that?"

Joan looked at her hands and noticed that she was wringing them again, a habit she had when she was uncomfortable. "Do you mind if I smoke," she asked, sheepishly. Sawyer offered her a cigarette which she politely declined. Drawing him into her conspiracy, she said, "I hope you won't tell my mother or Uncle Fred that I smoke."

Without waiting for a reply, she took a pack of Kools from her purse, grabbed a cigarette, lit it and took a long drag.

"Anyway, the entire time I was with him, he looked at me very intently, as though he was trying to fit me into a box or a fixed idea he had in his head. His questions were confusing a lot of the times and then, when I answered them, he would often misinterpret what I said and twist my words to fit into something he wanted to hear; and if I tried to correct him, he would start writing furiously on this note pad he had. He wasn't really listening to me, not really."

Sawyer was familiar with how attorneys led witnesses, and he figured that psychiatrists did much the same thing. Each wanted his respective client to tell him exactly what he wanted to hear.

Apathy, disorganized thoughts, delusions, hallucinations – the string of symptoms flooded his brain. "What 15 year old kid wouldn't seem to have any and all of those if her father and brother were dead, and she was accused of murdering them?"

Margie knocked on the door and, without waiting for a response, walked in placing the sandwich, coffee and potato salad on the corner of his desk, the only spot that wasn't covered with documents or note cards. "See you tomorrow," she said.

So focused was Sawyer on the reports from Dr. John Romano at Cincinnati General that he did not see Margie either come or go. "More psycho-babble," he muttered. He leafed through the pages quickly. Romano seemed to focus more on Joan's somnambulism and anxiety. He remembered studying a case in law school, "What was the name of that guy," he asked, as he walked over to his law books and, after some shuffling, found it. "Here it is," he smiled.

"Rufus Choate, ah yes." He then went to his filing cabinet and looked for the file "Criminal Law Class Notes."

Smith had always been a compulsive note taker and never threw anything away. If he had a weakness, it was simply that his method of filing was somewhat haphazard. He read aloud the first paragraph of a synopsis of his notes on the Tirrell case.

Maria Ann Bickford was a prostitute in Boston. On October 27th, 1845, one of her many wealthy customers, Albert Tirrell, with whom she had slept at the brothel, slashed her throat so severely that Maria's head was nearly severed. To cover the murder, he tried to burn the brothel. It seems he became enraged when she refused to give up her profession and be exclusive to him.

Tirell was defended by Rufus Choate an ingenious attorney who, once he learned that Albert was a known sleepwalker, used sleepwalking as his defense. Choate did not deny that Albert had murdered Bickford – but claimed that since, as a sleepwalker, he was not in control of his faculties, he should not be charged with the murder. The jury deliberated for two hours and found him not guilty.

Sawyer made his final decision regarding his defense.

*   *   *

As he read extensively and talked with psychiatrists, he became convinced that he could best defend Joan by admitting that, in fact, she had killed her father and her brother, but that those actions were the result of her sleepwalking. Sawyer didn't like the word "sleepwalking" because it was just too benign. It didn't fully capture the heart of his defense. His research revealed another phrase that was frequently used interchangeably with it—"Night Terrors."

Sleepwalking, he learned, was not all that uncommon in children and those occurrences were precipitated by puberty, menstruation, drugs, sleep deprivation, as well as other causes. The sleepwalker usually has his eyes open but does not respond easily to outside stimuli, remaining, instead, locked into the events of his nightmare. If he heard a gunshot and it were a part of his night terror, he would not awaken. The old adage of "Do not try to wake a sleepwalker because he might become violent" is just that, an adage. In fact, it is very difficult to wake a person who is in the throes of night terrors.

Most real violence committed by a sleepwalker occurs as a part of these nightmares, and the victim will almost always be one of proximity. Sleepwalkers do not find a knife, walk a mile to the house of someone against whom they have a grudge and commit murder.

The person who, while in the midst of one of these night terrors, commits a real and physical act will usually remember having had a bad dream but will not be able to recall the events with any clarity or specificity. This phenomenon of parasomnia has its mirror image in those individuals who can recall the dream but cannot associate it with any real event.

The other test of a person who has experienced these nightmares is that, very often, a close relative also is a sleepwalker who has nightmares. In Romano's report, it clearly stated that Joan's father had somnambulism, as well.

Sawyer Smith felt that, with the Tirrell case as a precedent and after viewing all of the psychological reports and synthesizing that information with his interviews and research and knowing that he could call experts in the field of dreams, he could defend Joan against anything the prosecution had. He was now immune to any evidence that they would bring to court.

He smiled, in spite of the fact that, as he looked at his lunch, he realized his potato salad had started to dry out.

Chapter Thirteen
Strategies At Stringtown
(September 1, 1943)

13

They all three loved the challenge of a difficult case; all three were well schooled in the law and in experience. What set them apart were their attitudes toward the job, their diverse personalities and their egos

Charles W. Riley was the pit bull of the three: once he sank his teeth into a case, nothing would deter him from its completion. He was not one to encourage plea bargaining or, in any way, to make the case's resolution easy for the defense. He had a loyalty to the law and an uncommon desire to see the guilty punished. If he took a case, he assumed the total guilt of the accused.

After reviewing the Joan Kiger story and talking with the sheriff and others, as well as considering the evidence which existed shortly after the murders in August, he had no doubt: it was cold blooded murder, premeditated, calculated and vengeful.

On the other hand, Raymond Vincent, although an excellent attorney in his own right, was not as passionate, did not take cases personally and could, at the end of a long day, enjoy a great meal and an excellent glass of sherry over a discussion of sports, politics, entertainment…. He could plea bargain without feeling that he had failed the court system; and if he lost a case, he did not perseverate over the fact that a guilty person was again walking the streets of his town. A case was a case and not a crusade. In spite of this more relaxed attitude, he would work incessantly to achieve his political ambitions; and of the three attorneys, Vincent was the only one acutely aware of this trial's implications to their futures: for a man like John Vest whose private practice in Walton could use a boost, being spotlighted nationally, as one of the individuals who was instrumental in the conviction of a cold-blooded murderer such as Joan Kiger, this trial would bring to his office high profile clients with deep pockets; and for an attorney who was more politically motivated, such as Raymond Vincent, a guilty verdict could propel him into such rarefied political air as a run for the governorship.

Because Vincent had identified these possibilities for himself, he felt the most pressure; and he intended to work day and night – and to convince his two friends and fellow prosecutors to do the same for the next few months, until they saw the judge's gavel fall and heard him read the jury's decision, "Guilty of Murder in the First Degree."

John Vest was somewhere in between. He may have been the most qualified as a prosecutor; and of the three, he was the most realistic, practical and well organized. He was also the best actor in front of a jury. It was he who could look a group of 12 individuals in their eyes and convince them that his point of view, whatever it might be, was the only logical and thoughtful one to be considered. And these three men were friends, having collaborated on other cases and having rubbed elbows socially over the years, not to mention their monthly attempts at golf.

So when the Boone County prosecuting attorney, Raymond L. Vincent, and his hand picked team of old friends gathered around a conference table in the Burlington courthouse planning their strategies for the upcoming Kiger murder trial, they met with the self assurance and determination that this case would be one of the few that Sawyer Smith would not win.

"This is going to be a tough one. No jury will want to convict a pretty, 16 year old girl of murder on circumstantial evidence. Somehow we have to overcome this natural reluctance on the jury's part," Vincent said.

"It looks like a slam dunk to me," John Vest countered. "We've got her fingerprints on the guns and her admission that she fired all three weapons, as well as her written confession that she shot into her parents' room and into Jerry's."

"It won't be easy," Riley spoke up. "Joan has already changed her story several times; and the mother, Jennie, sometimes corroborates Joan's story and sometimes doesn't. Which versions do we try to attack?"

Vincent asked the group, "Do you think a jury would believe Joan's story of a mysterious stranger being in the house, threatening the family?"

"Sawyer Smith can't prove that there was an intruder," Riley said.

"Can we prove that he wasn't there?" Vest offered.

"I think so," Riley countered. "Remember, in one of her stories, Joan says she shot at him. She told Sheriff Williams, 'If I had only hit him we could trace him.' The sheriff will testify that he and Deputy Rouse looked that house over for hours. There were no slugs in any of the walls, the woodwork or ceiling. How do you explain that?"

"Maybe Sawyer will say every shot hit the intruder," Vest commented, laughing.

Vincent was silent for a few minutes.

"What is Sawyer's greatest strength as a defense attorney? That's what we have to exploit."

"I worked with Sawyer on several cases. He likes to brag that he wins cases the moment he picks the jury," Riley said, pensively.

"That's good – so we have to figure out what he's trying to do as he selects jurors. We'll challenge enough of his choices to affect his game plan," Vincent said, "but we've got to think further ahead than that. Although we have enough real evidence to convict most murderers, it's still circumstantial. Who's going to believe that a girl who was 15 at the time of the murders would do it? There's no motive that we can identify. We've interviewed schoolmates, teachers, relatives, neighbors anybody and everybody who ever heard of the Kiger family. The profile we got was one of a typical, well adjusted family. The jury needs motive and we don't have one.

"Sawyer may even go with the insanity plea," Vincent continued. "I know I would. That's the most logical. The jury can find her not guilty and feel good about their decision. They can recommend that she be institutionalized and feel even better. They're helping the poor child."

"If she is found not guilty, goes into treatment but eventually is released—and let's be realistic—many of these nut cases are let out, we have a murderer walking the streets," Riley said, with distaste.

Again Vincent was quiet.

The discussion continued, but he stared vacantly ahead. He was in the midst of an epiphany; and as he continued to work out in his head his two pronged approach to the trial, Vest realized what was happening and therefore continued to facilitate the remainder of the morning's strategy session, until the eleven- thirty lunch break came.

Vincent was a complicated person who possessed a keen intellect and a fiery temper. He was not a man you would remember if you were to see him in a crowd. But when you observed him in a courtroom, in front of a jury, you would never forget his face—and you would never forget his forceful stride as he crossed the room or the arch of his eyebrows as he made a critical point. He was nearly Vest's equal.

This trial would be a battle of two local titans, Sawyer Smith and Raymond L. Vincent: men with expanding reputations, monumental egos and unlimited ambitions. There was more at stake here than the mere guilty or not guilty verdict. Just as important would be the way the game was played, the finesse, the bombast, the legal sparring, as they performed upon the stage. All this was what made the contest interesting, unpredictable and intellectually challenging. Both men prided themselves with being able to anticipate the next logical, legal maneuver and to have an answering gambit prepared.

The drive to the Stringtown Restaurant in Florence was a continuation of the courthouse discussion of how best to prepare for the trial.

As Estelle Ryle, the matronly waitress with a thickening waist and unkempt salt and pepper hair, began taking their orders, Vincent returned to the present. He had his trial strategy planned. It's strange how long stretches of ungratified planning can change so abruptly, as boredom is replaced by brilliance.

Vincent looked across the table, watching Vest slice his steak into neat manageable bite-size pieces. "John, I'd like you to prepare a case for us. Convince us that we should try Joan only for Jerry's murder."

Vest was the thinker, the step-by-step, logical follow-all-the-rules attorney of the group. He was dependable and thorough; and with Sawyer Smith as their opponent, they needed to turn over every rock and know, for sure, what was beneath; and because more trials are won by thoroughness than by genius, Vincent wanted his input.

"And Chuck, I'd like you to do the same for Carl. Convince us that we have the best chance of a guilty verdict by trying Joan for his murder alone."

"Why not try them both at the same time?" Vest asked. But he knew that Vincent had his reasons and that the plan he had would be what they would all agree to.

"Why not?" Vincent reiterated. "Look at the advantages and disadvantages of both scenarios. One, try Joan for both murders and what happens? You get a conviction or you don't.

"The advantage of bringing charges against her for only one of the murders is what?" He looked at the two men. "What is our advantage for trying Joan for only one murder?

"We don't have to prove she killed them both," Vest offered.

"True," Vincent said, "What else?"

"The trial will be shorter. Less physical evidence to collect and explain."

"Okay, keep going."

The men looked at one another.

Vincent took a drink from his coffee. "Let's look at it from another angle. What are our options if Joan is tried for both murders and is found not guilty?"

"We have none." Riley said. "It's all over, and I would absolutely hate to stop at that point. We have to find a way to protect ourselves from that."

"Right!" Vincent exclaimed.

"And what are our options if we try her for just one murder and she's found not guilty?"

"It all depends," Riley said, beginning to see Vincent's plan.

"And isn't that a better option than the first which, as you said, was none?"

Vest replied, "So if the jury finds her not guilty for one murder, we could then try her for the other murder."

"Exactly," Vincent said, satisfied with his logic.

"And more than that, if Sawyer uses the insanity defense and she is eventually institutionalized, we have the option, if she's ever released, of bringing charges against her for the remaining murder," Riley said, with growing excitement.

"Great idea, Ray" Riley exclaimed. "If the Stringtown sold booze I'd buy you a drink for that beauty."

Having decided to try Joan solely for *one* of the murders, they moved on to the next topic: how best to get Joan to reaffirm her earlier oral and written confessions. Since those days shortly after the murders, Joan and Jennie had both revised their stories, probably with the help of Sawyer Smith. Vincent had directed a team of investigators to look into the dynamics of the Kiger's interpersonal relationships only to come up with a disappointing profile: they seemed to be a normal, loving family with no obvious dissensions – no ugly warts that could be used to the prosecution's advantage. The typical strategy of law enforcement to divide and conquer had not worked. Although they had interrogated Joan and Jennie at length, often and separately, their stories, although on the surface at variance, eventually dovetailed – obviously because they had access to one another over the last few weeks – and their attorney had access to them both.

So, if divide and conquer was not working, what next? The facts suggested that Joan was the actual killer; but it was risky to rely on circumstantial evidence alone – and so far, that's all they had. Carl was shot numerous times at very close range and Jennie's story of a stranger firing from the doorway was obviously a cover-up. The jury would see that right away, but how would that aid the prosecution in their attempt to convict Joan for first degree murder?

As Vincent and his team finished the final pieces of their Stringtown steaks, Riley threw an idea on the table: since Joan and Jennie seemed so close and were attempting to rearrange their versions of what happened that August night to protect one another, why not arrest the mother also for the murders—claim that she either directly participated or was complicit in the planning or cover-up? Riley's theory was that when Joan realized her mother was going be tried for first degree murder and could receive the death penalty, there would be only one action on Joan's part which would circumvent this possibility. Joan would have to admit to being the only one involved in the deaths of her father and her brother.

If Joan confessed that she knowingly and without help killed her family, Jennie would be free.

Having made initial preparations for a winning strategy and having planned on how best to position themselves in case of a loss, the three well-fed friends headed back toward the courthouse.

Chapter Fourteen
The Lawyer and His Client
(December 15, 1943)

14

December 15, the day before the jury was chosen and the tenth meeting between Joan and Sawyer, he arrived in his Covington office at ten a.m. The Covington streets were already alive with holiday shoppers. Since Christmas was only ten days away, spirits were high; and in spite of war rationing, most goods were obtainable. The tide of the war was turning; and for the first time, victory seemed only a year away.

Joan arrived punctually, wearing a sweater that looked a size too small and a bright red skirt, making her appear much older than she was. Sawyer frowned at what he observed but stood up and embraced her, asking if she would like a soft drink. "No thanks. How about a cigarette?" she asked, with a self-assurance Sawyer had not seen before. This was not the same girl he had first interviewed some months ago. She was gradually becoming herself or at least the self Sawyer felt she was prior to the August 17 tragedy.

Sawyer thought back to the first time he met Joan. He had driven from his Covington office to the Burlington jail; and when he arrived, Elmer, Julia Kirkpatrick and Joan were in the living room preparing to have chocolate cake which Julia had just taken from the oven. Sawyer's mouth watered as he took in the smells of the house. They knew he was coming, of course, and somehow had learned that he was a chocoholic. Joan, too, loved anything chocolate, as evidenced by her consumption of the cake and her inattention to Sawyer. He mentally compared the Joan who now sat with him in his office with the girl he first met in the jail just a few days after the murders. As he entered the Kirkpatrick's living room, Joan did not even look up. She was pale and without make-up or fingernail polish. Her hair, though not disheveled, was not at all attractive. He recalled that when he introduced himself, she glanced unsmilingly at him and then focused her attention on the cake. It was, he thought at the time, as though she were in shock, and he decided immediately that he would arrange for her to see a psychiatrist. Her affect was flat and her energy level, as he perceived it, was almost that of a comatose person. The fact that the local officials had not had her seen by a doctor was inexcusable.

As Sawyer joined Joan for milk and chocolate cake, she sighed, averted his gaze and continued to watch Julia as she tidied up the room. Failing to engage her in any light conversation about the cake, about the fact that Elmer was allowing her to stay in their second bedroom or even about the weather, Sawyer decided to go right to the heart of his visit: he was having trouble mounting a defense for her due to the fact that she had confessed verbally and had signed a written statement, indicating that she had shot at both her father and her brother.

After considerable effort, he was able to draw her out, and Joan began a long discourse as to why she confessed. As she told the story, at about 1 a.m. on the night of the tragedy, when the various officials began arriving at the crime scene, Jack Maynard, a family friend, took her to her room and interrogated her for an hour. Following that, Sheriff Williams and Deputy Rouse queried her for another hour. Then she was searched; thank goodness, it was by her Aunt Eva; but she could hear the Sheriff, on the other side of the door, asking Eva to search different parts of her body. She felt humiliated, even though Aunt Eva kept apologizing, saying that this was the only way she could even see her. Joan was taken from that room and again bombarded with questions by the following additional people: Melvin Huff, Highway Patrolman; Earl Chrisrophel; Robert Tiepel; and Chester Fee, Covington policeman and others whose names she could not recall. She proceeded in a flat expressionless voice, barely above a whisper, saying that these men continued to question her until 6:30 a.m., at which time they took her to the Burlington jail. While at the jail, they relentlessly questioned her until, at some point that morning, she simply fell asleep and remained so for an hour. When she awoke, they began once again. By then, she was so tired that when they asked if she would sign a paper, she willingly said, yes. She did not even bother reading what she was signing, she was so exhausted.

All during this interrogation, she kept asking to see her Uncle Fred again, but the officers refused to allow her access to any family member.

As her story unfolded, Sawyer realized that, although she was taken to jail, the Sheriff had not placed her under arrest and had not charged her with any crime. More importantly, she was not taken before the Boone County Judge, as required by state law, but was held illegally until ten a.m., August 18.

In addition, most of the men who questioned her were from Kenton County and out of the Boone County jurisdiction and that such questioning was, therefore, illegal. Sawyer remembered his mind taking the entire story which Joan told and slicing it neatly into legal pieces of motions to quash, motions to strike and demurrers to the indictment.

"Mr. Smith?" He was jolted back to the present by Joan's insistent voice. "May I have a cigarette?" As he handed her one, he asked "Have you and your mom done your Christmas shopping yet?" trying to begin this last meeting before the trial on a lighter note.

"She's with Uncle Fred and Aunt Eva in your waiting room. Mamma is still limping badly; so we try not to do too much walking; yeah, we've about finished. Mamma wants to stop at Eilerman's and get something special for Uncle Fred and Aunt Eva. After all, they've been just wonderful to us. We've been staying at their house, and Uncle Fred has helped us arrange for bond money; Mamma told me he was the one who recommended you."

As she lit her cigarette, Joan smiled easily and inhaled deeply.

"I hear the doctors have just decided to leave that bullet in your mother's hip. How does she feel about that?"

Joan's smile faded. "She doesn't talk much about it," and taking another deep breath, she continued, "Mamma just doesn't want to think about anything that happened."

"Well, she'd better be clear about what she remembered about August 17, Sawyer said, emphatically. "She's absolutely going to be called to testify."

"You talked to her," Joan said, looking directly at Sawyer, "You know how she is."

"The only thing I'm concerned about," Sawyer replied, jabbing his forefinger on the desk, "is that your mother corroborate your story. Her telling another version of what happened is not going to help you; and in the few times I have met with her, she has changed her story three times!" Sawyer stood up, came around to the side of his desk and, sitting on its edge, said, "You and I have come to agree over the last ten meetings on these points: One, you did not shoot anyone. Two, you did have a horrible nightmare that night. Three, you saw, as a part of your nightmare, a figure in your house trying to harm your father. You also saw this figure in front of Jerry's bedroom door. Four, you found one of your father's guns and you fired at this figure. Five, when you saw that your father was shot, you went for help."

Joan nodded, extinguishing her cigarette in the green ashtray on Sawyer's desk, "Yes, yes. That's just about the way it was."

Sawyer Smith knew more than he was telling his client. In the discovery phase of the trial, he had learned that the prosecutor was going to call Wilson, the ballistics expert from Chicago as a witness; and he was aware that Wilson was going to testify as to which pistols fired which shots. The intriguing part of his testimony would be that one of the Colt .38's was fired eight times, meaning that it had to have been reloaded. Smith was sure that the prosecutor would use this finding to try to establish pre-meditation and to argue that someone who is asleep could hardly be expected to locate additional cartridges, reload the pistol and then continue her murderous activities. Because of this forthcoming evidence, Smith made his decision not to try to convince the jury of Joan's innocence; rather, his approach would be that in acting out her night terror, she unwillingly and unwittingly did, in fact, kill her father and brother. By freely admitting that Joan killed her family, Smith felt he could diffuse Vincent's argument and throw him off stride. Smith's strategy was to make it impossible for this jury, which he handpicked, to render a verdict of guilty. In addition, he had experts who would testify that Joan could have reloaded and fired again and again and yet remain in the midst of one of her night terrors.

"Now Joan, I don't know exactly how Mr. Vincent, the prosecuting attorney, is going to approach this case. I know how I would, but he may see things differently. We'll have to roll with the punches and adjust our defense, based on what he does. You just have to follow my lead, Okay?"

"Sure," Joan sighed, looking at her watch. "Anything else?"

Being a former prosecutor, he knew how a re-creation of the crime scene would impact the jury; and because of the distinct possibility that Vincent would do just that, Sawyer had to prepare Joan for what would, no doubt, be traumatic for her. He purposely waited until this meeting to broach the topic because he felt that revealing Vincent's probable strategy too soon would cause her extreme anxiety and be disruptive to the emotional equilibrium she had been able to sustain these past several weeks. He vacillated about having Jennie in the office when he told Joan about his supposition and, in the end, decided it would be best if Jennie weren't there. He had called her the night before, telling her what topics he would be covering with Joan, preparing her for the possible aftermath of the office visit.

"Yes, Joan. Just a few more things. What do you think the prosecutor's job is?"

Joan's furrowed brow revealed her puzzlement at the question. "You mean the prosecutor tomorrow? The one in my case?"

Sawyer nodded.

"Well, I guess it's to prove I'm guilty of Jerry's...." Joan always struggled with the word "murder." It seemed to get caught in her throat, creating a shortness of breath that would lead one to believe she was having an anxiety attack.

As the color drained from her face, she said, "...you know. That's his job. To put me away. Do you have any water?" she asked, looking around the room.

Sawyer walked over to a walnut credenza where Margie kept a pitcher of water full and loaded with ice cubes. She always checked on it in between appointments, without fail. As he poured Joan a glass of water, several ice cubes spilled over the lip of the glass pitcher and fell to the hard wood floor, just missing the carpet. Knowing the fit Margie would have with those water stains, Sawyer kicked the cubes onto the rug. He'd been at the receiving end of her admonitions all too many times.

As he handed Joan the slightly wet glass, he said, "Yes, that's right. The prosecutor wants to prove your guilt to the jury. He has to convince the jury that you are unequivocally guilty, without a shadow of a doubt."

Joan held the glass tightly and looked up at him with widening eyes.

"One way to appeal to a jury is to do something dramatic, something that would stir their emotions. Something like re-creating the murder scene."

The glass fell to the floor, shattering. Joan said, biting her lip, "What? The crime scene? What do you mean?"

"Joan, this is where you are going to have to be very, very brave. And Lord knows, you have demonstrated an incredible amount of bravery thus far. The prosecutor is likely to bring in your dad's and Jerry's beds with the bloodstained bedding." He looked at her intently, uncertain of what her reaction would be. As he looked into her eyes, he felt she had somehow slipped away from him.

"Joan! We will ask for you to be excused from that part of the trial. Do you hear me? You will not have to be present during that part of the trial."

Joan started to detach from herself. She began to observe this girl on a chair with a broken glass near her foot. "Joan." Sawyer began to shake her. "Joan." He had never seen such emptiness in someone's eyes.

The girl reached out for her.

"Yes, Mr. Smith. I'm here."

"Did you hear me? You will not have to be present during that part of the trial."

Joan shuddered and sighed deeply. "Oh. Okay."

Sawyer still had a few more things to go over with Joan, but knew she needed a break and, in fact, so did he. This last episode with Joan was quite disturbing, something he hadn't experienced with her before; and he hoped it was a one time only situation.

"Joan, how about we take a break for fifteen minutes? You can go to the powder room and freshen up a bit." Sawyer picked up the broken glass and tossed it in the garbage can and cleaned up the water. "Can I get you something to snack on? I think Margie has a stash of chocolate chip cookies somewhere around here."

"No, thanks. I'm not hungry; I'm sorry about the glass," Joan said, as she left the office.

Sawyer knew that Joan was tired of going over all of this. He was, too, but he knew also that, when she took the stand, it would be her demeanor and the conviction of her story which the jurors would most remember when it came time to deliberate. She had to be completely prepared.

Sawyer's plan was to introduce the possibility of a crime syndicate connection on the part of the Kenton County officials. He would talk about the gambling and the slot machines at Northern Kentucky's Beverly Hills, Glenn Rendezvous and other local night spots. He would call witnesses to testify that, on the night of the murders, Mrs. Kiger asked Joan to bring her the $1440.00 that was hidden under the couch in the library (in 1943 this amount was more than a year's salary for the average worker). Sawyer was also prepared to introduce two expert witnesses who had assessed and treated Joan after the murders: Dr. Walter Sprague, head of the Eastern State Sanitarium where, in late August, Joan had spent a month being observed and evaluated; the other witness would be Dr. John Romano, Director of the Psychiatric Clinic of General Hospital, in Cincinnati. Smith purposely chose these two experts because their final diagnoses corroborated his night terrors hypothesis. By beginning his defense with a number of the above theories, he felt that he might just sneak up on Vincent; and before he had a chance to rebut the Night Terror version, it would be permanently fixed in the jury's minds.

Joan returned to the office, having put fresh lipstick on, as well as rouge. She looked very pretty, but exhausted.

"We're almost done Joan, and I want to share with you my confidence that you are going to be judged not guilty. It's going to happen in one of two ways: one, not guilty because the prosecution could not show enough evidence necessary to find you guilty beyond a shadow of a doubt or, two, not guilty because the crime was done while you were in the midst of one of your night terrors.

"While you are on the stand, especially when Mr. Vincent interrogates you, you simply have to stick to the truth. The fact is you have no memory that, while you were in a waking state, you harmed anyone." Sawyer's tone became increasingly dogmatic.

"You remember that, in your nightmare, you fired at the intruder. Whether this actually occurred or not is up to you to decide but up to the prosecutor to disprove. That's your story. Stick to it. Don't let the prosecutor force you to admit that you actually remember killing Jerry; and as I have reminded you before, this trial is centered only on the death of Jerry, not your father. The prosecutor evidently feels that he has a stronger case and a better chance at a murder conviction prosecuting you for only the one death. Another thing: you must share with the jury a little about yourself; so I will ask you some personal questions, such as where you go to school, what your grades are and what your plans for the future are. They need to see you as a sixteen year old girl with dreams and aspirations.

"I've told you that the prosecution will be trying to find a motive for these murders. You have no motive. You, your parents and Jerry were a very happy and loving family. You were looking forward to your 16th birthday and being able to drive. You, in fact, were planning your birthday party for the week after the murder. Okay? Now, just a couple more questions and I'll let you go, Joan. These are questions Mr. Vincent will probably ask you.

"When you discovered that your father had been shot, you say you ran outside?"

"That's right."

"Okay, now think. Was the front door locked or unlocked as you left?"

Joan looked frustrated. "Mr. Smith, I don't know. If you were in my shoes would you know?"

"Now think carefully—picture yourself going down those stairs. You're frightened, you're in a hurry to get out of the house and you think the intruder might still be inside. You come to the front door. What kind of lock did it have?"

"A dead bolt and also a lock you have to open with your thumb and forefinger."

"Do you remember doing that?"

Joan looked at her right thumb nail, now healed, but she thought about trying to open the door with that injury.

"No," she exclaimed, "No, it wasn't locked."

'Okay so you went through the unlocked door, then what?"

"I just stood in the yard for a minute, and then I realized I needed to go to Mr. Mayo's house down the road to get help. I knew Daddy kept his car keys on a hook inside the front door so I went back. When I got inside, I decided I had to wash my hands and face. I knew I looked awful, so I went to the kitchen sink. While I was in the kitchen, I noticed that the side door was open, so I closed and locked it and ran out the front door and drove to Mr. Mayo's."

"Joan, you never mentioned before that the side door was open," Sawyer said, frowning at the new twist in her story.

"I just now thought of it," Joan said, shrugging her shoulders.

"Oh, okay, then what did you do?" Smith asked, somewhat troubled.

"I went back outside and drove Daddy's Oldsmobile over to Mr. Mayo's. It was only the second time I had driven alone. I didn't have a license, but Daddy was teaching me to drive."

All these memories started returning, and Joan quickly reached out for the girl. She began feeling that familiar numbness, a sure sign that the girl was leaving her. She just didn't have much energy to fight her; yet she knew she had to hold on just for a little while longer. Taking several deep breaths, she began to feel something ever so slight, an imperceptible undulation of sadness. I should still feel bad about what everybody says I did, she thought. And then suddenly, the tears brought them together and pushed the detachment aside.

This was the moment Sawyer had been waiting for, however. He was a superb lawyer not just because he could master the facts of a case. He won trials because he understood juries; and he knew that for this jury of 12 men whom he had helped pick based on the fact that they had daughters of their own, these men had to see Joan cry. That would be the difference between guilty and not guilty. And now, as he watched Joan sob, he knew he could help her, help her cry for the jury.

Reaching for his handkerchief, he gave it to Joan, patting her on her shoulder. "That's enough for today," he said.

He stood up, as did Joan; and putting his arm around her, he walked her to the door, saying, "You'll do fine, Joan, just fine. After I talk with your mother, the two of you need to go shopping this afternoon. Go to Coppins. Buy a nice subdued outfit or two, something that makes you look younger."

Sawyer continued into the waiting room with Joan. Fred and Eva Williamson and Jennie sat silently anticipating the conclusion of the meeting, having long ago grown accustomed to those periods when each would be distracted by his or her own worries or concerns. Fred stood up, greeting Sawyer warmly, knowing that Joan's future was in good hands, feeling an unexpressed pride in the fact that he was responsible for convincing Sawyer to take Joan's case.

"Well, Sawyer, are we ready for tomorrow?

Sawyer put his hand on Fred's shoulder, saying, "Almost, and with Jennie's help, we will be ready." He extended his arm to her and she grasped it with both hands and, with his help, was able to come to a standing position. She maintained that firm grip, as they headed back into his office.

"How's that hip doing?"

"It just doesn't seem to be getting any better," Jennie complained. "Dr. Ertel told me to keep walking on it; but gosh, it really hurts after a few minutes."

Sawyer helped her into the leather chair in front of his desk, then wheeled his own chair from behind the desk and placed it directly in front of Jennie.

"Jennie, this is our last talk before the trial and, probably, our last chance to review your testimony. You know that Vincent will be anxious to manipulate your version of what happened that night to his advantage. I think he's going to be surprised by our approach to the case, and he may not realize what our plans are until you testify. Let's go over some of the facts, as you remember them.

"I know. I know. I know what you want me to say, and I'll say anything that will help Joan."

"Jennie, I don't want you to testify with that attitude. Vincent will pick up on it right away. You have to have a story that you believe in—a story that you can tell time after time with no variations as to what happened that night. You have to decide what the truth is and stick with it. If you do that, Vincent will not be able to suggest changes in your story as he interrogates you. There has been absolutely no evidence that there was a stranger in the house, threatening your family. No sign of a break in, no guns, other than the ones owned by Carl and no witnesses. Joan says that she fired shots at this phantom in front of your bedroom and in front of Jerry's. There are no slugs and no ballistic evidence that substantiate that possibility, so Joan's story will be attacked by Vincent.

"I've thought about that a lot," Jennie said, the discomfort of the leather chair showing in her face. "You know, at first I said I saw a shadowy figure in the doorway. I described him; but after all you said and all I've read in the papers, I know that couldn't be true. I think my mind wouldn't let me see Joan in that doorway. She was and is too precious to me to accept that she could have done all that."

Jennie began crying.

Sawyer said nothing, knowing that she had to work all this out in her own mind. She had to believe what was true—that Joan was the shooter, the only shooter; for if she believed otherwise, Vincent would exploit that weakness. Vincent must not be allowed, through Jennie, to suggest a scenario at odds with the one which Sawyer would try to prove.

After a few minutes, Sawyer said, "Okay, Jennie, tell me what really happened that night."

She looked up, her eyes shiny from the recent tears, "Are you really sure its best to admit that Joan killed Jerry?"

"I am," Sawyer said, without additional comment.

"Well, I was awakened by Joan shouting about someone being in the house and by the sound of a gun being shot over and over. Our bedroom was totally dark. I smelled the gun smoke. My ears were ringing from the sound. Suddenly the bedroom door was pushed all the way open and Joan stood in the entrance screaming and pointing a gun in my direction. I lowered my head, pretending to be dead. Another shot. My hip felt like it was on fire. I looked up. The door was clear, but I could hear Joan shouting; and I heard shots coming from the hallway near Jerry's room. Then I thought I heard someone run by our bedroom door and down the stairs. I know that couldn't be because almost immediately, Joan appeared in the doorway again. It was at that point, I lost consciousness."

"Is that what you truly believe, Jennie," Sawyer asked.

"Yes, that's what I remember, as I look back on what happened."

"When did you ask Joan if she was having another nightmare?"

"I don't know. Some time later. I came to and she was in the room again. I called to her, asked if she'd had a nightmare. She didn't answer, so I told her to go to Mr. Mayo's for help. She handed me a gun and said something about my needing it in case that man came back. It was all her nightmare. I'm sure of it now."

Sawyer was satisfied. Jennie's story would now dovetail with his defense, a defense built upon the fact that Joan did, in fact, kill Jerry, but did so while not in control of her faculties but while in the midst of a night terror.

Sawyer stood up, reaching for Jennie's hand, ready to escort her back to the waiting room.

"Sawyer, I have a couple more questions." Jennie's tone of voice was suddenly a bit more forceful. She had been mostly compliant, almost deferential to Sawyer; but just twenty-four hours before the long awaited trial, the pressure was finally surfacing. For the past week, Jennie had not slept well and had no real appetite. Her resilience was wearing thin.

"Of course, Jennie," Sawyer said, stepping back, pushing aside files, as he sat on the corner of his desk. He unconsciously retreated to that same spot whenever he needed to concentrate very deeply on his client's words.

"First of all, how did Joan do when you told her about the possible re-creation of the crime scene? She seemed a bit dazed when she came out for a break."

Sawyer disingenuously said, "She did just fine. A little surprised at first, but I immediately told her that she wouldn't have to be there and that seemed to quell any fears she may have had."

Jennie sighed with relief. This was something she did not want to talk to Joan about. Sawyer assured her that, if she wished, they could both leave the courtroom together.

She went on, "I'm still disturbed about the indictment brought against me," Jennie said, remembering the shock she felt as she was served with papers. "How could anyone think I had anything to do with Carl and Jerry's murders? How can they do that? What evidence do they have? I had nothing to do with what happened, so how can they prove I did?"

Sawyer paused, a little puzzled, "Now Jennie, we've been through all this. We talked about it the day you were freed on bail. I told you not to worry about this maneuver on the prosecutor's part. I explained that he was just attempting to scare both you and Joan."

Jennie began to feel a slow rise of anger which revealed itself in red blotches on her neck. My God, she thought to her self, haven't we been through enough without lawyers trying to scare us? "Well, I am scared and so is Joan. She went into absolute hysterics when I was served. Is that what the law is all about? Scaring people?"

Sawyer always tried to maintain an emotional distance from his clients, so he would be better able to focus on his defense. One of his mentors, a professor he highly respected who taught criminal law, expounded vehemently on remaining as objective as possible in any and every case. Seeing him standing on the platform in front of the class with chalk dust on the sleeves of his jacket, Sawyer could still hear his words echo in his ears, "Never! Never have an opinion about any case you take.

Never! Be emotionless with each and every client. Focus on the law and only the law."

The Kiger case was a challenge for him in this regard. For the most part, he was able to keep very tight boundaries between his human side and his legal side, but there had been a few times when that boundary softened. And this was one of them. Here was a woman whose husband and son were murdered, probably by her daughter; and she, herself, would always be reminded of the pain of this tragedy every time she took a step.

"Jennie, I know that this has been a terribly difficult time for you," Sawyer explained. "I assure you, with every confidence, you have nothing to worry about. As soon as this trial is over, they will drop all charges against you. I'm positive of that."

"How can you be so sure?" Jennie asked, shifting her position in the chair.

"The only reason they've charged you is to put pressure on Joan to admit that she planned to kill Carl and Jerry all by herself, feeling that she would not want you implicated." Even though Sawyer had given her all this information just after he'd arranged bail for her, he did not feel any impatience or irritation with Jennie's continuing worries.

"I don't know. I don't know," Jennie said, almost to herself. "I'm just so very tired."

"Believe me, Jennie. Whether Joan is found guilty or innocent, the charges against you will be dropped." Sawyer stood up again. "Anything else?"

"Tell me what will happen to Joan if you are able to convince the jury that she did not mean to kill Carl and Jerry."

Sawyer returned to his chair, saying, "A number of things could happen. One: if Joan is found not guilty, she could not be tried for the same crime again; two: its no secret as to why the prosecutor chose to try her for Jerry's murder only. He was thinking ahead to his second trial."

"I don't understand," Jennie said.

"It means that he can go back and try Joan later for Carl's murder."

"Oh, my God! Oh, my God!" Jennie cradled her face in both her hands and began crying. "No. No. I can't go through this again!"

"Jennie, what you and Fred need to consider, if Joan is acquitted, is getting long-term professional help for her. Maybe the Menninger Clinic, in Kansas; maybe General Hospital, in Cincinnati; or maybe even the Eastern Sanitarium in Lexington, Kentucky. Joan will need ongoing therapy. Think about how you feel now and multiply that by ten. It's a testimony to Joan's strength that she has held up as well as she has over the past four months." Sawyer often wondered how Joan was able to withstand the hospitalizations, the interrogations, the ostracism, as well as her concerns over what her future would be like. In thinking back to her dazed state earlier, he wondered if she could hold it together through the rigors of the trial.

Jennie regained her composure. Her emotions had been under tight control since her visit to the cemetery just after she was released from the hospital, and she hated when they surfaced without warning. "I do think it's a good idea to get Joan help. She may look and act strong; but after all, she is only 16 years old. I worry about her. Can you work with us to arrange treatment for her in a really good hospital?" Jennie asked, as she extended her hands for help out of the chair—and, more importantly, for help in finding a solution for Joan.

Chapter Fifteen
Christmas Shopping
(December 15, 1943)

15

Leaving their meeting with Sawyer in a somber mood, Fred, Eva, Joan and Jennie walked to the car in silence. Every time any of them left his office, the same dark and foreboding murk seemed to hang heavy in the atmosphere. Leaning on Eva, Jennie and she walked slowly behind Fred and Joan. The sky was filling with winter clouds, and the air was crisp. Blustery winds would periodically gust between the walkers, causing them to huddle closer to each other for warmth.

Piling into the cold car, the women shivered. Fred told them to be patient as he turned up all the knobs on the heater. To any passer by, this group looked merely like four Christmas shoppers caught up in the silo of their own thoughts and memories.

The rumblings of a hungry stomach brought them back together. Uncle Fred laughed perfunctorily and suggested that they get something to eat. Eva, whose stomach sounded the alarm, was the first to suggest a restaurant somewhere between Eilermans and Coppins. Jennie chimed in that, after lunch, they could split up and do their shopping and then rendezvous at an agreed upon locale.

The group seemed to come alive as they nibbled on sandwiches, munched on French fries and drank cokes. In between bites, they chatted about the War but, mostly, about Joe and John. Jennie brought a few of their recent letters and handed them to Eva. Joan leaned over the table, intercepting the mail.

Surprised that her mother wouldn't have let her read these letters first, she held them tightly. "Mamma, I'll give these to Aunt Eva when I'm finished reading them."

Eva, a bit embarrassed, nodded her head and told Joan that would be fine.

Jennie took the letters from Joan's hand; and with some irritation in her voice, she handed them to Eva, telling Joan she could read them some other time. Trying to protect Joan, Jennie didn't want her to know that both of her brothers were having a difficult time and were experiencing some insomnia and depression over the loss of their dad and Jerry. And although they didn't go into great detail, it was obvious that they had their worries, concerns and doubts about Joan. Their grief was palpable with each and every word that was written.

Joan sulked and made loud slurping sounds with her straw, trying to suck every last drop of her cherry coke from the glass.

As they left the restaurant, they agreed to rendezvous at Coppins, in the shoe department, at 2 p.m.

Joan held Jennie by her elbow as they walked through Eilermans. The energy that permeated the store was uplifting – every counter displayed perfectly shaped Christmas trees, each with a different theme of decorations. The cosmetics counter had a plethora of crystal angels scattered over the branches of its tree while the jewelry department flaunted one dotted with intricately carved wooden figures, depicting the Twelve Days of Christmas. Trees loaded with candy canes, strings of popcorn or Santa and his reindeer could be seen on top of the many counters interspersed throughout the store. Shoppers were crowding the aisles, loaded down with their holiday plunder. In the background, Bing Crosby could be heard crooning "White Christmas" in that deeply resonant voice of his.

Joan looked over at her mother as she was intently examining men's ties.

Watching Jennie hold up one and then another, she felt a flood of affection for her.

Moving closer to her, Joan said, as she leaned into her ear, "Mamma?"

"What do you think of this one for Uncle Fred?" Jennie asked, as she selected a gray striped tie and held it up for Joan to see. She was lost in deciding whether or not she should even get Fred a tie, wondering if he really needed one.

"Yes, that's a nice one. Mamma," Joan began again, "I'd love to go see *Holiday Inn* with you. We haven't gone to a movie in such a long time, and I think that would be a good one, don't you?" Joan knew that her mother loved musicals and, in particular, ones starring Bing Crosby.

"Yes, we can do that," Jennie said, half-heartedly. "Now do you really like this tie for Uncle Fred? Naturally we'll get him some other things, too. I was going to get Aunt Eva a pair of pearl earrings with a matching necklace. I just don't know what we would have done without either one of them."

Joan sighed and a deepening sense of loneliness dampened her earlier holiday spirits. Although her mother had been very supportive of her and concerned about her well-being since the night of the murders, Joan felt as though an opaque veil had descended between them. There were many long silences as they went about their daily routines. Most of their interactions focused on the trial.

As she was paying for Fred's tie, Jennie told Joan she needed to sit down for a while.

Walking over to the shoe department, Joan saw a few seats that seemed to be removed from the hubbub of the shoppers. Her mother sat with a moan. Joan grimaced every single time she heard this sound coming from Jennie's lips. An image of her mother lying in bed, splattered with blood, inevitably flashed before her mind's eye.

Placing the shopping bag between her legs, Joan sat down. Both women gazed straight ahead with expressionless faces.

"Mamma," Joan placed her hand over her mother's. "Are you mad at me?" This was a question that had haunted Joan day in and day out. She finally mustered the courage to ask her mother directly.

Jennie's head jerked toward Joan. "What?"

"Well, we haven't really talked about that night—I mean, you know, just you and me. And I just get the feeling that you're mad at me or something." Joan started wringing her hands. "And I understand if you are, I mean, I would be mad if I were you."

Jennie looked around at the milling shoppers and then at Joan. Perplexed by this question, she assured Joan that she was not angry with her for anything and wondered where in the world she got such a notion.

Her voice cracking with emotion, Joan said, "Well, I mean you don't talk to me very much. You never want to do anything with me. And you wouldn't share Joe and John's letters with me. I would think that we should have read those together. After all, it's just you and me, now."

Jennie thought back over the last few months and, for the first time, realized that she *had* distanced herself from Joan. This realization caught her by surprise. A mother should be forgiving, not angry, Jennie thought to herself. But I guess I am angry with her. Her actions destroyed our family. But were they her actions, or was someone else there, too? This was the conundrum Jennie constantly struggled with. And now the internal bantering that she kept at bay surfaced, suddenly. One voice said, "Of course there was someone there. You saw someone." Another voice countered, "It was Joan who fired those shots. It was Joan you saw. Sawyer wants you to say it was Joan."

Seeing that her mother's neck was covered with bright red blotches, Joan asked if she was all right. Everyone in the family knew that the color of Jennie's neck was a give away to her unexpressed anger.

Once again reassuring Joan that she was fine, Jennie patted Joan's knee and said, "I'm sorry if I've made you feel bad, Joan. But let's not ruin the holidays with such talk." As she reached for her purse, a sharp pain flooded Jennie's entire pelvic area.

Slumping in her seat, Joan surveyed the crowd and caught the back of a familiar head. Not believing her eyes, she jumped up, nearly falling over the shopping bag that rested between her legs and broke through the crowd until she sneaked up behind a girl in a green coat whose brown hair looked disheveled and unkempt. Approaching her from behind, Joan put her hands over the girl's eyes and whispered, "Guess who?"

Mae turned around, gasped, and both girls excitedly hugged each other and danced in circles. Screaming in high pitched tones, they each shouted the other's name. Passers-by glanced at them in annoyance but, given the holiday season, were quick to forgive this ear piercing outburst.

Joan dragged Mae over to where her mother was sitting.

"Mamma, look, it's Mae! Can I go have a coke with her? Please? You can sit here, and we won't be gone long. I promise."

Jennie was relieved to end their earlier conversation and happy to see Joan so excited. There had been so very little joy for Joan.

"Hi, Mrs. Kiger," Mae said, as she and Joan held hands ever so tightly, each afraid that letting go might mean they'd never see each other again. "It's great to see you. How are you feeling?" Mae stopped short and wondered if she should have asked this usually benign question.

Jennie smiled and nodded her head. Seeing Mae stirred up the most unusual feelings within her. A part of Jennie was happy to see her, and another part of her was angry; it was this angry part that drowned any positive feelings she may have initially felt toward Mae.

The last time Jennie saw her was just before the murders. A strong surge of resentment welled up within her as she thought about the last phone call she had with Mae's mother. Even though she knew that Mae would not voluntarily remove herself from Joan's life, she still felt some anger toward her. Mae's absence was terribly painful for Joan, particularly now. Although Joan always made excuses for Mae, Jennie knew that she was deeply hurt.

This anger at Mae's abandonment of her daughter seeped over into a deeper layer of resentment. Looking into Mae's face, Jennie saw innocence. Here she was, a 16 year old girl who had a normal life, was enjoying her junior year, was going out with friends, driving, shopping for her gown for the upcoming Christmas Formal at La Salette and flirting with boys – what her own daughter should be doing, instead of talking to lawyers, psychiatrists, taking psychological tests and having nightmares. Looking into Joan's face, Jennie saw suffering. Mae had a father and a normal family. For a brief second, she hated her.

Covering up her feelings, she told the girls to go ahead but suggested that they be back in half an hour.

"Would you like me to bring you something to drink?" Joan asked, as she gave her mother a peck on her cheek – an action which startled Jennie. She couldn't remember the last time Joan had kissed her. Touching the spot where Joan's lips had left a slight wetness, she indicated that she would like a coke with no ice.

Mae and Joan left rapidly, arm-in-arm, chattering wildly.

Returning to the same restaurant and booth she sat at during lunch with her family, Joan ordered them both a cherry coke and a plain one to go.

After the waitress left, there was a brief but uncomfortable silence. Joan pulled a package of Kools from her purse and offered Mae one.

For the last several months, Joan had tortured herself wondering what Mae was doing, puzzled as to why she hadn't called or written her or visited her. The void left by her absence was cavernous and filled with despair. All of her interactions since that night had been with adults – her family, doctors, lawyers, nurses. The only girls she had any contact with were those at the sanitarium, and they were strange. Mae was the only person on the face of the earth who could assuage her doubt, her fears and her pain.

Sipping her coke and nervously flicking her ashes into the round glass ashtray, she looked Mae straight in the eye and asked her why she hadn't heard from her. Posing the same question she had asked her mother, she wanted to know if Mae was mad at her.

Mae looked incredulously at Joan, the question unexpected and puzzling. Mae grabbed her hand, and sobbing, explained that she could never be mad at her, never.

"I did write you a letter, Joan, just after it happened. Like the very next day." Having committed the letter to memory, Mae recited it. Then suddenly, her eyes widened as she tightly pursed her lips.

With tears in her eyes, she blurted, "My god damn mother! Damn my mother! She was supposed to mail it." All the arguments about Joan between her and her parents flooded Mae's thoughts. Although her mother never said anything demeaning about Joan outright, Mae felt an undercurrent of aversion whenever the Kiger name came up. Never did she ever imagine that her mother would steal and destroy a personal letter, especially one so important.

Trying to be as tactful as she could, Mae explained that her mother was greatly influenced by neighbors, especially that Mrs. Schneider who seemed to believe that…Mae stumbled for words. How could she tell Joan that most everyone thought she was guilty as sin--that she was crazy--emotionally disturbed?

Joan sensed Mae's distress, knowing full well what she was thinking and saved her from having to finish her sentence.

"Thanks so much for writing that letter, Mae. Having you recite it to me right now is much better than if I had gotten it months ago." So caught up in her own problems, Joan hadn't really given any thought to how that night had affected Mae. Imagining what she had to deal with at school and at home saddened her deeply.

"How are you?" Mae asked, sympathetically. "I mean like *really* how are you?"

"I'm fine. I mean *really* fine," she said, rather unconvincingly.

More silence. Billows of smoke obscured these moments of awkwardness.

Breaking the stillness, Mae told Joan that she wasn't afraid about having to testify at the upcoming trial. Their conversation shifted to their experiences with Sawyer Smith and his secretary. They giggled about how she was so perfectly dressed and coiffed but was always in a dither because she couldn't seem to find anything on her desk—a desk which looked like it had been struck by a hurricane.

"I liked your lawyer, that Mr. Smith," Mae said as she stubbed her cigarette in the overflowing ashtray. "He said they'd be asking me what we did and where we went before the murd…." Mae stopped short, having just as difficult a time saying the word "murder" as Joan always did. "You know. I don't care what anyone says, I know you didn't do it. You didn't, did you?" She quickly cupped her hand to her mouth, as though she'd said a curse word in front of one of the nuns at La Salette.

Joan looked at her watch and picked up the bill. "Mae, it's time to go. I can't leave my mother there much longer." When Mae reached for her change purse, Joan waved her hand and said she was buying and suggested that Mae could get the next tab. As soon as these words were said, Joan wondered when that would ever be.

Joan finally answered Mae's questions. "And yes, they say I did it. I didn't think I did, at first, but now….well, I don't know. Everybody keeps telling me that I did. I never told you that I was a sleepwalker. I guess I was too ashamed. It's such a weird thing. I didn't want you to think I was that weird."

Mae reached over and grabbed her hand as a tear trickled down her cheek. "Joan, no matter what, I would never think you're weird, ever." Then, her face lit up. Rumbling through her purse, Mae pulled out a large brown envelope that had been addressed to her.

"Here. Now *this* is weird! I had no idea I'd see you today, but this came in the mail just as I was leaving to go Christmas shopping. I didn't want to go back in the house, so I shoved it in my purse. It's your gift."

"Oh, Mae. I haven't gotten your gift yet," Joan said, guiltily. Once again she realized that she had been too self-absorbed over the past few months.

"Don't worry about that," Mae said, as she handed her the envelope.

Joan opened it and gasped, "Oh, my gosh!! It's an autographed picture of Bette Davis as Julie in *Jezebel*!" Joan stared at the glossy photo with Miss Davis' handwritten signature sprawled along the bottom. In awe, Joan touched her face as Bette gazed back in her low cut white ruffled ball gown.

"Thank you, so much!" Winking at Mae as they got up from the booth, she said, "Now don't you agree that she's much more beautiful than Joan Crawford?"

Chapter Sixteen
The Pot Bellied Stove
(August 18 – December 16, 1943)

16

Gulley's Store was a Burlington, Kentucky institution dating from 1918, when Lester Gully and his brother-in-law, Albert Petit first opened their all-in-one grocery; and all-in-one was no exaggeration. They would pump your gas, sell you farm tools, make you a sandwich, provide groceries for cash; or if you had no money until your tobacco crop came in, they would let you charge.

Since Gulley's was the only place within an hour's ride by horse or a twenty minute ride by car that provided for all the community's needs, the pot-bellied stove, at the back of the store, soon became the social gathering place for this close knit town. It was here that gossip was traded and cattle and farms bought or sold.

The store was a five minute walk for anyone employed by the variety of businesses in Burlington: the People's Deposit Bank, Smith's Store, Kirkpatrick's store, the hardware store, the Boone County Recorder, the Barber Shop, the Post Office, the Farmer's Mutual Insurance Company, Jess Eddins' Garage, the New Burlington School, which housed about 100 students grades one through twelve, the courthouse, the jail, Snappy's garage, McBee's Service Station, as well as Frank Milburn's secretive war factory – all in a town of 300!

When Boone County was formed in the late eighteen hundreds, Burlington was originally named Craig's Camp after John Hawkins Craig, one of the men who donated land which was to become the town of Burlington. The two major streets, Burlington Pike and Idlewild- East Bend Road crossed at the very center of the town and on each corner of the intersection a substantial structure was erected, three of which exist today: on the north east corner, the county courthouse, erected in 1898; on the southeast corner, the planning and zoning office (originally People's Deposit Bank); on the northwest corner, the Burlington Hardware Store, which started its life as a tavern; and on the southwest corner stood a building constructed in 1921 by Dudley Rouse. This corner of Burlington was well suited to accommodate, over the years, a General Store, a pool hall and, more recently, Smith's Grocery, run by Luther and Lucille Smith. The structure has been demolished and is now a parking lot for the Burlington Baptist Church. Lots of Baptists and lots of Democrats in this town.

In December, 1943, Gulley's store was a very active place. Every day at lunch, business men (and men is the correct terminology, for no lady would be seen at Gulley's around the pot-bellied stove) congregated here to share opinions on the upcoming Joan Kiger murder trial. If modern polls were employed with this group, the findings would reflect what was evident to any eavesdropper listening to the opinions shared at Gulley's: a 15 year old girl could not have shot her father and brother; and everyone agreed that if that high priced defense lawyer, Sawyer Smith, was going to try and say the killing was done while Joan was having a dream, he was one "desperate son-of a bitch."

As Sickem Weaver, the Boone County Recorder's typesetter so succinctly put it, "You don't shoot a gun 15 times without waking up."

No one in the store could remember how Sickem got his nickname. And even his parents, Nora and Lloyd Weaver, who ran a boarding house and sometimes helped prepare meals for prisoners in the local jail, were not forthcoming on that point.

Sickem stopped by Gulley's store every afternoon about 4 p.m., after working at the newspaper, on his way home to his parents' house, about as block away. Nora and Lloyd Weaver were God fearing Baptists who brought their son up to accept the strictest of interpretations of the Bible. Sickem provided his parents with such a sense of a job well done that they did not even think to ask themselves the question as to why, at twenty-nine, he had remained unmarried and, as far as they could tell, had no proclivity toward walking down either side of the aisle.

Another frequent visitor to the store was Alvin Boyers Renaker, the Vice President of People's Deposit Bank. AB, as he was called, was more of a listener at these gatherings; but he was a respected listener. Farmers joked that AB stood for "Always Broke" because he would lend money only if it was obvious that the borrower really didn't need it. He had neither time nor money for desperate people. His presence, however, did add a seriousness to the discussions because, simply by nodding as a speaker made his point, he gave credence to that argument; or by shaking his head, everyone knew that he deemed the line of reasoning spurious.

Lester Gulley rarely joined in because, in spite of the loafers and gossipers, there were legitimate customers; and he attended their needs. He carried around a long stick with pincers on one end and a mechanical trigger on the other which would allow him to reach even the loftiest shelves, some eight feet up, for whatever was needed. He had a high pitched voice and a laugh that was more like a chortle, but one rarely heard either so intent was he on his job. He carried a note pad in his apron and when a farmer asked, "Can I pay you when the crops come in?" Lester would just make himself a note as to who, what, when and how much and he would then ram the paper down on a long nail driven through piece of half inch poplar, placed conveniently on his counter top. "Pay me when you can," he would say.

When Lester Gulley died in 1970, the unpaid notes were found; and once totaled, his heirs learned that over a thirty year period he had extended over$10,000.00 in credit which was never repaid.

About once a week, Boone County deputy sheriff, Irvin Rouse, would stop at Gulley's. After all he was well aware that the Gulley's gossipers were also voters; and every day since Jake Williams had asked him, in 1941, to be his deputy, Irvin had been running for Sheriff. At that time, a sheriff could not succeed himself. Four years and out was the life of a Boone County Sheriff.

But Irvin was more than a political fixture at Burlington. He also coached a knothole team that in one season was undefeated and went on to the playoffs and swept the competition. Another baseball story they tell about Irvin, but never in his presence, involved his umpiring techniques when he would work the minor league games. This story highlighted one breach in his otherwise firm resolve to keep his law enforcement duties separate from his personal life: in the midst of a game, an argument with a player and his coach broke out. The argument escalated; and as Irvin's face turned red and his exasperation became apparent to everyone, he suddenly pointed his stub at the two and said, "This argument is over. Remember I'm the Deputy Sheriff of Boone County. Either you guys play ball or I'll arrest you both for disturbing the peace." If this had been a joke, it would have been a great line; but Deputy Rouse was totally serious.

When Irvin came into Gulley's, he would buy a Coke and amble back to the stove (even in the heat of summer, the stove was the heart of the store, a magnet around which all conversation centered). Holding the Coke in his left hand, he would grab different people around the neck and then, with his stub, jab them in the ribs. Irvin always enlivened the group with his antics and his humor—and a good joke whether physical or verbal usually placed a vote or two in his column.

Naturally, as the trial approached, everyone was interested in what he had to say; but since he was fairly sure he would have to testify, he was now reluctant to talk about what he knew.

"Come on, Sheriff. You think she did it?"

That almost always did the trick – got Irvin to talking. Calling him Sheriff was like throwing a honeycomb to a bear. He would become very tractable. But today he would only say, "Y'all come to the trial. You'll learn a lot more than I can tell you."

"Come on Sheriff, do ya think she did it?"

After the second soothing sound of that word, Sheriff, he loosened up a bit.

"Well now, think about it. What's the most important thing a prosecutor wants to show about the accused?" he asked, taking a final drink from his Coke.

"The gun!" Someone shouted.

"A witness!" Another offered.

Irvin grinned, "The most important thing is motive; I'm going to leave you with this question. If Joan did it, can you tell me what her motive was?" And with that he waved his stub and exited by the side door.

Lester took out his note pad, "One Coke, five cents, Irvin Rouse," he wrote and slammed it down on the nail.

Courtney Kelly, up until he was tapped for his new job, was also a part of the Gulley pot-belly stove regulars who had been coming here to the store so long they each knew what the other was going to say before he said it. Courtney had been many things in a career which was stifled by the fact that, like Sickem, he did not want to leave the town he loved, to work in Cincinnati or Covington. The drive was an hour each way, and, although the pay was good, a lot better than a schoolteacher makes, he could not even imagine doing it.

It wasn't that he didn't need the money. He was trying to raise five children and remodel an old house on the edge of town; and because of that, he, too, infrequently asked Lester Gulley for a little time. Yet, when Court died in December of 1983, he owed no man.

The position he accepted changed his finances and many other aspects of his life. Had he thought through the negative ramifications of this new job, he probably would not have taken it; but take it he did; and he was not a man to renege on an agreement. The short man syndrome worked and didn't work on Courtney Kelly. He was sure of himself, opinionated and could be overpoweringly persuasive. But he was a kind man who would do anything for his town or for the family whom he loved.

As the war continued into its third year, the draft board began calling up more and more young men in the area; and Court began to feel that his friends, as well as acquaintances, started to treat him with more deference

– more – he couldn't quite put his finger on the difference, more like they treated Ralph Stith, the local undertaker, part of whose job was coming to people's houses to pick up a deceased loved one. He felt the Burlington people were seeing him as one who would come to their houses and ship their sons and husbands overseas to die.

Even parents who had teenage boys began to avert Courtney's gaze for fear that he would notice their children and put them on his death list.

Being the head of the Boone County Draft Board was changing his life, reducing his circle of friends and making him, when he walked into Gulley's Store, often wished that he had not.

His saving grace and the reason he was not relegated to being the pariah that he sometimes felt he was rested with his eldest son, Calvin, who soon would also be in the service. The town understood that Court, too, would then be going to bed every night worrying about the odds of that telegram from the War Department coming the next day, saying, "We regret to inform you that your son...."

Edward Rogers was not a regular visitor or shopper at Gulley's; but since he lived in Belleview Bottoms, a river community six miles further west from Burlington on Highway 18, he would stop occasionally for groceries and farm supplies.

All of the Gulley regulars knew how worried Rogers was. His son, Edward Jr., was in the Pacific and had been involved in some of the fiercest battles of that theatre. Rogers would occasionally share what he knew of Edward's whereabouts, but it was obvious to all that the conversation pained him very much. The father's constant question was, "How long can Edward escape injury or death in the horrors of those Island invasions?" Still, as neighbors, everyone had to ask; and as parents themselves, many of whom had sons in harm's way, they knew the never ending pain of the Rogers' family.

The telegram that finally came to them was far from the first to come to Boone County, but the fact that it was not the first made it no easier. "Mr. & Mrs. Edward Rogers, Belleview, Kentucky, The Secretary of War desires me to express his regret that your son, Edward Rogers, Jr., has been reported missing and presumed dead on the battlefield of Okinawa. If further details or information are received you will be notified…."

Just as when one throws a stone in a pond and watches the ripples go on and on toward the opposing shore, so a death in a community continues to affect everyone. Judge Carol Cropper's daughter, Carolyn, became engaged to Edward, Jr., before he left in December, 1942, to be trained with the Thirteenth Armored Division and later with the 715 Amphibian Tractor Battalion. By January, 1944, he was in Hawaii receiving additional training before seeing action in the Battle of Siapan and Tinian. From there the winds of war took him to the Philippines and to the battles of Zamimi Shimi and Ie Shima. It was during the battle for Okinawa that he gave his life for his country.

The irony of Edward's death would not become apparent to the many who loved him until much later. The irony was that the military strategist had decided that Okinawa had to be taken at any cost in order to begin the final invasion of Japan. The Japanese knew it, the Americans knew it, and for that reason, the battle was one of the fiercest fought in the Pacific. Okinawa, before this decisive battle, had a civilian population of 435,000; and during the fighting, 140,000 civilians died, along with 66,000 Japanese soldiers who defended the island with such tenacity.

American losses were excessive, as well; so much so that the strategist calculated that over one million allied soldiers would lose their lives in an all out assault on Japan. In the brief pause of this war in the Pacific, as the leaders contemplated the horrors to come, a precipitous event occurred which made the taking of Okinawa moot and completed the irony of Edward Rogers' death: prototypes of Fat Man and Little Boy were successfully tested. The President of the United States was now faced with the decision as to whether America should drop the Atomic Bomb on Japan. By giving a "thumbs up," Harry Truman saved a million American lives and countless millions of Japanese soldiers and civilians alike. Invasion plans were cancelled; occupation plans were drawn up. The war was over.

Did Edward Rogers, Jr. and the thousands of other Allied soldiers, who died in this assault on Okinawa, die in vain or can one assign some special significance to this last great battle of World War II?

The patrons at Gulley's store struggled with a similar problem, but one on a such nationally insignificant scale that no serious comparison should be made: yet, the death of a million people or the death of two needs closure— requires the measuring stick of logic; and in the month of December, 1943, as the Kiger trial approached, everyone searched for some reason, some compelling logic, some overpowering motive to explain the deaths of Carl and Jerry.

Chapter Seventeen
The Sheriff's Office
(December 17 - 21, 1943)

17

Boone County Sheriff Jake Williams and his deputy, Irvin Rouse, would end each day, during Joan Kiger's murder trial, returning to the Sheriff's office located in the courthouse; and there they would sit around the commanding presence of a large oak desk and review the day's events, a bottle of Kentucky bourbon facilitating their review.

Jake's office was a quagmire of aging evidence, dating back to his time as Deputy Sheriff. Shotguns leaned against the wall, affidavits from one case or another were piled in the corners, yellowed newspaper clippings had been thumb-tacked to the wall; but in spite of the disorder, it was his home away from home, and here he felt especially comfortable.

This afternoon, however, he was a troubled soul; and when Jake was troubled, everyone around him knew it.

"Damn," he said, looking at Irvin. "Damn, that damn lawyer."

It was the beginning of crunch time for Sheriff Williams. He would soon be interrogated by the best there was. Sawyer Smith's reputation would put fear in any law man. He was that good.

"I know he's going to ask me to explain everything I saw and did. He's going to say that I screwed up the crime scene."

Jake was vulnerable in a number of areas, and he knew it. He went directly from farming in 1937 to becoming Deputy Sheriff when Frank Walton asked for him; and then, in 1941, he was elected to the position of High Sheriff of Boone County. He had no training in law enforcement and certainly no training in securing a crime scene.

If Sawyer were to ask Sheriff Williams to elaborate upon some of his more challenging cases, Jake would be hard pressed to cite anything more substantial than the arrest of old man Frybe for being drunk in Jack Holt's tavern or having to talk to Billy Short about all those cars up on blocks in his front yard. "Oh, yeah, then there was the time….oh hell, if I'd only had one good murder case in Boone County." But in his seven years as Deputy or Sheriff there had been none.

He knew Sawyer would be asking why he allowed all those people at the Kiger house to mill around for hours. Finally the sheriff said to Irvin, angrily, "Hell, they were all there before we even arrived. We did our best to keep them downstairs away from the bodies."

"Damn right," Irvin said. "But, you know, half of Covington's police force was there."

"How many would you reckon were there, altogether?" Jake asked.

"Well, let's count them. There was that neighbor, Robert Mayo, and his father."

"Yeah," said Jake. "And it was Mayo who called me that night. Said that Joan came to his house with her horn blaring. He also called the Grant County Sheriff, Lewis Henderson. Why in the hell he would do that, I don't know. The murders took place in Boone County. That makes it our case. And why call the state police? Mayo must have called them because State Trooper Huff was there, also."

"But that's not the worse part," Jake said. "Covington Police Chief, what was his name?" He paused, while scratching his head. "Al Schild, that's it. Al Schild. He brought along Covington's Bureau of Identification Chief, Lieutenant Tiepel. And there were also two Covington detectives."

And Irvin chipped in, "There was also the guy from the Covington City Manager's office. Remember him? I think his name was Christophel and, oh yeah, those nosy neighbor ladies; one of them actually picked up a shell casing! Remember that? And don't forget that Fred Williamson and his wife were there, too."

"Looking back, what really jerked my leash," Jake said, "was when that Jack Maynard, took Joan up to her room, locked the door and talked to her for over an hour. What the hell was goin' on up there?"

Jake stopped to take a slug of the Kentucky brew. "And that damn lawyer is going to ask me if we secured the crime scene. What a joke. Including the two of us, I count fifteen people in that house after the murders."

"Now wait, Jake. There was also that little old lady who lived next door. The one who said she was awakened by something that sounded like a backfire. And don't forget she brought her son-in-law with her. That makes seventeen. How the damn hell can you control a crime scene with that many people wandering around?"

*　　　*　　　*

The Sheriff wasn't the only one worried about the next day's testimony. Deputy Rouse was worried, also. He would be called, in large part, because it was he, along with Sheriff Henderson, who found the pistols and shell casings in the Rosegate cistern. As Sheriff Williams topped off Irvin's glass, they continued strategizing because they knew they were up against a bulldog of a defense attorney.

How Joan Kiger was able to get Sawyer Smith to defend her was a bit of a mystery. No mystery that her family would want him. After all he was known throughout the region as an attorney who won the majority of his cases.

"There are ways," Irvin said, after a long sip of his whiskey. "After all, they did come up with $25,000.00 as bail for Joan; and later in December, when her mother was also charged with the murders, they found bail money for her, too."

Originally both women were going to be tried for the murders of Carl and his son. Williams really never could understand why prosecutor Vincent waited until December 6 to arrest the mother. It was obvious from the very beginning that she was either shielding Joan or complicit in the murders. She should have been in jail right along side her daughter. At least, now, they were both going to be tried for murder, even though Smith was successful in asking Judge Yager for separate trials, Joan's to be the first. But the money puzzled them the most— the $1440.00 found under the couch, the bail money they had to come up with for both Joan and Jennie, as well as Lord only knows how much to hire Sawyer Smith! The sheriff's suspicions leaned toward a mob connection— how else could one explain access to all that cash.

"The most confusing part of your testimony tomorrow, Irvin, will be about the three murder weapons," Jake said, getting back to their preparation. "You've got to be sure where you found each gun, how many shots were fired from these guns and anything else that damn Sawyer is going to throw at you. Think you're ready?"

Irvin adjusted himself, nervously. He would do that when telling a joke or under pressure, and he could do it whether sitting or standing.

"God damn," he said, in exasperation, "One time I go through it all in my head, and I think I've got it right; and the next time I think about it, I'm not so sure. I wonder, would it be so bad if I wrote this stuff down and used my notes when Sawyer asked me questions?"

"Nope. I think the jury would have trouble believing you if you couldn't just tell your story without any notes. Now let's go over it one more time, and I'll be Sawyer Smith."

"Okay," Irvin said, as a man resigned to his fate.

Sheriff Williams, pretending to be Sawyer Smith, said, "Now Deputy, would you state your name and what you do for a living?"

"Oh hell, Jake, let's just skip over that part. Let's get to the pistols."

But Sheriff Williams persisted. "Deputy, I need for you to answer my question."

Irvin sighed and adjusting himself again, said, "Well, Okay. I'm Irvin Rouse and I'm the Deputy Sheriff of Boone County, Kentucky."

"And how long have you been Deputy?"

"Well, when Sheriff Jake Williams – is it Okay I call you Jake. Maybe I should call you by your real first name."

"Jake will be fine. That's what all the jurors know me as. After all, I've helped most of them out, one way or another."

"Okay, when Sheriff Jake Williams was elected in 1941, he picked me as his Deputy."

"Now, Deputy Rouse, can you tell the court what kind of law enforcement training you've had that would cause Sheriff Williams to choose you."

"Hell, Jake, you know I haven't had any. You know I worked for the Highway Department until my hand was crushed and had to be cut off."

"So, Deputy, are you saying that you did not have the necessary law enforcement experience for you to perform your job."

"Jake, damn it, he's not gonna talk like that. I tell ya, he's gonna ask me about the pistols."

"Wrong, Irvin. Get it through your head that he already knows about the pistols. The whole town knows about the pistols. It's been in every paper in the country. The jury knows about the pistols. He has you on the stand for a lot more reasons than those damned pistols."

"Well, what does he want," Irvin said, his face turning red.

"He wants to make you look like a damn fool." There, Jake had said it; and looking directly into Irvin's eyes, "He wants everything you say about that night to be up for question."

"You know, Jake, the Highway Department told me that because I got hurt on the job, I could come back there anytime; they would give me my old job. The hell with all this. I think I'm goin' back."

Irvin was sweating. The stub of his right arm was tingling. He could feel the pain in his missing hand. "What did the doc call that? Phantom something.... Phantom pain," he said. He rubbed the stump vigorously trying to make it hurt, trying to make the real pain overcome the false pain.

"Irvin whether you're my Deputy next week or not, you will be on the stand tomorrow; and Sawyer will be trying to corner you. So let's keep at this a little longer."

"Okay, but don't ask me about my training. You know I haven't had any. And, damn it, Jake, you haven't had any either. What if he asks you when you get on the stand about your training?"

"Oh, he will, Irvin. He will."

They continued going over the various scenarios that they expected would be thrown at them the next day. Finally the bottle was empty. Jake stood up and put his arm on Irvin's shoulder, saying quietly, "Get a good night's sleep, partner. Tomorrow's going to be a long day. He flipped the light switch and they walked out into the frigid night air.

Before going their separate ways, Irvin paused on the last step of the courthouse, not quite knowing how to broach the next subject. "There's something I need to tell you, Jake. Something I haven't told anybody. About a week after the murders, that Kiger neighbor, Mrs. Hitzel, called me. She said she was walking around the Kiger place and she noticed a hole in the screen of the front door-- said it looked like a bullet hole to her. I went out and took a look. It could'a been anything. A stick. An animal, a finger-- anything could have made that hole. I didn't think it was worth reporting. You see any problem with that?"

"Forget about it, Irvin. Just remember everything we've talked about, and I know you'll do just fine; and believe me, you don't want to take any notes in with you."

Jake extended his left hand to Irvin, something no one else had ever done; and with that handshake, the two friends headed home.

Chapter Eighteen
The Deputy's Dilemma
(December 18, 1943)

18

It was the second day of the trial, December 18, 1943, and Irvin Rouse was upset—upset with his wife, Doretta, the beautiful Barlow girl he married a decade ago—and upset with himself.

His day on the stand was getting closer; and he wanted to look professional, like a law man who knew what he was doing, a man no one would question as to what he saw and what he did.

He had asked Doretta to wash a pair of pants that went especially well with his deputy shirt, a shirt that had pre-sewn holes just made for his deputy's badge. Doretta brought him his freshly washed and pressed pants, and she brought him something else.

"Irvin," she said, "I don't know what this is, but it was in the washer when I pulled your pants out."

She handed Irvin a .38 slug.

Feeling his heart skip a beat, he inhaled sharply but tried to remain composed. Taking the slug in the palm of his hand, he let his mind drift back to August 17, when he had dug it out of the base of Jerry's bedpost.

Mindlessly, he had placed it in the watch pocket of those pants and had not thought of it since. Irvin always looked at his job with pride. He felt that he was the physician of law enforcement; he understood that the basic creed for a doctor was "whatever you do, do no harm." This misshapen piece of lead reflected the first of two mistakes he had made in the Kiger case; but fortunately for him, he knew his secret was still safe. Doretta's discovery would not warrant any further thought on her part.

The second mistake would not become obvious until much later, and he really wasn't sure it was his mistake but....

On August 17, when Sheriff Williams and Irvin walked Joan into the Burlington jail, Irvin was carrying a small overnight bag which Joan had packed; and as they approached her cell, he handed the bag to her. She reached for it with her right hand, and Irvin noticed a bandage around her thumb-- and red fingernail polish on her nails: "Hurt yourself?" he asked.

"Yeah," she said. "I don't remember how, but I tore my thumb nail off. It's really been hurting."

"Have Mrs. Kirkpatrick look at it," the Sheriff suggested.

That was the end of the conversation and the beginning of Irvin's angst.

Irvin wondered whatever happened to that thumb nail that Sheriff Henderson found by the cistern lid. It was not part of any evidence that had been collected. Did Henderson even remember the incident? Irvin had seen him a few times in the intervening months, and Henderson had not mentioned it. Irvin certainly was not going to bring it up. As the trial unfolded, day after day, and the evidence mounted, pointing to Joan as the killer, Irvin relaxed a little, feeling that neither the .38 slug nor the thumb nail was crucial to her conviction. Still, the "Do No Harm" mantra he had adopted as a law enforcement officer haunted his every waking moment. From the time he saw Joan, in the living room at Rosegate, wringing her hands and wiping them on her robe, he was convinced that she was guilty. He couldn't bear the thought of being responsible, in any way, for weakening the prosecutor's case. Fortunately, as Irvin assessed the trial thus far, the prosecutor was doing very well on his own.

He put on his newly pressed pants and his deputy shirt. Doretta would have to pin the right sleeve tightly around his stub as she always did; but before he called her for that, he placed the .38 slug in a cigar box where he kept his tie clasps and loose change, next to the ring he used to wear on his right hand. Both were reminders of mistakes he had made. The slug would provide no constant visible reminder of a lapse in judgment, as his missing hand did; but it was there, in the drawer, and there it would stay.

Just as the shell casing became Joan's constant companion, a reminder of that hour in her life which robbed her of the rest of her life, so the sight of the slug every morning when Irvin dressed himself reminded him of his guiding principle as a law enforcement officer – "Do No Harm."

From 1943 until his death in 1970 at the age of sixty-five, Irvin looked upon that slug every morning and it reminded him, for another day, of that motto he had taken upon himself so long ago; and it transferred easily to civilian life, following his four years as sheriff. Because of its positive influence on the rest of his life, he died feeling that from the moment that he tossed the slug into his cigar box, he had been true to his creed. Some years later when his wife, Doretta, died, the slug was still there in the house, in his cigar box. She had touched nothing; and when their children, Audrey and Gayle, came from Florida to auction off all of their parents' possessions, the slug met the same ignominious fate as did Maria Kiler's reminder of a moment in her life—a fleeting second of curiosity and then to the waste basket.

Chapter Nineteen
The Foreman
(December 21, 1943)

19

In a small room on the second floor of the courthouse, 12 jurors gathered to consider the fate of the school girl, Joan Kiger. The trial itself had been a short one, only five days, and the evidence was compelling. Probably the most disturbing of the five days was the fourth when the bloody beds, pillows, sheets and mattresses were brought into the courtroom and displayed. Vincent's forceful re-creation of the Kiger bedrooms brought home, as no testimony could, the brutal nature of the murders. Even though four months had passed since that August 17 night, the blood-soaked mattresses still had a smell that these farmers who were accustomed to slaughtering animals could identify.

Vincent had explained that for a single killer to shoot at the victims so many times suggested an anger and a rage so extreme that the intention of that night was not simply the death of the family but a scenario which represented a cathartic blood letting.

They were all glad to have the trial behind them, and they felt the verdict would be swift in coming. The evidence pointed to Joan: her own confession as related by the Sheriff and her written confession as presented by the prosecutor, Vincent, left no doubt that Joan murdered her father and her brother and, in all likelihood, tried to murder her mother.

After considerable small talk around a large chestnut table, Albert Dringenburg gave a shrill whistle. The chatter stopped and he said, "Let's get this over with. I've got two acres of tobacco I need to strip before the January market re-opens. Most of us have lots of chores to do. So let's vote and be done with it."

Lamar Congleton stood up. "Now, we can't rush this. The girl's future is at stake. Let's be sure we do the right thing. We all have jobs we should be doing. I've got 140 acres, fifty head of cows, forty hogs and seven horses, as well as tobacco that need stripping. My wife and thirteen year old son are trying to keep everything together, but let's not think just about us. We have a verdict to decide on and it isn't as simple as figuring out whether Joan did it or not. We have to base our decision on her state of mind, as well. You remember the instructions that Judge Yager gave us?"

"Hell, Lamar, how can you shoot fifteen times and not mean to kill someone?" George Heil broke in, laughing.

Next Byron Kinman spoke, "Look, everybody, let's just take a vote as to *whether* Joan did it. Then we'll have a second vote deciding if she was crazy or not when she did it. But now, before we do that, we've got to have ourselves a foreman, and I think Lamar here would make a good one. Any objections?"

Lamar raised his hand to protest, but everyone shouted him down. "You got it, Lamar. You're our foreman."

"Now can we vote?" Dringenburg asked.

"Okay, okay, Lamar said, "If I'm it, I'm going to see that we follow the Judge's instructions to the letter. Now this may be repetitive and it may be dull, but I'm going to read aloud Judge Yager's instructions to us. I think we all need to hear it one more time before we start deliberating. Since we all know each other, y'all just sit back and relax while I go through this. Then I think we should have an informal vote to get started. Is there anybody here who objects to doing it this way?"

No one spoke up and by the way they all leaned back in their chairs, Lamar figured he could begin reading:

INSTRUCTIONS TO THE JURY

Instruction No. 1: If the jury believes from the evidence in this case beyond a reasonable doubt that the defendant, Joan Kiger, in Boone County, Kentucky, on a day in August, 1943, and before the finding of the indictment herein, did unlawfully, willfully, maliciously and feloniously and with malice aforethought and not in her necessary or reasonably apparent necessary self-defense shoot and wound Jerry Kiger with a pistol, a deadly weapon, and that from said shooting and wounding the said Jerry Kiger did then and there die, then the jury should find the defendant guilty of willful murder as charged and fix her punishment at death or confinement in the penitentiary for life, in the reasonable discretion of the jury.

Instruction No. 2: If you do not believe from the evidence beyond a reasonable doubt that the defendant, Joan Kiger, has been proven guilty of murder as set out in Instruction No. 1, but believe from the evidence beyond a r reasonable doubt that the defendant did in the County of Boone, State of Kentucky, in August, 1943, and before the finding of the indictment herein, without previous malice and not in her necessary or reasonably apparent necessary self-defense, but in sudden affray, or in sudden heat and passion upon a provocation reasonably calculated to excite her passions beyond the power of her control, shoot and kill Jerry Kiger, you shall in that event find her guilty of voluntary manslaughter and fix her punishment of confinement in the penitentiary for a period of not less than two years and not more than 21 years in your reasonable discretion.

Instruction No. 3: If the jury believe from the evidence beyond a reasonable doubt that the defendant has been proven guilty, but that a reasonable doubt as to whether she is guilty of murder as set out in instruction No. 1, or guilty of voluntary manslaughter, as set out in Instruction No. 2, then the jury should find her guilty of voluntary manslaughter, the lower offense.

Instruction No. 4: If the jury believe from the evidence beyond a reasonable doubt that the defendant, Joan Kiger, shot and killed Jerry Kiger and you further believe that at the time she shot Jerry Kiger she was unconscious or so nearly so that she did not comprehend her own situation and the circumstances surrounding her, or that she supposed at the time she did said shooting of Jerry Kiger some member of her family was being attacked by robbers, then in that event you should find her not guilty.

Instruction No. 5: The words "with malice aforethought", as used in these instructions, mean a pre-determination to do the act of killing without lawful excuse, and it is immaterial how recently or suddenly before the killing such pre-determination was formed.

Instruction No. 6: The words "willful" and "willfully" as used in these instructions mean "intentional" and not accidental or involuntary. The word "feloniously", as used in these instructions, means proceeding from an evil heart or purpose, done with the deliberate intention to commit a crime.

Instruction No. 7: The law presumes the defendant innocent until her guilt is proved beyond a reasonable doubt, and if from the evidence any material fact necessary to establish her guilt, there is a reasonable doubt of her guilt, you should find her not guilty.

Instruction No. 8: Any verdict in this case must be concurred in by all members of the jury and the verdict if made may be signed by one juror as foreman.

Signed: Ward Yager,
Judge of the Boone Circuit Court

"Well, Lamar, now that we've heard all that for the second time, can we vote; or do you have more hoops we need to jump through?"

Lamar looked at the group, ignoring Dringenburg's comments:

"Okay, now, let's just have an informal vote. It won't count for anything, but it'll give everybody an idea of our startin' point. Is there anybody who thinks Joan did not murder her brother, Jerry?" Lamar looked around the table.

There was a brief silence. Finally Charlie White spoke up, "I think she killed 'em; but you know, her story about somebody being in the house needs to be talked about. Even the mother swore earlier that there was a stranger in the house."

"Oh, hell," Byron said. "When she got on the stand, that wasn't her story. You remember when Vincent questioned her, she admitted that back in August she thought there might have been an intruder; but on the stand, she said she figured it was one of Joan's nightmares."

Ed Black banged on the table. "Lamar, I'm sure glad you're on the jury. But I'll have to say, I'm getting tired of your mother-in-law's cooking. It's gettin' awful late. Can't we send out tonight for something from Stringtown or some place else?"

By the fifth day of this confinement, these farmers were worried about their families who had to shoulder all the work-load, and they were becoming restless. They needed to see the sun and the sky, and they longed for the feel of the wind across their faces; but during this week of being sequestered, they had been guarded day and night, either by Sheriff Williams or Deputy Rouse. Their only other contact with the outside world was when, three times a day, either Elmer Kirkpatrick or Sickem's mother, Nora Weaver, would bring their meals.

The 12 cots, covered with drab green woolen blankets, were lined up in an adjoining room in a jailhouse fashion, a mere foot of space between each. They were uncomfortable and devoid of privacy. The one bathroom was inadequate for the needs of the group, and the fact that they could not see their families was especially galling.

"I'm not going to vote on an empty stomach," Dringenburg said, changing his demands.

"And it's time they brought us some beer," someone else chimed in.

"Lamar, looks like we're going to be here for a while. It's already seven o'clock. Can't you get us something good to eat?"

Lamar went to the door and called Deputy Rouse in. He took their orders and exited quickly.

"Well now," William Heil said, "now we can't vote until Irvin gets back. I ain't leavin' here without one more free meal."

Lamar stood up again. "Okay, any more discussion on the stranger in the house theory?"

"I think we should review at it again," Byron said. "Look at all the damage done that night. And remember that Chicago gun expert, Wilson? He testified that one of the guns was shot six times, reloaded and then the killer just kept on shootin'. I don't think that makes sense."

"Damn right," Dringenburg interjected. "It don't make sense. You can't tell me somebody can do all that: shoot a gun 'til it's empty, reload, keep shootin', gather up all the shell casings, get the guns, move that heavy cistern lid and toss everythin' down in the water and do it all while she was asleep. It just ain't possible."

"Good," Lamar said, pointing at Dringenburg, "That's what we need to talk about. Did Joan murder her family while asleep and not in control of her actions, did she do it deliberately or is there a third explanation for what happened?"

Clyde Arnold, the only one of the 12 who was not a farmer, spoke his mind: "Her actions make me think it was planned,"

"You tellin' me she intended to kill her whole family?" Howard Abden, of Idlewild, asked, in disbelief.

"Everything we talk about is just a guess. Is it fair that we find Joan guilty by just guessing what happened?" Heil complained.

Deputy Rouse knocked on the door, and then entered, carrying two large bags, followed by JD Jarrel who had a case of Cokes and a pot of coffee.

"Hey, Irvin, where's my beer?"

Irvin looked up, spotted the speaker and said, "Now you know you can't have beer. You want Coke or you want coffee?"

"Ah, give me a Coke."

The 12 men around the table became quiet as they ate, their thoughts centered on rejoining their families and returning to their farm routines. Most had never been separated from either for so long, and they yearned for the comforts of life as they knew it.

Ed Black walked to the window, a cigarette in one hand and a cup of coffee in the other and looked down upon the town square. People were still milling about. He could see three men with their cameras, and there was a group of Burlington ladies, all dressed up, as though they were on their way to church.

"Come here, Lamar. Look at all this. They must think we're gonna walk out of here any minute with a verdict."

Albert Dringenburg overheard that comment. "Well, if we ever get around to votin' on it, we can walk out. What are we waitin' for?" he said, churlishly.

"Everybody finished eatin'?" Lamar asked. "Anybody need to use the toilet before we get started?"

"I gotta go," Black said.

"Me, too." Several others joined in.

"Okay, let's break for fifteen minutes," Lamar suggested.

They resumed their discussion thirty minutes later.

"You remember when Mae Klingenberg testified? She said Joan was planning her own birthday party on the week-end of August 21. Now why would Joan do that if she was gonna kill everybody?" Howard Abdon said, looking around the room for support.

"It makes her look innocent," Bill Hill suggested.

"No, I think she really honestly planned to have that party. I think something happened the week before or the day before the murders, something happened to push her over the edge. She had to be in a terrible rage to do what she did," Abdon argued.

Lamar opined, "Well, you know Vincent and his team looked for motive. They interviewed everybody who had contact with the Kiger family. There was no motive or he would have presented it. That's the weak part of his case. He could not explain why Joan would kill everyone and, especially, in such a violent way."

By now two hours had passed, and everyone was beyond ready to vote. There was little disagreement among the eleven farmers and one steel construction worker as to the guilt or innocence of Joan, but there was reluctance when it came to declaring that the crime was premeditated. Many of these men had daughters of their own and this fact created a soft spot in the logic which they brought to this table of judgment. It was not as though they were to decide the fate of some horrible degenerate. They were to pass sentence on a teen age girl much like the ones they had in their own homes.

"Any other discussion?" Lamar asked.

"Let's vote," several shouted.

"Okay," Lamar said. "The first vote will be simply on the basis of whether Joan murdered her brother and not on her possible motives or her state of mind or whether she was sleepwalking or awake."

Lamar gave each man a similar piece of paper. Five minutes later, taking his hat, he had each juror place his folded vote in it. Sitting at the head of the chestnut table, Lamar dumped the verdicts out, opened each one and read the decision aloud. It was unanimous. The jury of twelve men voted that Joan was guilty.

Lamar knew that his job as the foreman was to bring consensus to this jury, to help them arrive at a unanimous decision; but it seemed too easy. Everyone was so sure that Joan was guilty. Should he express his doubts? As a juror, as well as the foreman, did he have the right to move them away from this unanimity?

There were several things that disturbed him. One was the testimony of Dr. White, a Cincinnati pathologist, who said that Carl was shot at least six times from no more than 16 inches; and he had demonstrated how the killer must have leaned over the bed, getting very close and personal with the victim, something he did not think Joan would be capable of. And if Joan had to be that close as she shot, why was there no testimony of blood splatter on her pajamas or on her body? Also, what about Jennie's original statement, the one he'd read in the local paper in August shortly after the murder? She was quoted as saying that she saw a shadowy figure in the doorway firing at Carl and her and that she pretended to be dead so that he would go away. Yet, in the testimony this week at the trial, she admitted she was wrong then; and her latest story was that it was Joan, in a sleep walking state, who was the killer. Even in this version, she did not describe Joan as entering the room and firing at point blank range. It just seemed as though Jennie was changing her story either to protect Joan or to convince the jury of her guilt.

Vincent made a point of asking the Sheriff if Joan had the top of her pajamas tucked in or hanging outside. "Outside," the Sheriff had said, emphatically. That was telling to Lamar because he remembered Jennie's statement in August that she saw a shadowy figure with light pants and a shirt hanging outside his pants. Could it be that there *was* a stranger; and could Jennie now be changing her story in an effort to protect him or, at least, divert the jury's attention from the possibility that someone was there? Then again, was the shirt that she saw just Joan's pajama top? What further troubled Lamar was the fact that while Jennie was upstairs, critically wounded, almost hysterical, she asked Joan to go downstairs and get the $1440.00 and Carl's will which were hidden under the couch. Why, at this horrible time, would she want Carl's will or the money?

As the other men bantered back and forth, Lamar recalled reading aloud the judge's instructions to the jury a few hours earlier, and he knew that they must consider as evidence only what was presented to them during the trial; anything that they had heard or read at an earlier time was not to have any bearing on their decision. In the courtroom, the judge was emphatic about this; Lamar realized that if he followed these guidelines, he could not even bring up for discussion all the information he was recalling from the August newspapers. He did not want to be responsible for a mistrial!

"Okay," Lamar said. "Now we go to the next part of the verdict. Was she sleepwalking, in a night terror or somehow in a state that prevented her from making a logical, rational decision. Any comments on that part of the vote?"

"That's the part that bothers me the most," Black said. "How the hell do we know what was going on in her head when she pulled the trigger?" There was an undercurrent of agreement.

"Comments from anyone?"

"Well," David Houston said, "We had testimony from several doctors and psychiatrists who swore it was possible for Joan to do everything she did that night while in one of these sleep walking fits."

"Yeah, I believe that," White interjected, "My mother-in-law is a sleepwalker."

Lamar broke in with his first sign of levity, "I'll bet you don't ever spend the night in her house again." Everyone laughed.

"Oh, she's not so bad," he said, seriously. "So I don't think that'll happen." He continued, "One of the doctors testified that he was treating the father, Carl, for the same problem. Said he'd been sleep walkin' on and off all his life. Said it was hereditary."

"How come, "Gilbert Dalwick spoke up, with some determination, "that when they had Joan's two brothers on the stand, they swore they didn't sleep walk."

"It's just like when you breed cows, "Dringenburg explained. "Sometimes traits are passed from the heifer or the bull that you want in your calf, sometimes what you don't want is passed on, too. You know it don't affect all your herd, just some. And you know from experience, you can't control everything. It don't bother me that

Joan got it and the boys didn't. That's just the way it happens."

Lamar spoke up, "Does anyone have a problem with the idea that the sleep walking version of what happened eliminates the need to look at motive?"

No one disagreed.

"Okay, everybody ready to vote on the question that Joan is not guilty because she committed the murders while sleepwalking?" he asked.

Everyone was in agreement and they said, almost in unison, "Let's vote!"

Lamar passed his hat around again; and again, he read the verdict aloud. There were nine not guilt and three guilty.

"Oh shit, "Dringenburg said, "We're never gonna get out of this jail."

"I need a root beer," Clyde Arnold complained. "Who's got the string?"

Lamar tossed the ball of twine over the table to him.

This jury of practical men had devised a simple plan for getting contraband to their quarters. They had JD Jarrel and Lamar's son, Harold, stationed in a side yard below one of their windows. Whenever they wanted a Coke, a pack of cigarettes, a candy bar or something even more frowned upon by the Sheriff, instead of going to the door, waiting for the Sheriff or his Deputy to open it, waiting for him to agree or disagree with ordering the item and then having someone do a slow march to Gulley's, which would take an hour, they simply lowered the string to JD with a note as to what they needed and the cash to purchase it. Within a few minutes they would feel a tug on the string and the item was delivered. Lamar's son, Harold, was thirteen years old, and it was he who ran like the wind to Gulley's store and back. The faster he ran the larger the tip that would come from the window.

Lamar sighed, losing some of his optimism. "Three of us think Joan is guilty of premeditated murder. Nine of us think she was not in control of herself. A verdict of premeditation means she could be sentenced to death. Is there anyone who would like to share his thoughts on having Joan put to death?"

"'An eye for an eye and a tooth for a tooth' it says in the Bible."

"Vengeance is *mine,* sayeth the Lord," Abden retorted.

"Anyone else," Lamar asked.

"Well, I voted that she should not be held accountable for her actions," Byron said. "But I understand how someone could want to punish her after seeing the beds of Carl and little Jerry and hearing the Sheriff talk about how they weren't just killed, they were slaughtered. My God."

"Are we ready for another vote," Lamar asked.

Melvin Lucas was the only one of the 12 who had not voiced his opinion; but earlier, when he overheard Lamar comment to Byron about doing the "Christian" thing regarding Joan's verdict, he felt he had to respond. Mel was a very religious man, a member of the Sand

Run Baptist Church and a daily reader of the Bible; and he understood, better than most, the logic behind the emphasis that there be a separation between church and state. The other comments made by the group about "An eye for an eye..." and Heil's reply, "Vengeance is mine sayeth the Lord," angered him. He stood up, a shy man, unaccustomed to talking in front of people, but a man with something on his mind.

"I can't sit around here while we're judging the guilt of this young girl and listen to this talk about Christianity or hear quotations from the Bible. Can't ya'll see that this has no place here in the jury room?"

"I though you were a Christian," Heil broke in. "And if you are, why would you be talkin' like that?"

"This is not an Inquisition," Lucas replied. "We can't use religious doctrine to decide whether Joan is guilty or not. We have to use the law. We need to stick with what Judge Yager told us before we left the courtroom. He didn't say nothin' about usin' religion to help with our decision." Lucas was getting angrier as he spoke. His face was red all the way to his receding hairline. His gnarled hands had formed into fists, this topic obviously a passionate one for him.

"Look, Mel, if they didn't want us to base our findings, at least partly, on our Christian background, why did they make every witness swear to tell the truth, the whole truth, so help me God?" Byron asked.

Mel replied, "That's just so they would be under oath. So they'd know they'd better not commit perjury. It don't have nothin' to do with bein' a Christian. And Lamar, I think, as our foreman, you need to tell everybody to leave their religion on the other side of that locked door over there. We need to look at this case based on the law and the law alone."

Heil stood up. "Now, Mel, Lamar has a right to his opinion. Leave him alone. If they didn't want us to use our religion in here, Vincent or Smith would have asked us questions about what we believe in before pickin' us as jurors."

"But he did," Byron broke in.

"Vincent asked me if I believed in the death penalty. That's like askin' if I believe in 'an eye for an eye, a tooth for a tooth.' I couldn't forget my religious beliefs on anything I've ever done in my adult life. It's part of what separates me from an animal. We all came through that door with different experiences, including our religions beliefs. We're surrounded by all kinda stuff that's about religion. Look at the coins in your pocket. 'In God We Trust.' Listen to our patriotic songs. 'God Bless America.' Melvin, we can't leave any of these things that make us unique as a person or as a country on the other side of that door."

Byron was out of breath, unaccustomed to making such a long speech. He sat back in his chair, looking around the group for their reaction.

For a few seconds there was total silence within the room. The murmur of a conversation outside the locked door could be heard, and the raucous squeal of tires as cars stopped at the crossroads just beneath the courthouse windows provided evidence of a world beyond the immediate reach of these jurors. The droning of a solitary airplane across the night sky reminded them also of their aloneness—their need for home and family.

Finally Lamar felt he had to say something. After all, it was he who was inadvertently responsible for this line of thought. Too many of these men had overheard his conversation with Byron.

"You know, everyone who's been talking here makes a good point. I sure didn't mean to start an argument on religion. I was just hoping we could be fair with Joan. Give her a chance for a life as an adult if she was ever cured of whatever her problem is. I just didn't feel it was the ethical thing to do – sentence her to death, a 16 year old, no matter what she was accused of or found guilty of. It just doesn't seem like something we should do as Americans."

Dringenburg decided this argument was too good for him to stay out of. Banging on the table, he said, "Now look here. Are you religious people tellin' me if I was a….um…a..what do you call those people, people who don't believe in God?"

"An atheist," someone volunteered.

"Yeah, atheist. Are you tellin' me I couldn't be on this jury? That as an atheist, I couldn't make a fair decision?"

"Hell, Albert, you ain't no atheist. Why are you actin' like you are?" Charley White asked.

"That's not the point, " Dringenburg looked directly at Charley. "My point is do you have to be a Christian to make a decision within the law the way Judge Yager told us?"

Dalwick spoke up. "Well, if you ask me, I don't think you could make a good decision, especially a life or death decision, about a person if you didn't believe in God."

"So, what you're saying," Dringenburg interjected, smiling at this opportunity to nail down his point, "what you're saying is that only citizens who believe in God should serve on a jury. Where is it written that you can do that?"

"I'm not sayin' it's written anywhere. I'm just tellin' you how I feel," Dalwick replied, petulantly.

Lamar saw that this conversation was going nowhere. "Look everybody, can we just get back to what our job is? We can't keep going over this religion thing; and as far as I know, all of us are Christians, including Albert, here. So let's deal with the decision we have to make with Joan."

"Should we make a written statement that our decision was not based on our religion?" Heil asked.

No one was quite sure what he meant by that, and they looked at Lamar to field that question.

"The only statement we need to make," Lamar replied, "is either the one word guilty or the two words not guilty. Let's get back to that job."

"I'm all for that," Dringenburg said, enthusiastically.

That ended the discussion on religion.

Lamar asked the group if there were ready to vote again.

Albert Dringenburg felt he was on a roll, and he had always enjoyed being on center stage. "There's not any reason to vote again so soon. Nobody 's gonna change his mind that easy."

Lamar replied, smiling, "Now Albert, you've been the one who's so anxious to vote and get out of here. Why the switch?"

Dringenburg came from a long of line of farmers. His success was not due to a formal background in agriculture or a superior intellect but to being well-grounded in common sense and having the ability to evaluate the success of a particular crop or type of farm animal. Staying with what worked and taking few chances had kept him afloat financially. He was also a man who was more than bluff and bluster, although he used these two techniques to his advantage. Of the three whose vote was that Joan was guilty, he would be the one the rest would least suspect; and that's the way he liked it. He never wanted to reveal his hand too soon. This method of decision making, he felt, gave him an advantage. The final part of his personality which helped him cope with the adversities that came his way was his logical, unemotional approach to dealing with life's problems.

Several years ago he had paid $20.00 for a hunting dog; as Penny matured, he could see that she was well worth a week's pay; however, about a month ago, while out hunting with her, he stopped to eat the sandwich he had brought with him. Somewhat distracted by a quail darting out of the grass, he dropped the sandwich. Penny jumped on it immediately; and when Dringenburg reached to retrieve it, Penny growled and bit his hand, drawing blood.

He looked at Penny then at his bloody fingers and, unemotionally, said, "Well, Penny, this is your last hunt." Dringenburg wrapped a bandana around his hand and headed home, knowing exactly what he had to do. He found a bottle of peroxide and soaked the bandana in it and tied it again around his bitten hand. Then he called Penny, and they walked to the barn where he located a shovel and some rawhide.

Going back behind the barn past the manure pile, he dug a hole two feet square and two feet deep. He then tied Penny's front and rear legs together with the rawhide and placed her beside the hole, saying to Penny, "You know, if you bite me once you'll probably bite me again and, if not me, maybe one of my kids." With that, he lifted the shovel and smashed it against Penny's head crushing her skull. Still unemotional, he rolled her into the shallow grave and filled it in.

Basically, that represented the reason that he voted that Joan was guilty. It was obvious to him that she had murdered her father and brother; and whether it was in a rage or in a nightmare, it was still murder. She was too dangerous to be allowed to go free. Dringenburg's thinking was that someday her anger or her uncontrolled nightmares would target her future husband or children.

"You know, Lamar," Drinbenburg said, "I'd like to know who voted guilty. Is there any reason we can't know who they are? If we're all gonna have to agree on this here verdict, we need to know who needs convincin'."

Joe Black interrupted, "Well I don't mind tellin' everybody. I didn't vote that she was not guilty."

"So you voted that she was guilty," Lamar clarified.

"That's just what I said," Black responded, somewhat offended.

Lamar, remembering that he was the foreman, cautioned, "Now, listen everybody, you know you don't have to tell how you voted if you don't want to."

"I'd just like to hear a good reason for lettin' her go free," Dringenburg said, stubbornly.

Byron stood up. "Well, now. I think Lamar gave me all the reason I needed when we were talkin' over dinner tonight. He asked me, as a Christian, how could I not give the girl a chance. She's only 16 and has her whole life ahead of her."

"Yeah, like the chance she gave her six year old brother, "Heil replied, sarcastically.

"My question," Dringenburg asked, "is how are we gonna protect society from Joan? You know she's gonna do it again, sooner or later."

"Can't we recommend that she be put away until they find a cure for her problem?" Black asked, looking at Lamar.

"I don't know that answer," Lamar said, somewhat puzzled. "Let me write a note to the judge, and we'll have the Sheriff take it to him."

The discussion continued as Lamar gave the question to Jake Williams who was stationed just outside the door to the jury room. In fact, he was so close, that when Lamar knocked, Williams immediately opened the door and reached out his hand as though he knew Lamar had something for him. Could the Sheriff have been eavesdropping? Did it really matter at this point? Lamar shook his head, thinking, I'll sure be glad when this is all over.

About fifteen minutes later the Sheriff knocked on the door and then entered. "Lamar," he said, "the judge told me to tell you he'd consider any recommendation ya'll have as part of the verdict. Anything else?"

Lamar was expecting something from the judge in writing. "No, Sheriff. Not now. Thanks." Somewhat disappointed, he turned to the 11 men who sat staring at him, "You heard what he said. So we need to work on a recommendation we can all live with—one that will allow us to come up with one verdict."

Black took the floor. "If we can recommend that Joan get help and not be out walking the streets, I'd vote not guilty."

"I think that's fair," Byron said, "but we have to make a strong statement as to how we feel—a recommendation that Joan not be just set free, like she was innocent."

A murmuring and nodding of heads signified a general agreement among the jurors.

Lamar looked around, "Any other discussion?"

"Now, I'm ready to vote," Dringenburg said, "And I think we all are."

Lamar looked at Byron. "You went to high school. Would you and Albert write out our recommendation, and I'll be passing out the ballots again so we can start voting."

In a few minutes Byron got Lamar's attention. "I think we've got something."

"Good," Lamar said, optimistically. "How about reading it to all of us?"

Byron stood up, cleared his throat and began. "We, the jury, recommend that Joan Kiger be assigned to one of our mental hospitals or clinics for long term treatment and not to be released until the doctors can say, with absolute certainty, that she is no longer a threat to anyone."

"Okay, thanks, Byron. Now, if in our next vote, we get a unanimous decision, this recommendation will be included with our verdict and be given to the judge before sentencing.

"I'm sure we all have our doubts," Lamar said. "But we've got to come together with one voice on this. Whoever the three were who voted guilty, just think a minute. The clinic where she was treated might just agree to keep her. Shouldn't we offer her hope instead of death? Just give it some thought. Is everybody ready for the next round of votes?"

No objections were raised.

Once again, the papers, the hat and the oral reading of the vote of each of the 12.

Chapter Twenty
The Verdict
(December 21, 1943)

20

Joan walked out of the court house on December 21, 1943 with a brother on either arm: on her right was Joe, a Marine Lieutenant, and on her left, John, a Navy Seaman. At long last she was free. In only a four hour deliberation, the jury of twelve men had found her not guilty. Now she could return to La Salette Academy and finish high school, and she could complete her plans for college.

The Sisters at the Academy had instilled in Joan a yearning for knowledge, and long ago, she had decided to become a teacher. Now all that would be possible!

Chapter Twenty-One
Stanley's Reprieve
(December 22, 1943)

21

December 22, 1943, the day after the Joan Kiger murder trial ended, two men who had attended the proceedings every day, always sitting in the rear seats on the right hand side of the courtroom, returned to Chicago.

After the second day of the four day trial, these men began to stand out: two swarthy men in suits, talking to no one and listening intently to every word by every witness. Ninety five percent of the audience was local people, most were from Burlington, and the remaining five per cent, excluding the two men in suits, were newspapermen from around the country.

Once back in Chicago, these men reported immediately and directly to Joseph Rizzi.

"So, Domenick," Rizzi said to one of them. "What's the real story? Who killed Kiger?"

Dom glanced at the *Chicago Tribune* which Rizzi was reading. "You know what the paper says: the girl wasn't guilty. But we were there. We heard all the evidence; and I know it seems weird, but she had to be the one. This kid had to be the killer. She shot her old man. Sure, she testified about some stranger being in the house, said she shot at him; but believe me, she's a fruitcake. This goofy broad talked about going around the house shooting at this intruder and yelling about killing everybody in the house. The ballistics guy, from here in Chicago, swore that all of the bullets came from Kiger's own guns. Mr. Rizzi, she did it."

"I hope not," he said. "Stanley had damned well better be the one who made the hit. If we pay money to a politician for a few simple favors, he sure as hell better not be taking money from another family at the same time. And Kiger was. One of my snitches let me know that he had his hand in the Cleveland Syndicate's pocket, as well as in ours. I want the word to get out on the street that if you do that to us, you are going to be very, very sorry. I sent Stanley to take Kiger out; if he didn't do the job, we're going to look like a bunch of incompetents. Domenick, get in touch with him. Let's find out what the truth is: I also want to know why, if that damned Polock didn't kill Kiger, he kept the advance. Also find out why, after four months, he hasn't even shown his face around here."

"It may take a while. Like you just said, we haven't seen or heard from him since the shooting in August."

"How do you usually contact him for a hit?" Rizzi asked.

"We go to the Glass Tap in Jefferson Park and tell the bartender, Casimir, that Stosh needs to call home."

"Do it."

"Okay, Mr. Rizzi."

*   *   *

The Glass Tap was a hole in the wall on Milwaukee Avenue known for its bar made of glass blocks. Casimir had bought the place shortly after Scarface was jailed for tax evasion. He used to work for Capone, but since Capone's arrest he had been clean. Most of the patrons were now second generation Polish/Czech. Little English was spoken in the bar; and any time of day or night, one could hear "Na Zdrowié" coming from within.

Dom dropped by the Glass Tap the same afternoon to deliver Mr. Rizzi's message and, to his surprise, Stosh was sitting at a side table.

"Hey, Dom. Come on over. What you doin' slummin?" Stosh said, grinning.

"Where ya been? We've been looking for you, Stosh?"

"It's a long story," Stosh replied, rubbing his right shoulder.

"Finish your drink. Mr. Rizzi wants to hear what happened," Dom said.

"Oh yeah? How come?"

"He'll tell you," Dom said, matter-of-factly.

"Sure. Let's go." Stosh finished his drink quickly.

As they walked to the car, Dom noticed that Stosh was swinging his right arm in an exaggerated manner.

"What's the matter with your arm?" he asked.

Got shot by some broad," Stosh replied, smiling, suggestively.

"Hope it was worth it," Dom said, laughing.

The Windmill Restaurant was typical of this part of Chicago: an inconspicuous front door, a dark foyer, a hawk-eyed bouncer who knew everyone who was anyone.

Dom parked in front of 4530 N. Milwaukee Avenue, the long time home of the Windmill. Stosh opened the car door and started to get out, but Dom grabbed him by his left arm. "Wait a second," he said. "I need to give you a heads-up. Mr. Rizzi doesn't think you hit Kiger. I went to the trial. Looks like the girl bumped off her old man."

Fear and confusion showed on Stosh's face. "Would I take the advance if I didn't do it?"

"Beats me. So you tellin' me you *did* hit Kiger?" Dom asked.

"Pumped six slugs into him," Stosh said with some conviction. "Want to hear what happened?"

"No, no. Tell your story to Mr. Rizzi. I'm just saying, you'd better be prepared."

Dom and Stosh walked in and with a brief wave to the bouncer, continued through the dining room to a back side door which led to a dark hallway and a set of stairs. A single light bulb hanging from the second floor ceiling beckoned them up.

As they reached the top landing, a man in dress pants, a white shirt and suspenders stepped toward them;

recognizing Dom, he grinned and waved. "Here to see Mr. Rizzi?"

"Yeah," Dom said. "And he's going to be surprised at who I'm bringing. Tell him I've got Stosh."

The suspendered man disappeared behind a doorway and Stosh could hear garbled bits of a conversation. Shortly, the man reappeared, saying, "Hang out here for a few minutes. Mr. Rizzi's busy." And with that said, he pulled out a cigarette, walked over to the window in the hallway, opened it and stepped out onto the fire escape. Stosh could hear the hacking cough of a three pack a day smoker.

After about ten minutes, the door opened again; and a small, bespectacled balding man came out carrying a brief case and an arm load of files. "Excuse me," he said, in a whisper. "Could you open the downstairs door for me? I would hate to drop Mr. Rizzi's files."

About that time Rizzi came to the door. He did not look happy. "Where's Jacob?" he asked, looking at Dom.

"On the fire escape," Dom said, deferentially.

"Jacob! Get your ass over here! Help Benito with the files."

Then, looking at Stosh for the first time, he said, "Come on in, Stanley." Rizzi was a man who loathed informality when he was conducting serious business. "We've got some unfinished business, you and I."

Dom started in with him but Rizzi help up one finger, stopping him in his tracks. "Wait here, Domenick. This is just between Stanley and me."

Following Rizzi into the well-lighted office, lined with filing cabinets, maps thumb tacked to the wall and an eight foot oak desk dominating the rear of the room, Stosh wondered what this unfinished business might be, ignoring the suggestion made by the ache in his right shoulder. The desk was a clutter of papers, a typewriter and two telephones. Three chairs were facing the oak desk in a semi-circle and there were, what appeared to be, old blood stains on the bare oak floor. The windows had full length shades pulled down, revealing none of the bustling world on Milwaukee Avenue.

Mr. Rizzi was an educated man, a little rough around the edges, but always very polite. "Sit down. Sit down, Stanley," Rizzi said, pointing to the rows of chairs. "Can I get you a drink?"

"Sure, I'll take a beer."

Rizzi walked to one of the corners where an ancient refrigerator sat humming noisily. He pulled out a bottle and handed it to Stosh. Rizzi, speaking softly, said, "So, we haven't seen you since you took care of Kiger. How did that go?"

"Mr. Rizzi, it's the damnedest thing I've ever been involved in."

"So you did the job?" Rizzi asked, with a tinge of doubt in his voice.

"Yeah, sure. Sure I did. Don't I always?"

"Stosh, Kiger was shot with a .38 – you carry a .22. What's the story?"

"You see, Mr. Rizzi. I broke into this place about midnight. Went in the side door by the kitchen. The strangest thing was, I saw this .38 on the kitchen table, loaded. I thought, why not use the guy's own gun? So I picked it up. And then, since I always like to plan for a second way out of a house, just in case, I unlocked and opened the front door. Then I go upstairs. I listen. Lots of snoring was coming from this middle room, so I figure that was Kiger. I go in and I've got this .38 ready. I get real close to the bed. I use my cigarette lighter just long enough to see Kiger. He was lying on his back so I emptied the gun into him –six shots—and then, just as I turned to leave the room, I heard this broad screaming and shouting. She was standing in the doorway. I pushed by her and ended up in some kid's room. She came after me, shouting, saying she was going to kill everybody—that she was going to kill herself. She was one crazy bitch."

"Stosh, you telling me you let this little girl scare the crap out of you?" Rizzi said, sarcastically.

"It wasn't the girl. It was the fucking gun."

Rizzi took a sip from his drink and nodded, anticipating the rest of the story.

"So she kept pumping bullets into this kid's room. One of them caught me in the shoulder. Then she turned around and walked back into Kiger's bedroom still screaming and shooting. I got the hell out of there as fast as I could. But, Mr. Rizzi. I did take out Kiger," Stosh said, emphatically, with beads of perspiration forming on his upper lip.

"What about the gun? What did you do with it?"

"What gun?" Stosh asked, confused as to what Rizzi was thinking.

"The .38 you said you used to kill Kiger."

"Oh, well, hell. When that bitch hit me with a slug in the shoulder I ran down the stairs with it; but before I got to the front door, my hand got so numb, I dropped it."

"You wear gloves?"

"Of course, Mr. Rizzi. You know me."

"Okay, I've heard enough," Rizzi said, snapping his fingers. Looking toward a row of filing cabinets to his left, he barked, "Salvatore, bring Domenick and Jacob in here." From behind the cabinets, a skeleton of a man appeared, tall and gaunt, eyes sunk back in his head, disheveled red hair turning gray. He shuffled toward the front door.

"My bookkeeper," Rizzi said, as an explanation of the man's presence. "We learned a lesson when Capone got sent up for tax evasion. Now we pay our taxes; or at least, we cover our asses." He laughed at his own joke.

Rizzi looked up at the three men. "I think it's time for Stanley to remove his shirt. I'd like to see this so-called shoulder wound."

"Wait, Mr. Rizzi, I don't need help taking off my shirt." Stosh started to unbutton the front, but Rizzi looked up at the men and said, "No, No. You need help. Give Stanley some help."

Dom held one arm and Jacob held the other. Sal seemed to be anticipating his part. He opened his pocket knife slowly and, looking Stosh in the eye, ran the knife from Stosh's throat to his belly button, neatly cutting the shirt open. Blood trickled into Stosh's pants from the long cut in his chest and abdomen. As they ripped the shirt off, he winced. The damage from the slug was still all too real.

Rizzi was standing by his desk, adjusting his reading glasses. He motioned for Stosh to come over. Examining the injury closely, Rizzi took his hand and rubbed across the scar. "Who took the bullet out, Doc Jedniak?"

"Yeah," Stosh said, puzzled as to why he had to be roughed up just to check out his story.

"Well, that's easy enough to verify" Rizzi said, patting Stosh on the back. "Sit down. Finish your beer. Here, use my handkerchief; we don't want blood on the floor." And then looking menacingly at Stosh, he said, "You know, you should have checked in with us."

"I can see that now," Stosh said, as he gingerly wiped away the ribbon of blood on his chest.

"Domenick, give Stanley your shirt," Rizzi ordered.

Dom did not hesitate. He carefully removed his shirt and within minutes, Stosh was fully clothed and finishing the last of his beer. Rizzi waved the three men away, and they sat eyeball to eyeball.

"The *Tribune* says the boy, Jerry, was killed and the mother was shot. Did you do that, too?"

"It had to be that crazy bitch. I read a little about it while I was waiting for the heat to blow over. I can't explain anything that happened after I left that madhouse.

I know the only one I shot was Kiger. I read that Kiger's wife might have done it."

Rizzi smiled, nodding in agreement. "Well Stanley, I'm glad we had this little talk. We'll be seeing each other again, real soon."

And with that cryptic comment, Rizzi waved Stosh out of the room. As Dom escorted him down the stairs, he contemplated his future. Was he now vindicated? Was he a dead man? The interesting part of working for the North Side Gang was that sometimes you couldn't be sure.

Sal shuffled back into the room, still carrying his knife. Going to Stosh's shirt, now lying at the base of Rizzi's desk, he picked it up, wiped the blade clean and said, "Mr. Rizzi, earlier, I made a notation under the five hundred dollar advance we gave Stosh, 'Job Completed,' as I usually do. Should I change that?"

Rizzi thought a moment. "No, Salvatore, leave it for now; call Doc Jedniak; find out if and when he took that slug out of Stanley and, most importantly, ask him if it was a .38. I suspect we may have to revise your 'Job Completed' comment—but let's just wait and see what happens. There's no hurry."

Chapter Twenty-Two
Home At Last
(May 3, 1941 – April 15, 1944)

22

Joan felt an increasing resentment ever since the day she was found not guilty. Just as she was looking ahead to returning to school and spending time with Mae, her mother told her she would be going to the Menninger Clinic in Topeka, Kansas, for an evaluation and treatment for her nightmares. This news almost brought her to her knees. For the first time, she refused to cooperate with her mother and Uncle Fred. These psychiatrists, nurses and therapists were driving her crazy. If I wasn't crazy before, I sure will be if I keep having to talk with these people, Joan thought to herself.

"What more do you want from me?" she shrieked at her mother and Uncle Fred.

Glancing at each other with surprise, they were speechless at this outburst. Jennie's neck began to redden with blotches. She didn't need this aggravation from Joan. She had enough to cope with right now.

"Joan," she said sternly, so much so, that her tone startled her daughter, "you are going to have to trust us. Sawyer says it's very likely the prosecutor is not finished with you. There's the matter of your father's death and who's responsible for that. I'm not asking you, I'm telling you. You have to go. Dr. Ertel says that Menninger's has a national reputation for helping people who have horrible nightmares, so you are going there. Don't argue with me!"

"Do you have any idea what it's like to talk to these shrinks? All they do is ask stupid questions and look at me like I'm a freak. I just can't talk about that night, about how I feel about you or dad or Jerry one more time. This isn't helping me, it's making me CRAZY!!" Joan shouted, defiantly crossing her arms and holding them tightly to her chest. "I just want to go back to my old life. I thought I was going to return to school and that this was all over." Surprised by her own ire, Joan felt a surge of adrenalin.

Jennie was wondering when this moment would come. Her daughter had been compliant and cooperative with every thing that was asked of her. Jennie could tell over the past few weeks that Joan's frustration was getting closer and closer to the surface.

"We've both been through a lot, Joan; and although I haven't had to go to these clinics like you have, I have had my own struggles." Jennie sighed deeply and sat down at the kitchen table, taking a sip from her coffee. I, too, so wish I could go back to my old life, as well, she reflected, silently.

As Joan looked squarely into her mother's eyes, she knew the conversation was over.

"We'll be leaving in the morning," Uncle Fred said, "so you'd better start packing; and Joan, I'm sorry that you have to go through this, but your mother is right-- you just have to trust us. We want the best for you."

Joan retreated to her bedroom where she sat at her vanity, wondering how this all began in the first place. Suddenly, a wave of resignation flooded her body, and she recognized that this was how it had to be. Just do it, she said to herself; then, finally, life will return to normal. This nightmare will be over. What more could they ask of me?

*   *   *

After three long months at Menninger's, Joan finally returned home. Even though her mother was able to visit her occasionally, their time together was stilted and frequently uncomfortable. As she began to unpack, she could feel a swell of relief rise up. It's finally over. She recalled with pride that she had done whatever they had asked: taking her medications, interpreting inkblots, going to group sessions and mingling with the other patients. Although she had found her therapy with Dr. Menninger mostly helpful, their discussions were often times painful and frequently heightened her anxiety. The hypnosis sessions were the most uncomfortable. Joan fought the entire experience. She would not give up control. She knew the hypnotherapist was asking leading questions about the night of August 17, and it was easier to go along with his suggestions than to relive what actually happened.

During the second week of her stay, she found herself afraid to drift off to sleep at night because of the violent nightmares she would experience, nightmares so terrifying that she would awaken with a pounding heart and a deep feeling of dread in the pit of her stomach; however, in spite of all of this emotional upheaval, Dr. M, as she called him, told her that she was making progress. By the time she was discharged, she finally began to believe him. The nightmares had decreased in their intensity, the girl had left; and, for the most part, she was better able to manage her anxiety.

During her entire stay in Topeka, she so desperately wanted to return home; and finally, she was here. Looking around the room of her youth, she once again felt safe. There were so many large and small reminders of happier times. A smile came to her face as she gazed upon El Capitaine, a stuffed grenadier, which her brother had won for her at Coney Island. The grenadier proudly sat on her bed and aided in her reflections as she relived that trip to Coney with her family, in 1941, when she was 13 years old. She could still see El Capitaine perched on a ledge with other stuffed characters, all eagerly waiting to be chosen by any passerby who had the knack and the strength to knock over a trio of wooden milk bottles with one of three baseballs.

"Daddy, can you knock those milk bottles over?" she excitedly asked.

He tried to get that wonderful prize for her; but at best, he could knock only two of the bottles down. Her brothers, Joe and John, also tried but with no better luck. Seeing the disappointment on their faces, she re-assured each of them that she really didn't want that grenadier anyway and told them she would much rather have some cotton candy, a treat that wouldn't require any skill on their part.

She laughed out loud as she recalled that late the next day Joe came home and proudly presented her with El Capitaine. He explained that he knew how disappointed she was that none of the Kiger men could win the prize, so he went back with five dollars and stayed until he finally knocked the milk bottles over. And she vividly remembered him saying, as he handed her the grenadier, "And besides, I know you don't like cotton candy!"

As she continued to look around her room, her gaze rested upon the brass table lamp where she did most of her reading. She and Mamma had gone to Main Street, in Covington, looking for an antique desk lamp; and although Mamma had said "Twenty-five dollars was way too much," she smiled and whispered to Joan, "Honey, you're worth every penny."

It was so peaceful to be home, away from the doctors, nurses, bright lights and ever present boring music; and even though she liked Dr. M, she was glad that she would never have to see him again. This relief, signaling the beginning of her long- postponed return to reality, was tinged with worry, however. Had she really passed the tests? What were the results from the hypnosis? What would the doctor recommend? Would she be able to return to school? Could she pick up the pieces of her shattered life?

As she lay on her bed, clutching the grenadier, her mind drifted back again to an earlier time: her two older brothers, Joe and John, were home, safe. Given their age differences, Joan looked up to her brothers but never felt very close to them. They, however, felt very protective of her and would, to her irritation, frequently pinch her cheek or give her bear hugs, calling her "Jo Jo," a nickname she vehemently disliked. Whenever she complained to her parents of their intrusion into her personal space, they would laugh and tell her that that was her brothers' way of showing her how much they loved her. Angered by their insensitivity, she would retreat to her room where she would play with her paper dolls and create a world where she had complete control.

These moments of disdain for her two older siblings became more and more infrequent as she came to adore and admire them, wishing the two would let her become involved in their lives.

Jerry, on the other hand, was another story. Joan thrived on being the "baby" in the family and the only girl. Her birth order and gender seemed to gain her special status with everyone. So on the day that her mother excitedly told her she would be a big sister to a baby boy or girl, Joan, at the age of eight, became very angry. Going into a tantrum, she hit the floor kicking and screaming, hollering that she didn't want a brother or a sister. Shocked by this aberrant behavior from her usually compliant daughter, Jennie had to spank her and sent her to her room. Sobbing into her pillow, she vowed to herself that she would simply run away when this unwanted creature invaded the family. Taking her suitcase out of her closet, packing some clothes and a few of her favorite toys, she shoved it under her bed, wanting to be ready when the dreaded day arrived.

However, when her mom and dad brought this bundled screaming baby boy home, she felt an indescribable surge of overwhelming love fill her heart as she gazed upon his bright red face. Struck by the size of his teeny hands and matchstick fingers, she spontaneously and vigorously hugged and kissed him.

"Oh, Joan! He's just a baby," her daddy said, gently pulling Jerry from her arms. "As his big sister, you have to protect him and be very careful until he gets a little bit older."

Joan liked the idea of being the protector, at least until Jerry began showing signs of having a mind of his own. As he began walking, he wanted to go everywhere with her. Annoyed with his desire to cling to her, she would often ignore him or yell at him to leave her alone. There were other times when she would coax him into the library at Rosegate where she would have him snuggle up to her on the sofa, and she would, with great theatrical expression, tell him stories – his most favorite being Jack and the Beanstalk. Whenever she reached the part where the giant bellowed, "Fee-Fi-Fo-Fum," Jerry would shriek and cover his face with his hands. Joan would howl with laughter as she pinched his belly, lowered her head into his face and in her deepest voice repeated, "Fee-Fi-Fo-Fum, I smell the blood of an Englishman."

Her ambivalence for her little brother grew. There were times she would die for him and other times she wished he would just disappear. But underneath these mixed feelings was a deep affection and fondness for the little person who seemed to think she was absolutely wonderful.

The family's favorite recreational stop was Coney Island. Joan had so many fond memories of their times there. All this, however, was but the lull before the oncoming storm of World War II.

And it was during this earlier time, the spring of 1941, that her worry-free joy of living began to change; it changed because of her secret habit of listening in on the kitchen conversations of her parents, a serendipitous discovery precipitated quite by accident: Joan was looking for an earring that had fallen to the floor onto the heating duct and, as she tried carefully to retrieve the jewelry, she was surprised to discover that she could hear voices from the kitchen below. She experienced a perverse pleasure in eavesdropping, an act that allowed her to be privy to more information than a teenager generally hears. The heating duct from the kitchen below came directly into her room and seemed to amplify the conversations. Usually, what she heard was idle chatter about the family's finances or about Uncle Fred, Aunt Eva or the neighbors; but this discussion, between her parents in the spring of 1941, was Joan's first hint of the concerns which, as the years went by, would affect her more and more. Joan did not originally understand the seriousness of her father's predicament; but by the end of the next year, she would.

He had accepted money from several questionable groups of people, both of whom indicated that there were no strings attached to these contributions; rather, that these were monies to help him with his political ambitions. At first, all seemed innocent enough; but by the end of the second year, she could hear the tension in her dad's voice as he tried to deal with the pressures both groups began to exert.

By the summer of 1943, Joan was beginning to piece the puzzle together. There were these two factions who were asking for her father's support. One group was from Cleveland and the other from Chicago. Her father was most worried about those from Chicago.

"Jennie, I tell you, they're squeezing me like a vice. They both have been giving me money for my campaign for Mayor, and they both expect me to help them. Cleveland wants me to stop the move by our city to tax slot machine profits; Chicago wants me to make it politically possible for them to set up slots in Erlanger. If one knew I was talking to the other, I'd be in deep trouble. If I stop dealing with one group, I don't know what they'll do. How the hell did I get in such a mess?"

Joan's mother's voice was low and inaudible; but her father, upset with whatever she said, boomed back.

"Damn it. It's too late for that. We've spent the money. We'd have to sell Rosegate to pay them back. What the hell have I done?"

Even though she pressed her ear to the grate, she could still not understand her mother's words.

"No, no, you can't reason with those bastards. They want -- what they want. If I could just satisfy them both, we'd be off the hook. How in the hell can I do that? I'm not a crook. It's just not in me. I can't be bribed or bought."

A brief silence. "Well, at least I never thought I could be bought."

This memory spilled over into another. She reminisced about when her father first started carrying a gun, first starting sleeping with one under his pillow and when he began insisting that all the windows and doors be closed and locked, no matter how hot it became inside the house.

Something was gnawing within her. She needed some answers – answers to questions she had been mulling over and over during her stay at Menninger's. Her recurring nightmares revealed ominous figures invading Rosegate; and as she desperately tried to defend her family, the gun she was firing would snap harmlessly, time after time, leaving her totally vulnerable and her loved ones unprotected. The intruders always pursued her throughout the house; she could never outrun them. They continued to fire shots at her. She could smell the gunpowder and then, suddenly, her body would recoil as the bullets penetrated her back. In every one of these Night Terrors, she would try, unsuccessfully, to scream as blood spurted from her chest. Unable to continue reliving these experiences, Joan shuddered and broke off her thoughts. It's time, she said to herself, and she went downstairs to talk with her mother about these dark phantoms.

"Is Uncle Fred still here?" she asked, glancing around the kitchen. Jennie shook her head. "He went to get Aunt Eva and he'll be right back."

Joan knew that her questions would place them both in uncharted territory. "Mamma, would you tell me the truth if I ask you something?"

Jennie was unloading some groceries, her hip still reminding her of the bullet wound. Standing for more than five minutes was intolerable. She moved over to the kitchen table and sat down, heavily.

"Joan, you just got home. It's been a long trip. Don't you want to rest?"

"Mamma, will you tell me the truth?" Joan asked, again.

"Of course. You and I have always been honest with each other, haven't we? What's the matter?"

"Well, you know how Daddy was always worried that someone was going to kill him?"

Jennie became uncomfortable with where this conversation was going. "Yes. But I don't see…."

"Well, I have to ask you, was it the Syndicate he was afraid of?"

Jennie flinched. Standing up, grimacing in pain, she began rapidly to remove items from the grocery bags. Without giving Joan eye contact, she asked. "What do you know about those people?"

"I know Daddy started carrying a gun after they scared him." Joan watched her mother closely for any non-verbal reactions.

"Your father was trying to get them to leave him alone," Jennie said in a flat tone of voice, wondering why Joan was asking these questions now.

"Tell me the truth, Mamma. Could the Syndicate have killed Daddy?"

Jennie stopped short, started to say something but then changed her mind. "Honey, don't you know who killed Daddy?"

"Well, I was at that Topeka Clinic a long time; and the more I talked to them about that night, the more I *do* remember seeing somebody in your bedroom. I told them a lot of different things. But every time I went over what happened, I could see this man in the upstairs hallway going into your bedroom. He was a tall man and he had a gun; I know I shot at him."

Jennie swallowed hard. "Joan, that's all in the past. We just want you to get well. Don't keep going over all that. I don't think about it anymore." Her last words were coupled with a deep sigh.

Helping Jennie put the last of the groceries away, Joan felt that her mother was withholding something from her. She sensed, however, that any further probing would anger her; so she changed the subject to another topic that deeply worried her.

"Mamma, will I have to keep going back for more tests? I don't want to leave here anymore. Please tell me it's all over."

"I don't know what's going to happen," Jennie said, putting her arm around Joan. "Your Uncle Fred said we should be getting a report from Menninger's pretty soon, and that will help us decide what to do next."

Joan hugged her mother and held on longer then most of their hugs lasted. "Mamma, you know I wouldn't do anything to Daddy or to Jerry or to you." Looking into her mother's eyes, she so desperately wanted Jennie to acknowledge her innocence.

Jennie took a step back but faced Joan, "Honey, let's wait for the report. I love you. Uncle Fred, Aunt Eva and I are going to see that you get whatever help you need."

Jennie went back to the groceries. Joan returned to her room.

*   *   *

Fred had just gotten off the phone with Jennie, having told her about Menninger's recommendation. Realizing how upset she was, he decided to drive immediately to her house. It was at that point that Jack Maynard rang his doorbell.

Fred was not expecting him and was, at first, anxious to rush him through his conversation so that he could be with Jennie. Jack's visit was to forewarn Fred about tomorrow's newspaper headlines which were going to expose a $20,000.00 defense fund for Joan, raised by many of Carl's fellow politicians, as well as friends and interested citizens, in case she were indicted for Carl's murder.

The thing that puzzled Fred, as Jack continued to explain the situation, was why and how a group of people would donate so much money on such short notice. Fred understood that politicians don't usually make significant contributions unless it furthers their careers or covers their asses; and from what he knew of this group, it was the latter and not the former which made them so generous.

The two chatted about Vincent's tenacity and his determination to retry Joan. Fred expressed his gratitude, indicating that Jennie would probably need a defense fund since she had spent all of her resources on Joan's recent trial. They parted with a plan to meet again within a few days.

As he left his home and turned south on Dixie Highway, Fred realized that today was not the time to share this information with Jennie. Having to decide how best to react to Menninger's recommendation that Joan be institutionalized was enough of a shock for his sister-in-law.

Because of the year-long travails of Joan and Jennie, Fred had sorely neglected his business, the Williamson Camera Shop, in Covington, on Pike Street. The "Closed For The Day" sign had been in the window far too often. He had intended to go there today to catch up on some repairs, but his love for Jennie and Joan dictated otherwise.

He parked in front of their Crescent Avenue house, took a final drag off his Camel, and headed for the front door.

*   *   *

Joan was in a deep sleep and was jolted out of her slumber by a ringing telephone. As she tried to rouse herself, she heard a distant mumbling from her covert conduit of family secrets that sounded like her mother's voice. As she sleepily rubbed her eyes, she heard muffled weeping. She bolted out of bed, frightened by the sounds of grief. Joan thought that, maybe, for a change, she could help her mother; so she dressed quickly and ran downstairs. Jennie was sitting at the kitchen table, her head on her arm. She was crying, uncontrollably.

"Mamma, Mamma, what's wrong? Who was on the phone?" Joan felt a strong urge to hurt whoever did this to her mother.

Jennie did not look up and she continued to sob. Joan pulled a chair close to her and patted her head, empathy causing tears to flood her eyes.

"I'm all right. Go on back to your room." Jennie didn't have the strength to deal with Joan at this moment.

"Mamma, let me help you. What's wrong?" This distance between them was wearing Joan down. Her mother was unreachable except for the very mundane occurrences in their post August 17th lives.

"I'll be all right. Just go to your room, Joan. Go to your room," Jennie said, sitting up and trying to gain her composure. Taking several deep breaths, she squeezed Joan's arm and feigned a smile. "It's okay, honey. You go on."

Joan reluctantly obeyed her mother. "All right. But let me know if you need anything."

Joan and Jennie's relationship had gone through numerous permutations, especially so, after the murders. During those first weeks, they had little contact, and they both felt estranged from each other. When they were finally able to re-unite, they initially maintained a polite distance, neither of them sure what to expect from the other. During the pre-trial meetings with Sawyer, they tested the waters with one another to see how the other would respond, treating each other tenuously. During the trial itself, however, their bond tightened. They began to feel a special connection as two women who had experienced a shared trauma. Their grief was a silent creature that always clung to them and kept them ever mindful of what they had been through. For Joan, it was an overwhelming remorse for what she thought she had done, and for Jennie it was an excruciating awareness of what had been taken from her. As a mother, however, she could not direct her rage toward her daughter; and as a daughter, Joan could not let herself feel the guilt and shame of someone who may have robbed a mother of her husband and son. They both knew that those feelings, if expressed, would destroy their relationship.

So, Joan went upstairs, turned on her radio and walked around her room confused: "I thought I'd be happy if I could just come home," she said aloud, thinking of her experience at the clinic; "but I wonder now if I'll ever be happy again—if things will ever return to normal." She looked around for the book that Mae had left for her to read as a welcome home gift; but before she could find it, she heard the front door open and she recognized Uncle Fred's voice, as he walked into the kitchen.

Joan drifted toward the voices and pressed her ear hard to the cold grate.

"Jennie, I'm so sorry."

Then her mother's voice, still unintelligible.

"I know. I know, Jennie. But we've got some tough decisions to make, and we have to make them now. I've been carrying this report from the Topeka clinic around for a week, trying to decide what to do. Sawyer was right. The Boone County prosecutor does plan to indict Joan for Carl's murder. We've got to protect her some way. I talked with Sawyer this morning, and he has come up with a strategy that I think will work."

Jennie's voice....

"Look Jennie, neither of us can afford to do that. That's why I want to have Sawyer help Joan."

Jennie's voice…

"No, there *is* no hope. Dr. Menninger's report's states that Joan is insane, permanently insane. They're recommending that she be placed in an institution for the rest of her life."

Sobbing, from Jennie….

"Well, Sawyer told me what we have to do. There's no other way."

Jennie's voice…

"Sometime in mid-April, but we have to move very quickly."

Joan was stunned. Pulling herself up from the floor, she couldn't believe what she was hearing. Were they saying that she was crazy? "I'm not crazy," she said aloud, indignantly. There had to be some mistake. Joan reflected on the last few months. Thinking back to her days at the clinic, she had tried to be the model patient. She cooperated with everyone, participated in every session with Dr. Menninger and in every group session. How could they say she was crazy? Her body began to feel increased levels of anxiety. Her breathing became shallow, her heart rate increased and her chest felt as though it would explode. She began pacing, making complete circles in her room, stopping only long enough to light a cigarette.

"Joan," Jennie called from the bottom of the stairs. "Joan, please come down here."

When she stepped into the living room, Joan saw that her Uncle Fred was standing next to the fireplace while her mother sat in the worn wing back chair her dad used to commandeer to read the evening paper.

"Joan, you are going to have to go to the College Hill Sanitarium in Cincinnati for a short while." Fred walked over to her and reached out to put his arm around her. Joan stepped away and sat down on the couch farthest from her mother. Fred was hurt by this rebuff but continued, firmly.

"The prosecution wants to try you, now, for your dad's death. Sawyer believes that we need to have one more evaluation prior to the hearing and that you need to be where Vincent can't subpoena or arrest you."

Joan interrupted, "Hearing? What hearing?"

"There is going to be a Lunacy Hearing regarding your mental health, and we need to keep you away from the prosecutor's subpoena as long as possible.…" Uncle Fred's words became a verbal blur as she tried to process what this meant. Joan sat, staring into space, trying to grasp this new twist to her life.

Jennie was surprised that Joan didn't protest about this piece of news as she did when they forced her to go to the Menninger Clinic in January, and she assumed that it was due to the fact that Fred was explaining that the current plan was a legal maneuver rather than a sanity issue. Fred and Jennie had already agreed that they would not tell Joan the results of the Menninger Clinic's final evaluation. One thing at a time.

Lunacy Hearing? Joan thought to herself, as she headed toward the stairs up to her room. I thought I was getting better. Things *are* better for me; but they still think I'm a lunatic? She had clearly missed Fred's point regarding this legal maneuvering, so focused was she on her mental state and the information she had gleaned from her secret eavesdropping.

"Insane? Permanently insane…" she said, paraphrasing what she heard her Uncle Fred say through the heating duct. What about school? My friends? What about college? She shook her head, confused by this turn of events. Her anxiety began to be tempered by her anger. "I haven't done anything," she screamed. "I'm normal!" She stood before her full length mirror and shouted at her reflection. "I'm normal! I don't deserve to be locked up. I didn't kill anyone!" She wanted to separate from herself, but she could no longer do that. In fact, Joan had not seen the girl for some weeks. Picking up her hairbrush, she threw it at her image; and with the shattering of the glass, Joan fell to her knees, sobbing. The crying went on for so long that she started to gag, and eventually she fell into a deep sleep.

*   *   *

"Joan? Are you all right?" Jennie tried the door, but knew it would be locked. "Joan?"

"Yes, I'm all right," she said, barely able to open her eyes. It took her a few minutes to shake the heaviness she felt; and as it began to fade, her anger quickly spread throughout her body and transformed into rage. It became intolerable. Sitting up on the floor, she saw a few jagged pieces of the mirror near her feet; and picking up the largest one, she dug the edge into her forearm and made a straight line. The sting of her flesh slicing open made her drop the sliver. The blood slowly rose to the surface of the wound and began flowing more profusely. Her anger dissipated, and she felt a hiatus from its hold on her. No, she said to herself. Stop. Remember what they said at the clinic. This is not going to solve any problems.

Standing up, she looked at herself in the cracked mirror. Joan's arm was dripping blood. Strangely enough, the arm of the girl looking back at her was not bleeding. She was startled to see this image of herself. Wrapping a scarf around her arm, Joan unlocked her bedroom door, went to the bathroom, washed and then bandaged the wound. "I know I'm not crazy," she said aloud. "I know I'm not."

Going back to her closet, she pulled out the same suitcase that she had unpacked when she returned from the clinic and began furiously cramming clothes into it until it was full; then she forced the lock closed and sat on her bed. Her emotions were becoming too powerful. The anger turned into a sinking sense of hopelessness and dread. "I need a plan. I'm not going to let them put me away."

*   *   *

Joan had been home for only a few weeks, and, once again, her fate was being decided by the legal system. It was early Saturday morning, April 15, 1944 and Uncle Fred and Aunt Eva picked her and her mother up at their Crescent Avenue home and headed toward her Lunacy Hearing at the Covington courthouse.

"We really didn't have to be present at this hearing, but I thought it best that we at least attend the reading of the verdict," Fred said.

Her mother and Aunt Eva were silent. Joan observed everyone, trying to determine what each thought would happen today. Finally Joan spoke to her uncle.

"Are they going to send me away again, today?" she asked, lifelessly.

Uncle Fred looked at Jennie and then, turned to Joan who was in the back seat, replied, "Joan Marie, today the jury will tell us whether they agree with the clinic's report. If they do agree, then Judge Goodenough will decide what should happen to you."

"What could happen?" Joan asked.

"Well, the judge can do whatever he wants to. He could have you go to General Hospital, in Cincinnati, or he could have you go back to Topeka for more treatment. He could even make your mother or me your guardian and let us decide what you need. He has a lot of choices open to him. I don't have any idea which one he'll pick."

Joan sat quietly as they made the ten minute trip to the courthouse. She thought back to the conversation between Uncle Fred and her mother. Uncle Fred's words repeated themselves in her mind. "She's insane. Incurably insane. She has to be put away for life." Joan was determined not to let this happen to her. The thought of being in an institution day after day, year after year, was beyond her comprehension. For the past few days, depression filled her body. Its presence made breathing difficult. As the hearing approached, the despair tightly clung to her. She had no desire to push it away.

By the time they reached the courthouse, she had developed a plan, a way to circumvent being institutionalized.

They entered a long narrow room with pews like a church. Fred had timed their arrival perfectly. A group of people were sitting off to her right, facing her. The Judge entered from a side door and everyone stood up. She heard, as if in a fog, a voice saying, "Judge Joseph E. Goodenough, presiding." Comments were made from the front of the room by several individuals who had their backs to her. The Judge said "Very well" and looked at the jury to his left.

She turned in the direction of these 12 old people who were looking back at her. Ten women and two men. What do they know about my life? she thought. Why should they decide what happens to me? Finally, one old lady stood up and read from her notes: "We find Joan Kiger of unsound mind and a danger to herself and to anyone who is around her."

The lady sat down, looking quite smug. Joan looked over at Judge Goodenough. He nodded slightly, then, turning to Joan, said, "Based upon the testimony of Dr. Charles E. Kiely and upon the recommendations in the report from the Menninger Neuropsychiatric Clinic, as well as the decision of today's jury, I hereby commit you for the remainder of your life to the Central State Hospital for the Insane, in Lakeland, Kentucky. Your sentence begins immediately."

Bang! The gavel fell once. The Judge rose and left the room. Uncle Fred leaned toward Jennie and patted her on the arm. Ambivalence rose up within Jennie as the verdict was pronounced. A part of her knew Joan needed more treatment, but her mother's intuition couldn't accept that she was insane. Now her entire family was lost to her.

Joan froze at the sound of the gavel. Even though she predicted this outcome for herself, the Judge's final words pierced her last thin hope that she could resume a normal life. Aunt Eva was the only one to give her any eye contact, but it was the gaze of someone watching a condemned criminal as she headed toward the gallows.

Two deputy sheriffs approached Joan, one on her left and one on her right. Neither of them ever had to deal with such a young murderer, let alone one who was deemed insane. Gazing at her with curiosity, they held her arms tightly, and Joan did not struggle. They were surprised that this deviant girl, whose name and face had taken center stage in all of the newspapers and dominated the local gossip circles over the past months, looked like any normal teenager.

Annoyed by the flash of the bulbs, the pressing reporters and the swell of voices in the courtroom, shouting, "I knew she was crazy." "She should have gone to prison," Fred felt particularly protective of Joan. She looked terribly vulnerable. "Deputy," he said, "let me take Joan to the car." And with that, he shielded Joan with his body, holding his hand to her face, as they headed out of the courtroom.

Deputy Menke escorted them to the rear of the building where their cars were parked and yelled for the reporters to leave. More bulbs flashed amidst the shouts of the press, "Joan, how do you feel about the verdict?" "Mr. Williamson, I'm sure you're not through with this yet. What are you going to do next?" "Mrs. Kiger, will you appeal?"

Ducking into the squad car, Joan, Jennie, Fred and Eva were breathing heavily. Their adrenalin had been working overtime since the verdict was announced. The deputy leaned in, before getting behind the wheel, and said, "I'm Deputy Richard Menke; and the judge has assigned me to accompany y'all to Louisville." He looked at Joan's face and was overtaken with pity. As a matter of fact, as he looked into each of their faces, his feelings of compassion intensified. The car was deadeningly silent.

As they headed out of Covington on Highway 42, Fred leaned forward from the back seat and said, "Would you let Joan go to her house to pick up a few things?" He was unprepared for this outcome, having no idea that the police would immediately escort Joan to the clinic; and he was sure that Joan would think that he had set her up, when, in fact, he was as surprised as everyone else at the turn of events.

"I've got my orders," Deputy Menke replied, sternly. "We go straight to Louisville." Sounding tougher than he really was, he was determined not to let his emotions interfere with his job.

Joan pleaded. "Deputy, just let me get a few books and some clothes. I won't be long. Please."

Menke looked at Joan in his rear view mirror. His mind vacillated between following through on his orders or giving in to this young girl.

"Can't your mother bring your things when she comes to visit?"

Fred responded. "We're not sure when we'll be allowed to see Joan."

Menke was silent as he struggled with what to do. Finally, he said, softening somewhat, "Okay, but if anybody ever asks, we didn't make this stop." From the day the story broke, Menke never could get his mind around the fact that a 15 year old girl could brutally murder her father and brother.

As they pulled up in front of the Crescent Avenue home, Joan gazed at her house which held so many warm memories. Tears spilled onto her cheeks. I'll never see you again, she said to herself, with real affection. Barely whispering she muttered, "Forgive me for what I'm going to do."

Entering by the front door, she stopped in the kitchen for a Pepsi, and then went upstairs. Everyone stood around, waiting. "Hurry up, Joan," her mother said, impatiently. Grateful that the officer was willing to stop, Jennie didn't want to keep him waiting long.

Before Joan closed the door to her room, she heard her mother asking if anyone wanted coffee or a soft drink. Two years ago Joan's father had installed deadbolts on every door, inside and out, so fearful was he of a break-in. Joan now flipped the knob on the deadbolt and heard it click reassuringly in its slot. A burst of elation pushed the depression aside.

She looked around her private sanctuary, at all of the books, all the records, her radio, her dressing table with its lipsticks and nail polishes and, of course, El Capitaine. Holding him gently, she placed him in the center of the room. Then going to her bookcase, she picked up *Black Beauty*, her collection of *Nancy Drew* mysteries, and other of her favorite books, opened them and arranged them around El Capitaine. Then gathering several newspapers from her bottom dresser drawer, she crumpled them and placed them over this funeral pyre. Pulling a cigarette from her purse, she lighted it, inhaled deeply and threw the match on the crumpled papers. As the fire grew, she sat hypnotized, staring at her beloved El Capitaine.

She heard voices coming from downstairs, and she smiled, as the panic on the first floor grew. "Smoke! I smell smoke! Check the other rooms." Recognizing Deputy Menke's voice, she heard the fear as he yelled, "I'll check upstairs."

As if in a dream, she was aware of the Deputy banging on her bedroom door. She did not move. The smoke surrounded her. Once again she inhaled deeply. A few more minutes and it would all be over. The flames had jumped to the overstuffed chair in the corner and they were nearing the curtains. She could no longer even see the door. Just a little longer. Just a little longer.

*   *   *

The next thing Joan remembered was that she was outside. The fire truck was there. The neighbors were standing around, watching the pumper as it sprayed water into her upstairs bedroom. She heard a fireman exclaim, "Turn the hose off. It's out. Come on in. Let's clean this mess up."

Joan tried to touch her hair to fluff it out, a habit she had developed since letting her hair grow long, but her hands would not move. Looking down, she realized that she was handcuffed to a chain around her waist. She began to scream, banging the handcuffs on the police cruiser which she was leaning against. Deputy Menke came running over, "Settle down, Joan. Settle down. Get in the car." Furious that she had put him in a very tenuous situation with his superiors, he opened the back door and shoved her roughly in, and then sat beside her in silence. Had he misjudged this girl? Eyeing her carefully, he pondered to himself, she doesn't look crazy, but that sure was one damn crazy thing to do. His mind darted back to what he would have to tell the chief. He realized that his promotion would be a thing of the past.

In a few minutes, Fred came over, "Deputy, I think we can leave now. The Fire Chief said they would take care of everything."

The Deputy replied, "Okay, Mr. Williamson. You get back here. I'm going to have to handcuff you and Joan together. I can't take any more chances, and I don't want her trying to jump out." As they left Covington, heading south, Joan's mind was racing. Over and over, she said to herself, I'm not going to be locked up. I'm not going to be locked up; and that refrain stayed in her mind as they passed Florence, heading ever closer to the Central State Hospital for the Insane.

About an hour into the trip, Joan said, "Uncle Fred, I need to go to the bathroom. Can we stop somewhere?"

Looking at the deputy, Fred said, "What do you think? Can we stop at a service station? We probably all need a break."

Menke just wanted to get this girl to her destination. He was feeling uneasy. "Well, I suppose so. But you and Joan are going to stay handcuffed. And Joan, don't do anything stupid."

Because she was handcuffed to Fred, she had to scoot across the seat and exit on his side of the car. They walked together around the side of the service station toward the restroom. As she approached the door, she looked at her uncle and said, "Uncle Fred, how are we going to do this?" Because of the fire incident, Fred wasn't sure just how stable Joan was, so he asked her if she was going to cooperate all the way to Central State. Nodding her head, Joan assured him she just wanted to go to the bathroom.

"Deputy Menke. Come over here. Get these cuffs off Joan so she can use the rest room." Fred looked at Joan, sternly.

"Look, I understand the problem, but, Mr. Williamson, you've got to promise me that you are going to stay right here until Joan comes out." Glancing over at Jennie who was standing near the gas pumps, he called to her and asked her to go the toilet with Joan. "Her mother will also serve as back-up. Don't let her out of your sight!" Fred nodded his agreement, and Menke removed the cuffs and left them dangling on the chain around Joan's waist. Followed by Jennie, Joan went inside the restroom, rubbed her wrists which had been chafing from the cold steel; and as she retreated to the stall, she stood there desperately searching for a plan, any plan that would keep her out of the asylum. The filling station was close to the road, and she could hear and feel the huge trucks as they rumbled by, headed for Louisville.

She and Jennie exited the restroom; and true to his word, Fred was there, nervously waiting for her. "Where's Deputy Menke?" Joan asked, looking over Fred's shoulder.

"He's on the other side, in the men's room," her uncle said, pointing toward the road. "He'll be right back."

Joan saw this as her chance. With a surge of adrenalin, she bolted from her uncle's grasp and, as fast as she could run, headed toward the highway and toward the oncoming truck. Jennie screamed. Fred yelled. The driver laid on his horn and edged his truck toward the side of the road; and as Joan changed directions to intercept him, he jerked it back toward the center of the highway. She could feel the weight of the truck as the road began to shake. With her heart pounding furiously, she shut her eyes, knowing that, at last, she would be free. A strange sensation of euphoria began to envelop her.

The force of the impact knocked her off her feet. She rolled down the side of the embankment, Deputy Menke on top of her, cursing vehemently.

Looking up, she could see the truck continuing on its way. The Deputy had tackled her at a full run, knocking her and him out of the road and into a ditch. She was muddy, out of breath and very angry. It seemed that no matter what she planned, the asylum would be there waiting for her.

* * *

When the doctors at the Menninger Clinic had diagnosed Joan as having dementia praecox, they were focusing on the reports of her actions of the night of August 17th and did not expand their considerations to include the remaining 99.9% of who she was, a bright, energetic outgoing teenager with a loyal circle of friends, many interests and detailed plans as to how her future would play out. The disease which they had assigned her manifested itself through hallucinations, flatness of affect, lack of focus and an inability to interact with others.

Emil Kraepelin, a German psychiatrist in 1893, coined the name dementia praecox to explain symptoms of erratic behavior which were not treatable and which led to an irreversible decline in mental function; and when the doctors at the Menninger Clinic placed this label on Joan, it sealed her fate. The court system understood that there was no hope for her future and that she could not be allowed to remain free and unsupervised due to the possibility that she might, once again, lash out against anyone close to her or even against herself.

In 1944 the decision made by Judge Goodenough to institutionalize Joan for the rest of her life was one that he felt protected everyone concerned; and when the asylum's doors finally slammed shut behind her on April 15, she realized that the world she woke up to on August 15, the day before the murders, would forever be beyond her reach.

*   *   *

The Lunacy Hearing and the sentencing which Raymond Vincent witnessed stymied his plans to retry Joan. He had previously laid the groundwork for the next trial by asking Kentucky's Attorney General, Eldon S. Dummit, to rule on the constitutionality of such a move.

Dummit's opinion was that the prosecutor could proceed. Vincent, along with Walton attorney, Charles Riley, then issued a public statement, outlining the prosecution's beliefs:

TEXT OF STATEMENT

"Joan Kiger switches from nightmare to insanity in the face of impending trial for the murder of her father.

"First it was an intruder, second it was a nightmare-- now it's insanity.

"The statement in the press has been called to our attention wherein a psychiatrist is reported to have said that Joan Kiger did not have a nightmare when she killed her father and brother in Boone County, Ky., in August 1943. We think that statement is absolutely correct. However, the statement says that Joan is suffering from a disease known as dementia praecox. This part of the statement, we are convinced is prepared propaganda.

"The statement says that Joan is reported to have told the psychiatrist all of the details of the fatal shooting of her brother and father. No doubt this is correct. The statement says Joan told the psychiatrist that she lay and thought about the murder for two hours before actually starting to fire the shots from three revolvers.

"We are fully convinced that this statement is true, because it was proved in the trial by seven or eight substantial witnesses that her bed had not been slept in. Therefore, she could not have had a nightmare.

"The statement says that Joan deceived her lawyer and a jury of 12 men in Burlington, Ky. Apparently she did deceive the jury, but every other person acquainted with the facts believed then and still believes that it is a cold blooded murder.

"The statement says that Fred Williamson, Joan's uncle, was notified two weeks ago of the doctor's report. However, no mention of this report was made until activity in the case began at the April term of the Boone Circuit Court on Monday of this week.

"The statement says that her uncle, Fred Williamson, has conferred with officials in regard to committing her to an institution. Of course, this is part of the planned propaganda to keep Joan from meeting justice at the hands of a Boone County jury in a second trial.

"In other words, Joan's advisers were fully convinced that she could not, on another trial, face a Boone County jury on the flimsy defense of a nightmare.

"In our judgment, it was therefore determined to have some psychiatrist state that Joan was of unsound mind, and, thereby create sympathy for her and thus avoid the penalty for the cruel, cold-blooded, unjustifiable murder of her father.

"All the circumstances of Joan's life show that she is a perfectly normal girl; she has attended school and made her grades in a normal way. On numerous occasions she visited the homes of her girl friends. None of her teachers or her friends ever detected anything unusual in her life.

"The murder of her father was cold-blooded; planned in advance, and carried out in the minutest detail. She got the pistols, killed her father; one pistol was hard to discharge, she took the bullets out of it and placed them in another pistol; shot 15 shots into her father's and brother's bodies and the bed. Then according to her premeditated plan, she hid the pistols in the cistern; held a conference with her mother as to what to do next, then went for help, all the while contending that an intruder had committed the murder.

"From August to December, her story was that an intruder had entered her home and she shot at the intruder. When this was proved in the trial to be absolutely false, she then dug up the flimsy defense of the nightmare. When she and her advisers realized that she could not face a trial on the flimsy defense of the nightmare, it was planned to have a psychiatrist allege that she was insane.

"Nothing was even suggested of her being insane until the present term of the Boone Circuit Court, when it was thought that she would possibly face another trial for the cold-blooded, premeditated and unjustifiable murder of her father.

"The officials are standing by, watching the developments in this case, with the determination that no person, influential or humble, politician or otherwise, can commit two bold cold-blooded premeditated murders in Boone County, Ky., without ultimately facing a jury on all charges."

Signed, R. L. Vincent, commonwealth attorney;
C. W. Riley, county attorney, Boone County.

This statement was meant to be but the prelude to the indictment of Joan for the murder of her father; but shortly after its issuance, the pit bull of the Kiger case, Charles Riley, became seriously ill and had to withdraw.

John Vest, the second of the triumvirate, was assigned as a judge to the Campbell County courts to hear the case against The Beverly Hills Country Club's gambling activities. Within a year, Riley had died of a heart attack, leaving Raymond Vincent with an increasing case load and few qualified local attorneys to assist him.

When Judge Goodenough sentenced Joan, on April 15, 1944, to the Central State Hospital for the Insane, the odds of pursuing her further became somewhat remote; and with Vincent's loss of his team, the Kiger case was relegated to but an interesting footnote in Boone County's legal history.

Chapter Twenty-Three
Farewell To Rosegate
(October 9)

23

It was an absolutely stunning October day; the sun was just burning off the light fog as Jennie and Fred left her Crescent Avenue home for Rosegate. Joan had been discharged from Eastern State Sanitarium and placed in the care of her mother. And although Joan wanted to attend the auction, Jennie sensed her underlying agitation about the event, so she asked Eva to spend the day with her.

As Fred and Jennie pulled away from the curb, they waved to Joan who was getting ready to rake leaves in the front yard. As they headed toward Rosegate, Jennie's happiness over Joan's return slowly changed to a sense of dread that filled her body. She was familiar with this sensation because it revealed itself every time she took Joan to the hospitals or doctors. This nauseous dread was becoming all too real. For some strange reason, she believed that these feelings were a sentinel for her profound grief; so although she despised the first waves that reverberated in the pit of her stomach, she also was grateful.

As she gazed out the car window, she struggled to keep her grief at bay – something she had trained herself to do these past months. Touching it in any way, she feared, would release a surge of uncontrollable emotions—emotions so strong that they would swallow her up completely.

"Fred, how long do you think this will take?" she asked, only as a way to ground herself. Talking seemed to silence her pain, both emotional and physical; for whenever her grief began to creep to the surface, the wound in her hip throbbed with increasing intensity.

"It's hard to say, but I'm guessing we should be out of there around 1:00 or 2:00."

"Oh," she said, still staring at the window, not allowing her eyes to focus on the passing scenery for fear that it would remind her of the many shared family experiences at Rosegate—on the lake, in the garden and around the dinner table.

"I know this is going to be difficult for you, but you have to sell Rosegate for a lot of reasons, the most pressing being Sawyer's fees," Fred had explained.

In her mind that was the least pressing reason to sell Rosegate, although the most practical. She knew she would never go back there after today; she desperately needed to exorcise it from her life, and this personal goodbye was her way of doing just that.

When they arrived at Rosegate, there were already at least 50 cars parked in the field and along the side the road.

"Do you want me to drop you off?" Fred asked, matter-of-factly. From the time he first learned of the murders, he never once showed any signs of emotion to Jennie. He was a firm believer in handling life's problems with strict logic and responsible action, the one exception occurring on the night of the murders.

"Yes, just drop me off," she said, flatly.

As Jennie stepped out of the car, she was struck by what greeted her at the front gate – a milling crowd, staring, elbowing each other, pointing at her and whispering all too loudly, "There she is. There's Joan's mother. I never thought she would show up...."

Over the past months Jennie had learned to turn a deaf ear to this prattle and to continue with the business at hand, and today's business was the auctioning of her beloved Rosegate.

She stood quietly by the gate, not attempting to enter the yard, until Fred had parked the car and joined her. Looking for him in the crowd, she wondered what she would have done if she were alone. Eva and he had been her anchors throughout this entire ordeal. It was they who had visited her almost everyday while she was recovering from the gunshot wound in her hip. It was they who accompanied Joan to the hospital to visit her, and it was they who comforted Joan at the funeral of Carl and Jerry. It was Fred who arranged for bail for Joan, and, bless him, it was Fred who contacted Sawyer Smith and convinced him to defend Joan. And now, he had helped arrange for this auction.

355

Remembering Joan's birth, she could see Fred's beaming face as he held her for the first time, there, in the hospital; and she remembered his words, "Jennie, this is the most beautiful girl I have ever seen. I know I will always love her. This is better than a kid of my own!" He was squeezing Joan so hard and smothering her tiny face with kisses that Jennie had to yell at him. "Fred! She's just a baby! Take it easy!"

As Fred approached the gate, Jennie took a few steps toward him and reached for his arm. He guided her past the onlookers and into the house itself. Once inside, Jennie pulled back and stopped. The rooms were bare now, all the furniture having been moved outside to be inspected by potential bidders prior to the auction. It almost reminded her of the day Carl brought her here for the first time. He was so elated.

"Well, what do you think?" he asked. Whenever he got excited, his speech became very rapid and seemed to increase a decibel. Without waiting for a response, he blurted, "I think it's just what we need. We can spend week-ends here with the kids...."

When she walked through the front door with Carl dragging her into the living room, she vividly remembered how much she fell in love with Rosegate. While he was desperately trying to sell her on the idea of a second home, she had already made up her mind. She held back her reaction, however, and remained noncommittal because she didn't want to make it too easy for him. Waiting to be convinced that the decision he had already made was one she agreed with was a game they often played with each other. "This is an awfully big house and 20 acres to boot. Can we afford it?" she asked, knowing full well, he wouldn't have brought her here if he didn't have the funds.

Retracing those steps from that initial visit, she found herself in the kitchen. Her mind replayed the very first morning they had breakfast at Rosegate. She could still hear the chatter among Carl, Joan, Joe, John and Jerry, as the smells of coffee, frying bacon and eggs wafted in between the laughter. Sunny-side-up eggs were the family's favorite; scrutinizing the platter, they would squabble over who would get the most perfect egg with the same competitiveness they exhibited over who caught the biggest catfish. The boys demanded that the egg's golden liquid be unscathed so as to better soak into Jennie's hot biscuits. The ladies would laugh and say, "You men! We don't care. We'll eat the broken eggs." Jennie would always make sure she purposely cracked the yokes on at least three of the eggs, so the family could engage in their egg yolk banter.

There were so many pleasurable mornings in this kitchen. Every time Carl bit into a steaming biscuit covered with sausage gravy, he would announce to the family with a full mouth that their mother made the absolute best gravy in Kentucky.

A noise in the backyard returned her to the empty and silent kitchen. Looking out the window, she noticed some people wandering around outside the tool shed, examining the tools that were neatly leaning against the front wall.

"Looks like we're gonna have good weather today," Fred said. "That's a blessing." And with that barely out of his mouth, he stepped outside the back door and lit up a Camel.

Jennie eyed the tool shed and Carl's face flashed before her.

"Right here is what I love about this place! My very own tool shed!" He was pushing her out the back door toward his long sought after dream.

"Are you buying the house just for the tool shed?" Jennie asked, laughing. The memory of Carl sizing up the building and placing his imaginary tools in it brought a brief smile to her face. It lasted for only a moment, being interrupted by her new found companion of the past few months, those interminable feelings of dread. She blinked and shook her head.

"Fred, you smoke too much," she shouted out the back door, as a way to dispel these thoughts.

She turned around and walked to the library. Looking at the bare walls, she could see where the pictures of family vacations, birthdays and anniversaries once hung: Anniversaries--the 24th wedding anniversary-- black and white images flooded her mind's eye ….

"I can't believe it's been 24 years," Carl said, as he brought her a glass of champagne and placed it on the antique oak library table they had bought just a few weeks ago. "Twenty-Four years! Well, Jennie, would you do it all over again?" he asked, taking a sip of Dom Perignon, a gift from his friend, Jack Maynard.

"I suppose so, but I always wonder about that last boyfriend of mine. The one before you," Jennie said, smiling, waiting for Carl's reaction.

"What?" He bellowed and they both started laughing. Every single anniversary Carl always asked the same question, and she always gave the same response. They toasted and kissed.

"If you're feeling romantic," Jennie winked, "forget it! On our anniversary seven years ago, I gave in to that twinkle in your eye; and it miraculously turned into an eight pound four ounce baby boy. We're too old for any more surprises like that!"

As their anniversary approached, they decided to have a celebration at Rosegate, inviting the family and all of their friends and, of course, some of the people Carl worked with.

"Let's have a party this year 'cause next year, for our 25th, I want to take a trip. We can go to California," Carl said.

Jennie hired Estelle Ryle, who worked as a part time cook and waitress at the Stringtown Restaurant, to prepare the meal for her party. Wanting to enjoy the evening with Carl and their guests, she decided to forgo the stress of menu planning and meal preparation.

As Jennie and Carl sipped their champagne, the house began to fill with the smell of fried chicken, mashed potatoes and gravy and creamed corn. Estelle made the best fried chicken around. As a matter of fact, it was her chicken recipe that gave Stringtown its reputation. The anniversary cake was made by Eva, who took on the job of making the celebratory cakes for every family event. Her vanilla layer cake with creamed cheese frosting was everyone's favorite. She balked, however, whenever anyone wanted to "drown" her cake with ice-cream. "Eat it pure," she always said. "Eat it pure."

As Jennie remembered, her thoughts became dark. The party guests arrived, toasts were made. Earlier in the day, Carl had driven Joan and her best friend, Mae, to the trolley which would take them to the dock of the Island Queen on the Kentucky side of the river. They had boarded the Island Queen to Coney, expecting to return by late afternoon in order to join in the anniversary celebration. As the guests started to bid their good-byes and head for the door, Joan was still not home.

Jennie remembered that Carl was very worried and agitated that night. "Where the hell is she?" he said, as he paced around the library. After all of their guests had left, Jennie called Mae's house to see if they might be there; but Mrs. Klingenberg thought they were at the Kiger's. "Where the hell is she?" Carl repeated over and over.

Jennie wanted to call the police, but Carl stopped her, saying, "I'm going to drive to Coney Island and see where the hell she is." Interjecting, Jennie said, "Carl, that will be a waste of time. Coney Island will be closed. We need to call the police."

"We don't want the police involved," he said, adamantly. "I'm going to call Jack Maynard. He'll know how to handle this."

Although she didn't agree, she knew better than to argue with Carl when he was in such a frenzied state.

"You go to bed and try to get some sleep. Anyway, with all this commotion Jerry's up, so get him back to bed. I'll take care of this," he told her, as he walked her up the stairs.

Jennie's memories of the rest of that night were a blur; but she would never forget the sound of the phone ringing at 8:00 a.m., of listening to the sound bytes of Carl's angry voice shouting and cursing and then of hearing the phone slam down.

"Jennie, Joan called. She's at Mae's house and will be home later," Carl shouted, disgustedly, from the bottom of the stairs.

"That girl is getting a little to big for her britches," he exclaimed, as he walked into the bedroom. "She has no idea, no idea…."

Jennie was greatly relieved to know that Joan was safe. Lately Joan had become more defiant—an entirely new trait for her. As a little girl, she was always eager to please and was very compliant. Oh, well, Jennie thought. The boys weren't so difficult, during their teen years, but Joan is going to test us for all she can. Thinking back to her own adolescence, Jennie smiled, as she remembered skirmishes she had with her mom and dad. I guess I wasn't the easiest teenager either, she mused.

When Joan returned home later that day, Carl, Jennie and Jerry were picking tomatoes in the garden. Jennie wanted to get to Joan first and take her upstairs because she knew Carl was going to explode when he saw her. But Jerry began shouting when he caught a glimpse of her stepping off the Greyhound bus. "Joanie! Joanie!"

Carl immediately looked up and stormed over to Joan, grabbing her by the arm and roughly walking with her to the house, yelling the entire way. Jennie followed behind, telling Jerry to go to his room.

Pointing his finger in her face, Carl shouted, "Do you have any idea what you put your mother and me through? What the hell is a matter with you? Ever since you started hanging around that Mae you've become a different girl. Smoking, lipstick…and then this," he pushed Joan down on the couch. His face was red and his tone became increasingly hostile.

Jennie became frightened. She had never seen Carl in such a rage before, not in all their 24 years together. Joan began back- talking her dad, trying to defend herself; and as the first words came out of her mouth, Carl slapped her on the face. Joan screamed, more in shock than from the actual sting on her cheek.

"I forbid you to hang around Mae. Do you hear me?" his shouts bringing Jerry to the top of the stairs, crying.

Joan bolted from the couch and stood eye-to-eye with Carl. "You can't make me stop being friends with Mae! She's all I have! The only person who understands me. She's my very best friend."

Carl slapped Joan again, only this time his hand print glowed red on her cheek. Joan quickly brought up her arms to protect her face because she could see that her dad was going to smack her again.

Jennie stepped in, grabbed Carl by the shoulders and yelled in his face, "That's enough! Do you hear me? That's enough! What's wrong with you? Joan, go upstairs right now."

"Upstairs…upstairs….." She began to tremble as she looked over toward the hallway where the stairwell beckoned, hoping to trap her into reliving those violent memories.

"Jennie?" Fred walked into the room.

She turned to him.

"Just checking in on you," he said.

What would I do without you? she said to herself She knew better than to share her gratitude with Fred because he just become irritated whenever she did.

"That's what family is for," he'd say, brusquely, and change the subject.

A booming voice just outside the library window caught her attention. As Jennie looked out, she noticed that the auctioneer had lined up the two automobiles that they owned: a 1940 Oldsmobile and a little 1938 Ford Coupe, the car that Joan was to drive when she turned 16.

"I see they're about ready to starting auctioning off the cars," she said.

"Yup. I'm sure you'll get a good price for them," Fred said, as he lit up another cigarette and leaned over to look.

Jennie remembered that every Saturday during the summer Joan would back the Ford out of the barn and park it up close to the cistern, where she could pump water into a bucket and spend an hour or so washing and polishing "her" car. Wanting to insure Joan's safety, Carl had been able, somehow, even during this war rationing period, to locate five good tires for the Ford. Knowing how he felt as a teenager with his first automobile, he wanted Joan to be proud of her car as she drove her friends around; so he bought new seat covers, as well. It was difficult to know who was more excited at the prospect of her driving – she or her dad. And now, Joan would never drive that little Ford, never go to a prom and never have a completely normal life again. Never....

As she continued into the living room, she realized she would have to walk by the stairwell. No way around it. Hesitating, she fixed her gaze on the fireplace in the living room as she limped passed. She couldn't make herself even look at it. Picking up the pace of her steps didn't protect her from a kaleidoscope of smells, images and sounds as they filled her body. Gunpowder, an endless stream of gunshots, Joan's high pitched shrieks, Carl's lifeless body, cursing, doors slamming, her own screams, the pain, a shadowy figure in the door way, terror and chaos. What was happening? Jerry, my God, Jerry.....

Putting her hands over her ears, she hurriedly made her way through the house, looking for Fred. He was standing out back talking to some people. "Fred, Fred," she shouted. When she saw that she had startled the group, she caught her own panic and, in spite of her pounding heart, pointed to the lake behind the barn and said, "Excuse me, Fred. Can we walk back there by the lake?" The water always seemed to calm her.

Fred took her by the arm; and because of the constant pain in her right hip, they negotiated the open field slowly, stopping several times. As he stepped out onto the boat dock, Fred lit up another cigarette.

"You know. You *do* smoke too much and Eva agrees with me," Jennie said, as she gazed at the lake. This was by far her favorite spot at Rosegate. When Carl took her on that first tour of the place, the lake mesmerized her. As a matter of fact, the lake was something each member of the family enjoyed.

Joe, John and Carl would awaken before sunrise with Jerry lagging behind, rubbing his sleepy eyes. With their steaming thermoses of coffee and a plate of doughnuts, they would load up the fishing boat and sit in the middle of the lake in silence, for hours, hypnotized by their bobbers, waiting to find out who would get the biggest catch. It didn't matter if it was a bass, blue gill or cat fish, it just had to be the biggest. Jerry would always snuggle right next to Carl, look up at him, admiringly, and squeal with excitement when his dad's bobber disappeared.

As she gazed upon Carl's fishing boat, she was jolted by the memory of Joan's first sleep-walking incident. Jennie was distressed when Joan woke her from a deep sleep to tell her that she had found herself, mysteriously, sitting in the boat in the middle of the lake. Although she tried not to show any emotion by the event, Jennie was very disturbed that her daughter had inherited her father's penchant for night-time wanderings.

One would expect that this return to the double edged sword of loving memories and clashing terror would precipitate a flood of emotions. Yet Jennie stood stoically on the dock, thinking of what life would be like once this last vestige of her past was gone. The recent anguish and shock she had experienced, as she came to grips with the fact that everyone that she held dear had been taken away, was henceforth walled off deep within her indomitable will to survive. Now even the outward symbol of her past happiness, her Rosegate, was to be removed from her life.

Fred was convinced that Rosegate had to go: on the emotional level, he knew Jennie could never stay in this house again and, probably, after today, should never re-visit the place; on the financial level, it was imperative that Jennie sell. She still owed Sawyer Smith and there were Carl's bills--debts she was just now becoming aware of. The will, which she hadn't bothered to read until after the tragedy of August 17, revealed that Carl had only about a thousand dollars in War Bonds, the Crescent Avenue house and the cars. The $1440.00 that was hidden under the couch at Rosegate had been taken by the Boone County Sheriff, and she wasn't sure she would ever get that back. Once again Fred had to step in, take action and provide Jennie with sound advice and become a bastion of strength upon which to draw.

The loudspeaker interrupted Jennie's reflections. It was Rel Wayman, the auctioneer, calling the bidders around him. Standing on one of the hay wagons, he explained the rules of bidding, the method of payment and the order in which everything would be auctioned. Rosegate would be the final item at the auction. It's going to be a long morning, Jennie thought, wishing for a cup of coffee.

As if reading her mind, Fred asked, "Jennie, would you like some coffee?"

"I'd love some," she said, smiling easily, for the first time since this trip to Rosegate had begun.

They walked over to a large card table where chocolate and glazed doughnuts, steaming coffee and sandwiches were displayed. Napkins, paper plates and plastic silverware were neatly placed at the opposite end. A young girl, about Joan's age, ran up. "Mrs. Kiger, could I get your autograph?" she asked, excitedly.

Jennie looked at Fred, puzzled.

Fred stepped in. "What's your name?" he asked the nervous but smiling girl.

"My name is Joan, too. I thought it would be really neat if I had the mother of Joan Kiger sign my autograph book. I came to the auction for that one reason."

Fred gently took the girl by the elbow and guided her away from Jennie. He was annoyed by this insensitive kid but maintained his composure.

"Honey," he said to her, "Do you realize Mrs. Kiger has gone through a terrible ordeal? Her husband and son have been murdered and Joan has been hospitalized. Do you really want to remind Mrs. Kiger of all that?"

The young girl called Joan looked confused. "Well, maybe not." She hesitated, than said, "Who are you? Maybe you can sign my book?"

Fred signed the book and the girl walked away, her head down, trying to read what he had written.

"That was unexpected," Jennie said, forcing a smile.

Fred bought two coffees and two glazed doughnuts; and as he turned to Jennie to hand her a steaming cup, she said, scanning the front yard, "Gosh, look at the trees, Fred." The yard was filled with oaks and maples – their leaves brightly colored, as they danced their final farewell to summer, pirouetting in the breeze. "You know," she continued, "I changed my mind. I want to be here when Rosegate, itself, is sold. If you could just pull our car a little closer, I could sit there and still hear the auction. Taking a long drag off his Camel, he asked, "Are you sure you want to do that?" He was a bit confused since Jennie had been adamant earlier that she just couldn't bear to watch Rosegate go up for sale.

"Yes, I'm sure," Jennie said, limping toward the car. Earlier, as she walked through the house, she realized that she needed to be here right now. She wanted to say goodbye one last time to everything and everyone that she had loved. After all, she hadn't been able to say good-bye to Jerry and Carl. She so desperately wanted to go to their funerals but the doctors forbade it.

The day Fred and Eva picked her up from the hospital, the first thing she said to both of them, as she was helped out of a wheel chair and into the car by an orderly, was "I want to go to a flower shop and then to the cemetery."

Eva touched her arm, gently. "Jennie, the doctor said you needed to go straight home and rest."

"You heard me. No debating on this one," she said firmly, glaring at both of them.

They knew by the tone of her voice that she meant business.

Once at St. John's Cemetery, Fred helped Jennie out of the car, feeling her weight press against him, as he grabbed her right arm. Cuddling the two bouquets of red roses as gently as she did Jerry when she first held him on the day he was born, Jennie slowly walked toward the grave sites which were located near the road.

With help from Eva, Jennie arranged each bouquet against the headstones. Bowing her head, she whispered "Hail Mary, full of grace, the Lord is with thee...." With the sound of the "Amen," she removed one flower from each bouquet and said aloud, "These are for Joan."

Fred felt a tinge of embarrassment at being privy to such a special moment. Eva moved closer to Jennie and put her arm around her. The two women stood there, holding on to each other as only sisters can in such a moment of shared pain. Fred heard the sobs, the inaudible words; then, as if conjoined, they started to walk toward him. Jennie suddenly stopped, turned to look back and then asked Eva to help her get closer to the headstones. She ran her fingers gently across the engraved names – CARL KIGER; JERRY KIGER – she began to cry. The grief grew as each tear fell; and it was then that she took hold of herself and shouted within, No! No! I will not feel this.

A leaf fluttered and, upon its descent, touched her face. Yes, she thought, I needed to be here.

*   *   *

The last several months had been difficult for him. With great personal angst he realized that his work was in his blood – more a part of him than he ever imagined. It was when he read that the Kiger house, Rosegate, was up for auction that a voice in his head whispered, "Buy Rosegate. That way, you'll never forget your promise."

*   *   *

Fred was to be the bye-bidder at the Rosegate auction, so his presence was a necessity. He and the auctioneer had discussed the possibility that no one would want to bid on a house and farm where such brutal murders had taken place so recently. His job, then, was to bid up the property at least until it reached

$12,000.00, the price Carl had purchased the place for, a few years ago.

Fred and Jennie sat, pensively, drinking the coffee and half-heartedly nibbling on the doughnuts as they listened to the car radio, waiting for the sale of the farm to begin. Finally Fred opened the door, saying to Jennie, "I think we need to go over." It was perfect timing for, as they approached, they could hear the auctioneer review, once again, what the rules of bidding were, followed by a description of what was being sold. Wayman explained that the farm consisted of 20 acres, a barn, a chicken house and a tool house. "The house itself," he said, "for those of you who haven't had time to tour it, has four bedrooms, a full bath in every bedroom, a large living room, dining room, library, kitchen and pantry, along with a full basement and a 33 ton stoker coal bin.

"Everybody ready? Here goes!"

He began the auctioneer's chant, starting the bidding at $10,000.00.

Fred raised his hand and when the bidding finally reached $12,000.00, he was able to relax. His job was over. He looked around the crowd, trying to see who else was doing the bidding. By this time the price had risen to $13,000.00, and only two men were left: a heavy set young man in work clothes and a short, slightly built man with a swarthy complexion dressed immaculately in a dark blue suit, wearing a grey fedora. At $13,500.00 it looked as though it was over. The auctioneer chanted, "Going once, going twice…." But the man in work clothes reconsidered and shouted out, "$13,700.00." The man in the dark suit came back immediately with "$13,800.00."

Again the auctioneer began his chant, "Going once, going twice...."

And once again the young man raised his hand and shouted, "$14,000.00."

"Sold!" The auctioneer exclaimed. "Thank you all for coming. Remember, next week on Big Bone Road, the old Taylor farm's for sale. See you at 10:00 a.m.! This completes today's auction."

"Wait a minute!" the man in the dark blue suit shouted, muscling his way through the crowd and toward Wayman, who was still standing on the hay wagon. Although many thought Rosegate to be a house of horrors, this bidder saw it as his refuge from a dissolute past life and a constant reminder of his promise to begin anew; he was not going to let this opportunity pass so easily.

"Wait one damn minute! You can't shut the bidding off like that. What the hell are you trying to do?"

Wayman saw the grey fedora bobbing rapidly in the crowd headed his way, and he sensed trouble was coming with it. He caught the eye of the Deputy Sheriff who was standing by the Ford he'd just auctioned; and using the speaker system, he said, "Deputy, bring your men over here. I need some help."

The man in the suit stopped immediately. "Sorry," he said with a very obvious sense of loss in his voice and clearly a look of sadness in his eyes. "I don't want trouble, but I was ready to bid $14,500.00. You can't just close the bidding because you feel like it."

Wayman glared at this stranger who clearly didn't understand Boone County's attitude toward outsiders. Responding in an adamant tone, he yelled, "This house is sold, mister." And without taking a breath, he once again barked for the Deputy.

Completely baffled by this turn of events, the dispirited bidder spun on his heels and headed out of the yard toward his car– a Buick with Ohio plates.

The young man who had won the bidding came up to the table where the cashier was sitting: "I've got my check ready," he said, excitedly. "How do I make it out?"

"Congratulations," the cashier offered. "We'll need to see your Driver's License first."

The auctioneer came over, "I'm Rel Wayman. Great farm you bought. This is the fourth one you've bid on, isn't it?"

"Yeah," the new owner said. "I thought I'd never find a farm, and $14,000.00 was as high as I could go. If there had been one more bid, I'd been out."

"I know, I know," Wayman agreed. "That was pretty obvious to me."

"I'm surprised you remembered me," the new owner proffered.

"It was your eyes, I remembered. I could see how badly you wanted a farm, and I figured you'd looked long enough," Wayman said, smiling, satisfied that he'd helped a young man come a little closer to rural bliss.

"You bet I wanted it! This will be just great for me and my family. I own the Independent Linoleum and Carpet Company in Covington. I can use all this extra space to store my stuff. My name is Bill Miller."

About that time, the deputy came over, "Mr. Wayman," he said, somewhat confused. "You need some help?"

"No, everything is okay now. But for a second there, I wasn't sure."

"Well, you know I'm the only deputy you hired today. Who were you talking about when you said bring your men over here?"

"Don't worry about it, deputy. But I would like for you to stay around here a little longer."

"Sure, at one dollar an hour, I'll stay all day!" he said.

*　　*　　*

As they drove away, Jennie pulled down the visor so she could check her make-up and put more lipstick on. Her lips felt dry and cracked. Looking into the mirror, her peripheral vision could see the crowd thinning from the Rosegate yard. People were chattering, laughing. As Rosegate grew smaller and smaller in the distance, she detected a thin veil of gloom falling over the roof, the shutters and the yard. She quickly focused on the face staring back at her in the mirror, and she noticed that her mouth was colorless. As she put on her favorite Max Factor lipstick, her eyes met her own gaze. The grief and sadness she beheld startled her. She allowed herself to touch her reflection—but for only a moment. "How about if we pick up Eva and Joan and go to lunch?" she asked Fred, as she adjusted her position on the car seat to relieve the pain in her hip.

Chapter Twenty-Four
The Nightmare Is Over
(April 5, 1991)

24

In a facility for the terminally ill in Louisville, Kentucky, on April 5, 1991, an on-duty nurse went to check on a cancer patient, a 63 year old woman named Marie Kiler. Marie had been in the home for some time and had never had a visitor or a phone call. Her only contact with the outside world was a monthly bank statement: a dying old lady for whom the spark of life had long since been extinguished. This is a person, the nurse thought, who had died, emotionally, many years ago; and she wondered about Marie's life. Whom did she love; who loved her? How had she come to this, a ward for the dying, and, obviously, no one here to mourn her passing. Yesterday, Marie had, with her frail hand, pulled the nurse closer to the bed so she could whisper: "Remember, I want my body to go to The University of Louisville. It's in my will."

And now she was gone. The nurse was preparing to cover the body with a sheet and call the doctor to have him certify the time of death when she noticed that the old lady was clasping something in her right hand. Curiously, the nurse opened Marie's hand. A pistol casing fell onto the sheet, a casing so shiny, that it had to be brand new; yet, it was not. It was shiny from being handled thousands and thousands of times over nearly half a century.

The nurse's curiosity lasted only long enough for a cursory examination of the casing; then she tossed it in the nearby trash can and, turning abruptly, left the room, heading for the doctor's office to report yet another death in this house of the dying.

Epilogue

In 2003, sixty years after the tragic and horrific night of August 17, 1943, The Boone Country Historical Society decided to resurrect the events of that fateful year as it related to the murder of Carl Kiger and his son, Jerry. Following their research of the case, they made the decision that the information uncovered could best be presented in the form of a court trial. They titled their play, aptly, "The Murder Trial of Joan Kiger."

After the passage of 60 years, the eye-witnesses to the murder or even those who attended the trial were, with a few rare exceptions, deceased. The Historical Society had to rely, for the most part, on the newspaper archives. Using this source, they were able to collect enough information that they felt confident that the re-creation of the trial would be fair and impartial.

Since Joan Kiger was only 16 in 1943, there was even a strong possibility that she was alive and could be found. She might even be willing to share in this endeavor. However, in spite of an exhaustive search on the part of the members, no information on Joan was forthcoming.

It was as though, when she walked out of Kentucky's Central State Hospital for the Insane, she entered a world beyond the reach of any prying reporter, relative, police or well-wisher.

As a last ditch effort to determine Joan's whereabouts, Asa Rouse, a prominent Walton attorney and member of the Historical Society, hired a Texas detective, a tracer of lost persons. Asa was not hopeful, but one never knows.... In a short while a packet from the detective arrived. He had found Joan! But the Society had looked for and the detective had found Joan too late: She had died in 1991.

The information the Society received from the detective went on to reveal little known facts of those missing years: Joan had changed her name from Joan Marie Kiger to Marie J. Kiler and had graduated from The University of Louisville in 1958. At the age of 31, she began a teaching career in Louisville's public schools, eventually receiving a Guidance Counseling Certificate and finishing out her career counseling youngsters.

Her fervent prayer was that she could remain anonymous—a face in the crowd –and for almost 50 years she had been successful. As the decades passed, this very attractive young lady grew old. Her beautiful auburn hair turned grey, and her hopes of marriage and children were never realized. The secretive trips to her apartment in Louisville by her mother gradually diminished as Jennie, herself, became more enfeebled.

Eventually, Joan's one link with the past ended, and she was left alone—alone with the horrible memories of that night so long ago.

*   *   *

The murder trial of Joan Kiger briefly touched a nation, but soon the war news resumed its rightful place in everyone's mind. There were some individuals and places, however, which were changed forever.

- On April 16, 1944, Joan was judged to be insane by a Kenton County circuit court jury comprised of ten women and two men and was ordered, by the judge, to be committed to Central State Hospital for the Insane. The reason for this decision, according to their verdict, was that "she might try to destroy herself or anyone near her." Just four months later, on August 26 (one year and 11 days after the murders) Joan was released from Central State to the care of her mother. One of her psychiatrists, Dr. Kimbell, made this statement: "Joan is not insane. Prolonged custodial care is not the answer to her problems." The Kiger family physician, Dr. Ertel, continued to treat her.

- In 1944 Ouster charges were brought against Campbell County Sheriff Lee B. Kesla. John

Effort pleaded guilty for secreting slot machines at Beverly Hills. Red Masterson pleaded guilty on a similar charge regarding his club, The Merchant's Café. Pete Schmidt did also for his Glenn Rendezvous, as did Samual Gutterman, at The York Café.

- The Beverly Hills Country Club was destroyed by fire on May 28, 1977, taking the lives of 167 patrons and employees.

- A new jail was built in Burlington, relegating the original one to office space.

- Rosegate was sold in 1943 by Jennie Kiger for $14,000.00 to help her pay legal expenses. It was later demolished.

- The official transcript of the murder trial taken by court stenographer, Leila Wilhoit, after being sent to the state capitol in Frankfort, Kentucky, was lost.

- The murder weapons, themselves, disappeared.

- On Monday, January 3, 1944 the newly elected Covington City Commissioners voted not to renew the contract of City Manager, Jack Maynard.

- Sheriff Jake Williams had a massive heart in 1944, killing him immediately.

- State Police investigator, Melvin Huff, was gunned down in front of The White Star Café in Cold Springs, Kentucky, in 1948.

- Boone County Attorney, Charles Riley, who assisted in the prosecution of Joan Kiger, died of a heart attack in 1945, at the age of 54.

- Sawyer Smith, the lead attorney for the defense, on the other hand, died at age 86, in 1969 in The St. Charles Nursing Home.

- Judge Carroll Cropper died in 1976, at the age of 79. Two years later, Kentucky Governor Julian Carroll officiated at the dedication of the Interstate 275 Bridge between Boone County and Lawrenceburg, Indiana, naming the structure The Carroll Lee Cropper Bridge.

- Jennie Kiger died of breast cancer in 1979, at the age of 83 in Mississippi, where she had moved to be near her son, Joe. Fred and Eva Williamson had also moved there and were at her bed side for a final farewell to Rosegate.

- Joseph Kiger, a professor at the University of Mississippi, died September 17, 2006; and for his entire life, he refused to speak of his family or of the fate of Joan.

- Judge John Vest, who was involved in the Kiger murder investigation, returned to Campbell County to hear proceedings in the gambling and political graft and contempt charges against the owners of Beverly Hills Country Club.

- Raymond L Vincent died November 24, 1976 at the age of 77.

- Lamar Congleton, the jury foreman, died February 27. 1992 at the age of 94.

- Ward Yager, the judge, died in February of 1967 at the age of 76.

- Byron Kinman, one of the jurors, some time after the trial, married Sheriff Williams' daughter, Glenrose, who had been appointed by Judge Cropper to complete the term of her father when he died, suddenly, in 1944. Kinman then went on to serve as sheriff of Boone County following Irvin Rouse.

- Albert Dringenburg, another juror, every year until his death, on the anniversary of Jerry Kiger's birth, received an anonymous card describing what Jerry's age would have been and highlighting what Jerry would probably be doing. The final handwritten comment, which never changed from year to year was "How could you find the murderer of this beautiful child innocent?" A picture of Jerry was always included.

- Elmer Kirkpatrick, the jailor, died in 1959 at the age of 79. His son-in-law, Lamar Congleton, was the jury foreman.

- Fred Williamson, aka Uncle Fred, the good guy of the story, the man who held the fragile Kiger family together after the Rosegate murders: he and his wife, Eva, moved to Mississippi along with Jennie so that they could be close to Carl and Jennie's son, Joe, who was a professor at the University of Mississippi. Eva died in 1981, two years after Jennie; Fred, who had helped manage the affairs of these two sisters for so long and who had nursed them through their final illnesses, died shortly after his beloved wife.

Rosegate Murders Timeline

In addition to a straight forward time line, reflecting events as they are presented in this novel, the summery below also includes occurrences which the Boone County Sheriff's department and the prosecutor were aware of but which were not necessarily covered in *A Dream Within A Dream*.

1919	Carl Kiger and Jennie Hoelscher were married.
1936	Carl becomes Covington City Commissioner.
1939	Carl is appointed Vice-Mayor of Covington.
1940	Carl purchases Rosegate (titled in Jennie's name).
1941-42	John and Joe Kiger join the men and women fighting in WW II.

1943

August 3   Covington citizens complain to the city
                  commissioners that because Carl is living
                  at Rosegate, in Boone County, he should
                  no longer be Vice-Mayor of Covington.
                  They also raised the question as to how
                  a man who makes $125.00 a month can
                  afford to pay $12,000.00 for a second
                  home.

August 15   In the afternoon Carl takes Joan and her
                  friends to a trolley so they can visit Coney
                  Island.

August 15   The Kigers entertain friends at their 24th
                  Anniversary party. Joan does not come
                  home from her earlier outing to Coney
                  Island.

August 16   Individuals at a Ft. Mitchell restaurant,
                  while at lunch, overhear two men talking,
                  saying that they don't intend to keep
                  paying Carl Kiger in order to operate
                  their slot machines. They said that the
                  $1500.00 paid the previous month would
                  be the last payment made.

August 16 - 17   Carl and Jerry are murdered in their beds
                  and Jennie wounded. The Boone County

Sheriff, as well as Kenton County officials, converge on Rosegate.

August 17   Jennie is rushed to St. Elizabeth's hospital. Jack Maynard places an around-the-clock the guard on Room 231.

August 17-18   Joan is questioned for 16 straight hours by officials from both counties. Eventually, on the 17th she is taken to the Boone County jail.

August 18   Joan is formally arrested and appears before Judge Cropper.

August 19   Joan visits her mother at St. Elizabeth's, accompanied by her two brothers, John and Joe, her uncle Fred and his wife, Eva. They are escorted by Sheriff Jake Williams.

August 20   Joan attends the funeral and burial of her father and brother. All Covington city offices are closed.

August 21   Joan turns 16 while in the Burlington jail.

August 23   Joan is released on $25,000.00 bond. She goes immediately, at the recommendation of Dr. Ertel, the Kiger family physician, to the Cincinnati General Hospital Psychiatric Unit for an evaluation.

August 23   Cincinnati City Manager Sherrill learns of Joan's placement, calls Dr. Romano, the medical director, and orders him to release her, stating that because Joan is out of state and since Dr. Romano did not clear the admission with the city, the patient must be discharged. (Also, no doubt, Sherrill knew this case would create national attention and would strain the staff at the hospital as well as usurp their time when they would most likely be subpoenaed to testify.)

August 24   At the recommendation of Dr. Ertel, Joan is taken to the Eastern State Sanitarium, in Lexington, Kentucky where she is evaluated by Dr. Walter Sprague. She remains there until the middle of September.

December 6   Jennie is arrested for the murder of Jerry, but is immediately released, after posting a $25,000.00 bond. The charge was that she was complicit in the murders or gave directions to Joan regarding her actions.

December 17 The murder trial begins. John L. Vest, prominent Walton, Kentucky attorney gives the prosecution's opening summation of the case to the jury.

December 18 Sheriff Williams, Deputy Rouse and others testify as to the events of the night of August 16-17.

December 19 Prosecution ends its case by setting up the bloody beds of Carl and Jerry. Joan asks to leave the room during this phase of the trial.

December 20 Sawyer Smith opens for the defense presenting his nightmare theory. Joan testifies for two hours.

December 21 Jennie testifies and admits there was no intruder. She says that is was Joan who committed the murders. The case goes to the jury at about 6:00 p.m.

December 21 The jury delivers its verdict at 10:45 p.m.

1944

January –April Joan is in Topeka, Kansas at the Menninger Neuropsychiatric Clinic for extensive testing and treatment, following her trial and at the suggestion of Sawyer Smith who realized that Prosecutor Vincent would eventually attempt to try her for her father's murder. Sawyer was already planning his next defense for Joan which would be a plea of insanity.

April 2 Fred Williamson receives a report from the Menninger Clinic stating that Joan suffers from Dementia Praecox and is insane.

April 10 Joan is admitted to the College Hill Sanitarium in Cincinnati, Ohio to shield her from Vincent's subpoenas and in preparation for her Lunacy Hearing in Covington, Kentucky on April 15.

April 12 R. L. Vincent and Charles Riley issue a statement which questions Joan's innocence and the nightmare defense theory and accuses Sawyer Smith of using this as a ploy to keep her from being indicted for the murder of her father.

April 13	John L. Vest, Boone County assistant prosecutor states that it would do no good for Kenton County to try to provide proof that Joan was now of unsound mind. What really matters, he said, was the state of her mind at the time of the murders.
April 13	Friends of the Kiger family and politicians in Covington raise $20,000.00 to aid in Joan's defense, should she be charged with her father's murder. (One wonders why these politicians would be so interested in making sure that another trial did not take place.)
April 14	R. L. Vincent and Charles Riley announce that they may seek a new indictment against Joan, since the Kentucky Attorney General, Eldon S. Dummit had ruled that Joan, as well as her mother, could be re-tried.
April 15	Judge Goodenough, presiding over Joan's Lunacy Hearing, had appointed Dr. Charles E. Kiely as an unbiased expert who then reported to the jury on Joan's condition. The jury also read the report from the Menninger Clinic. During

these proceedings, Raymond L. Vincent was in the audience merely, as he said "as an interested citizen." And he was not happy when he heard the jury's verdict or the judge's decision that placed Joan at the Central State Hospital for the Insane.

April 22   Joe and John Kiger were granted emergency leave from the European and Pacific theatres of war to visit Joan at Central State Hospital. Jennie, as well as Fred Williamson and his wife, Eva, also visited her. (For emergency leave to be granted during war time suggests that something very unusual had happened at the hospital – something such as a suicide attempt.)

June 3   Joan was transferred from Central State to Eastern State Hospital in Lexington, Kentucky. Central State Superintendent, Isham Kimbell, stated that Joan's presence was too disruptive to the orderliness and efficiency of the hospital. He explained that visitors were coming in large numbers to meet with Joan, to get her autograph and to have pictures taken with her.

June 10	Joan calls Dr. Kimbell, pleading with him to let her return to Central State, citing that she hated the rules and the stuffiness of the Lexington facility and how, in contrast, she loved working with the youngsters at Central State and playing on their softball team. "Butch," as Dr. Kimbell nicknamed Joan, won him over and she was allowed to return to Central State.
August 26	Joan was released from Central State Hospital for the Insane, Dr. Kimbell making this statement: "Joan is not insane. Prolonged custodial care is not the answer to her problems." Joan was released to the care of her mother, Jennie.
June, 1958	At the age of 31, Joan receives a Bachelor of Science degree from the University of Louisville under the name of Marie Kiler. She then begins teaching in the Louisville public school system.
June, 1979	Jennie Kiger dies of breast cancer at the age of 83, in Mississippi, where she had gone to be near her son, Joe. Eva, Fred and Joe were at her bed side to witness the end of the Rosegate tragedy. Her body

was returned to Ft. Mitchell, Kentucky and buried along side her husband, Carl and her son, Jerry, in St. John's Cemetery. in Section II, plot l7, of her parents' family area (the Hoelscher family).

June, 1988   Marie Kiler retires as a guidance counselor.

April 5, 1991   Joan dies as Marie Kiler, of cirrhosis of the liver, at the age of 63. She lived at 4100 Town Road in Louisville, Kentucky. Marie left her body to the University of Louisville.

Sources

Information used to re-construct the story of Joan Kiger is a composite of facts as reported in the Kentucky Times Star, The Kentucky Post and the Boone County Recorder during the fall, winter and spring of 1943-44, as well as information gleaned from court documents and public records some of which are included in this book. Additional information for the story comes from interviews with senior citizens in Boone County who were privy to the trial itself and/or to the major figures in the trial.

The two books *Images of America: Burlington* and *Images of America: Boone County* were also of great help. And finally, viewing the re-creation of the jury trial which the Boone County Historical Society called "The Murder Trial of Joan Kiger," provided the flavor and tone of the times and gave an interesting depiction of the pace and character of the trial itself. Two men who were the impetus behind the Historical Society's recreation of the trial, Judge Bruce Ferguson and attorney Asa Rouse, were very willing to share information gleaned from their research.

Court Documents From
Sawyer Smith and Raymond Vincent
(Motions to Strike, Affidavits, Indictments, Motions to Quash, Demurrers, etc.)

BOONE CIRCUIT COURT

COMMONWEALTH OF KENTUCKY,   PLAINTIFF,

VS.   MOTION TO QUASH AND AFFIDAVIT

JOAN KIGER and JENNIE KIGER,   DEFENDANTS.

- - - - - -

Comes defendant, Joan Kiger, and moves the Court to quash
and suppress all the evidence of Melvin Huff, Highway Patrolman,
J. T. Williams, Sheriff of Boone County, Earl Christophel, Covington Policeman, Robert Tiepel, Covington Policeman, Irvin Rouse,
Deputy Sheriff of Boone County, Chester Fee, Covington Policeman,
Jack Maynard, Covington City Manager, and all other persons who
were permitted to ply this defendant with questions, or who had
her plied with questions or the answers thereto, at the time and
place hereinafter mentioned, because this defendant, Joan Kiger,
was taken into custody by said officers about 2:30 o'clock A. M.,
August 17, 1943, at her home, and after Carl Kiger and Jerry Kiger had been shot, and this defendant was from said time, until
6:30 o'clock P. M., August 17, 1943, detained, kept in custody,
and members of her family were denied the right to see her, and
she was denied the right to see or converse with relatives or
friends, and during said period of sixteen hours she was contin-
uously plied with questions relative to said shooting and other
incidents in her life; that during all of said time there were

County Court, and judge of the Juvenile Court of said County,
and by said Juvenile Court Judge duly ordered to be proceeded
against in accordance with the criminal laws of this State,
and the charge against said defendant, Joan Kiger, being referred by said Juvenile Court Judge to the Boone Circuit Court,
and the Grand Jury thereof, for prosecution by indictment,
as is more fully set out in the certified orders of said Juvenile Court attached hereto and made a part hereof, said
crime and felony herein charged being contrary to the form
of the Statutes in such cases made and provided and against
the peace and dignity of the Commonwealth of Kentucky.

Commonwealth Attorney
15th Circuit Court District of Kentucky

404

Defendant states that the room in which she slept and lived, her home, was searched, and all of her personal effects of every character and kind examined and searched by said officers, or some of them; that she was taken into another room of the residence, and her body, and the clothing she wore, and every part thereof searched from head to foot.

Defendant states that she was plied with questions by said officers, and during a part of said time in the presence of other persons, and at a time that said officers had stated to her that she was only wanted as a witness; that she was kept at said home in custody of said officers, as above set out, from about 2:30 A. M. until about 6:30 o'clock A. M., at which time said officers took her from said home to the county seat at Burlington, Kentucky, a distance of about nine miles, and kept her in custody and continued to ply her with questions, without permitting her to have any sleep or rest, until she became so exhausted that she fell asleep while said officers so had her in custody, and slept for approximately one hour, and when she awoke one of said officers was still with her and had her in custody; that during said time, as a result of said plying with questions, she was required to and did sign a written statement, which she believes the prosecution has in its possession, and that no warrant of arrest was issued for her until about 10 o'clock A. M., August 18, 1943.

Defendant says that each and all of said acts above set out were and are illegal, and without legal right or authority, and all of defendant's answers to said questions, as a result of such plying and illegal acts, were wrongfully and illegally obtained, and all of said evidence of the above named witnesses should be quashed for the following reasons:

II.

Defendant states that her legal and constitutional rights were violated by the acts above set out in that the same was and is in violation of Section 11 of the Constitution of the State of Kentucky, which provides that in a criminal case no person shall "be compelled to give evidence against himself", and in violation of Amendment V to the Constitution of the United States, which provides that in a criminal case no person shall be compelled "to be a witness against himself".

III.

Defendant states that the searches and seizures above set out, and all evidence relating thereto, was and is in violation of defendant's legal and constitutional rights in that the same is in violation of Section 10 of the Constitution of the State of Kentucky, which provides "that the people shall be secure in their persons, houses, papers and possessions from unreasonable searches and seizures", and in violation of Amendment IV to the Constitution of the United States, which provides that the right of the people to be secure in their persons, houses, papers and effects against unreasonable searches and seizures shall not be violated.

IV.

Defendant's legal rights were violated in that Earl Christophel and Robert Tiepel, when acting as such officers, or pretended officers, were acting illegally, as above set out, and in addition thereto, each of them derived their only authority as officers from the fact that they are police officers in the

-3-

BOONE CIRCUIT COURT

COMMONWEALTH OF KENTUCKY,   PLAINTIFF,

            VS.   SPECIAL DEMURRER   No._____

JOAN KIGER and JENNIE KIGER,   DEFENDANTS.

- - - - - - -

        Comes defendant, Joan Kiger, and demurs specially to
the indictment herein for the following causes:

        (1) The Court is without jurisdiction of the defendant,
Joan Kiger, because said defendant was only fifteen years of age
at the time of the alleged offense set out in the indictment, and
this Court is without jurisdiction.

        (2) The Court is without jurisdiction of the subject
matter of this action because this defendant was and is such in-
fant.

        WHEREFORE, defendant, Joan Kiger, prays a judgment of the
Court.

                                    _____
                                    Attorney for defendant,
                                        Joan Kiger.

407

BOONE CIRCUIT COURT

COMMONWEALTH OF KENTUCKY,   PLAINTIFF,

VS.   DEMURRER   No._____

JOAN KIGER and JENNIE KIGER,   DEFENDANTS.

- - - - - -

     The defendant, Jennie Kiger, demurs to the indict-
ment herein because the same does not state facts sufficient
to constitute an offense as against this defendant.

     WHEREFORE, defendant, Jennie Kiger, prays a judgment
of the Court.

Lawyer N Smith
Attorney for Defendant,
Jennie Kiger.

BOONE CIRCUIT COURT

COMMONWEALTH OF KENTUCKY,   PLAINTIFF,

VS.   MOTION FOR SEVERANCE   No._____

JOAN KIGER and
JENNIE KIGER,   DEFENDANTS.

- - - - -

Comes defendant, Joan Kiger, and moves the Court
for a separate trial herein.

WHEREFORE, defendant prays a judgment of the Court.

_____
Attorney for defendant, Joan
                        Kiger.

409

Dr. R. J. Ectt
Robt. Vinyard
Earl Christopher
Wm Murphy
Jim Dixon
John Jack Baymont
Dr. J. Bowins
C. M. Wilson
Alfred Steed
Robt. Mayo
Robert Mayo Jr.
Mrs. Robert (Michigan?)
Eugene Metzer
Guy Banister(?)
(J. C. White)
Sgt. Huff
Louis Hutchinson
Mr. Williams
(Dann Ross)
Art Knight
Wallace Grubb(?)
Lawrence Leonard
E. H. Guinn
Mrs. E. Wheton
Dr. M. A. Yroten(?)

No. 2591.
Commonwealth of Kentucky

Indictment for

Willful Murder

Vs.

JOAN KIGER & JENNIE KIGER

A TRUE BILL.

_____
Foreman, Grand Jury.

Presented by the foreman, in
the presence of the Grand
Jury, to the Court and filed
in Open Court, this __ day
of December, 1943.

_____ Clerk.
Circuit Court

Bail $25,000.00

We the jury hereby find the
defendant John Kiger, according to
the evidence presented, Not guilty.

Lamar H. Congleton
Foreman.

The defendant Reun. Gran Kiger
honing been tried and found
not guilty, it being the stronger
case the case Reun against
Jenny Kiger is hereby
dismissed This Dec 8/1943

R.L. Vincent
Com atty

Witnesses in Kiger Case.

=B=

Brugh, Bob - 1da

=C=

Carpenter, Lucy - 5da
1.28
Christopher, Earl - 5da

=G=
1.28 mi
German, Wm. M. - 1da
Grubbs, Wallace - 1da

=H=

Hetzel, Eeugene - 5da
1.72
Huff, Melvin - 5da
52.72
Henderson, Lewis - 5da
Kirkpatrick - 20

=M=
1.28 mi
Maynard, Mrs. Jack - 5da
Mayo, Robert Sr. - 5da
Mayo, Robert Jr. - 5da
Mayo, Mrs. Robert - 5da

=N=

Nunnelly, Dr. S. B. - 1da

=R=   ✗ 1.28
Rouse, Irvin [Schild, Alfred] - 2da.
        5da   S=

=B.C=

=W=

Williams, J. I. - 5da
Walton, Noel - 5da
Wilson, C. M. - 3da
White, H. E. - 5da

=Y=

Yelton, Dr. M. A.
5da
Yelton A D - 2

do
not
destroy
com O.B #2
Page 275

413

SAT DEC 18 - England

Kiger Trial Jury List

Lamar Congleton of Burlington

M.M. Lucas of Bulllittsville

Byron Kinman of Belleview

Edward Black of Idlewild

William Hill of Idlewild

David Houston of Richwood

George Heil of Limaburg

Albert Dringenburg of Florence <

Clyde Arnold of Florence

Charles White of Petersburg

Gilbert Dolwick of Constance

Howard Abdon of Idlewild

THE FACE OF THIS DOCUMENT HAS A COLORED BACKGROUND · NOT A WHITE BACKGROUND

1090430

91 09327

FORM VS NO. 1-A
(Rev 5/80)

COMMONWEALTH OF KENTUCKY
DEPARTMENT FOR HEALTH SERVICES
PROGRAM OF VITAL STATISTICS

118 _____

FILE NO.

CERTIFICATE OF DEATH

008350

AMENDED 5-7-91 evb

DECEDENT	1. DECEDENT'S NAME (First, Middle, Last) MARIS J. KILER born Joan Marie Kiger	2. SEX Female	3. DATE OF DEATH (Month, Day, Year) April 5, 1991
	4. SOCIAL SECURITY NO. 406-34-4037	5a. AGE Last Birthday (Years) 63	6. DATE OF BIRTH (Month, Day, Year) August 21, 1927	7. BIRTHPLACE (City/State or Foreign Country) Covington, Ky.
	8. WAS DECEDENT EVER IN U.S. ARMED FORCES? No	9. PLACE OF DEATH (Check only one)		
	10. FACILITY NAME (If not institution, give street and number) Christopher East Nursing Home	10a. CITY, TOWN, OR LOCATION OF DEATH Louisville	11. COUNTY OF DEATH Jefferson Co.
	12. MARITAL STATUS Never Married	13. SURVIVING SPOUSE	14. DECEDENT'S USUAL OCCUPATION Teacher	15. KIND OF BUSINESS/INDUSTRY Education
	16. RESIDENCE - State Kentucky	County Jefferson	City, Town Louisville	Street and Number 4200 Browns Lane
	Inside City Limits Yes	Zip Code 40220	18. RACE White	19. Education 17
PARENTS	20. FATHER'S NAME Carl Albion Kiger	21. MOTHER'S NAME Jennie Boelscher	
INFORMANT	22. INFORMANT'S NAME Kiger Dept Records	23. MAILING ADDRESS Health Sciences Center - Louisville, Ky 40292	
DISPOSITION	24. METHOD OF DISPOSITION Donation	25. PLACE OF DISPOSITION Univ. of Louisville Anatomy Dept, Louisville, Ky.	25a. LOCATION
	26. SIGNATURE OF FUNERAL SERVICE LICENSEE	27. NAME AND ADDRESS OF FACILITY Univ. of Louisville Anatomy Dept. Health Sciences Center - Louisville, Ky 40292	
CERTIFIER	Signature and Title	29. DATE SIGNED 4/18/91

THE BACK OF THIS DOCUMENT CONTAINS AN ARTIFICIAL WATERMARK · HOLD AT AN ANGLE TO VIEW

Printed in the United States
132492LV00001B/116/P

9 781438 912080